Inflicting Mayhem

Inflicting Mayhem

Dakota Destruction Book 3

Millie Copper

Copyright © 2023 CU Publishing LLC
ISBN-13: 978-1-957088-28-0

Written by Millie Copper

Edited by Ameryn Tucker

Proofread by MDC Proofreading

Cover design by Dauntless Cover Design

Also by Millie Copper

The Havoc in Wyoming Series

When a series of coordinated attacks devastate the United States, the people of Bakerville, Wyoming, must come together to survive. Unfortunately, not everyone has the town's best interest at heart. Some are striving for personal gain during the apocalypse.

The Montana Mayhem Series

A group from Bakerville, Wyoming strikes out on their own while searching for the desires of their heart. Unfortunately, the road will not be easy, and sometimes the heart is hardened and deceitful.

The Dakota Destruction Series

After a series of coordinated attacks devastate the United States, Katie and Leo sacrifice everything to help their country. But some things aren't as they seem. Is it time to go home and start fresh, or can something good come out of this terrible situation?

Wyoming Fall Series (In The October Fall World)

In the blink of an eye, an EMP changed everything for Lauren and her family. Now they are in a fight for survival, trying to keep their loved ones alive as society collapses around them.

Nonfiction Books

Millie has penned seven nonfiction, traditional food focused books, sharing how, with a little creativity, anyone can transition to a real foods diet without overwhelming their food budget. Many of her books also include preparedness and food storage tips.

Find these titles at:
MillieCopper.com

Join My Reader's Club!

Receive a complimentary copy of *Looming Mayhem: A Dakota Destruction Prequel.* As part of my reader's club, you'll be the first to know about new releases and specials. I also share info on books I'm reading, preparedness tips, and more. Please sign up at:

MillieCopper.com/Join

Chapter 1

Merissa

"Hey there, pretty lady. Where're you rushing off to?" I keep my gaze fixed ahead, just as I did yesterday and the day before. Ignoring the two troublemakers lurking on the corner seems like the wisest course of action.

Their decision to stake out this particular spot near the hospital remains a mystery. The fact they choose to loiter in the darkness and cold only adds to the puzzle.

If they show up again tomorrow, I'll report it to Captain Williams. I have a sneaking suspicion they might be connected to the issue with the new synthetic drug, Ploy. Whoever named it Ploy might be onto something, considering its side effects: memory impairment, anxiety, hallucinations, and even death.

"Move along," a gruff voice commands.

I turn my head to see a tall man in a heavy-duty snowsuit striding toward the thugs on the corner. He sports a giant sidearm strapped to his leg and carries a slung rifle on his back.

"Who's gonna make us, old man?" the shorter punk challenges, while the other slinks away.

The tall man stands even taller. I narrow my eyes as I realize it's Ritchie Kasubowski, also known as Bowski. Although I don't know him well, he lent a hand when the ration center exploded a few weeks ago, and I've seen him around since then. He steps closer to the short guy, who takes a stumbling step backward and lands on his bottom.

"You were saying?" Bowski asks.

I release a low chuckle and shake my head. Even though I should continue on my way, I can't help but stop and watch the spectacle.

The guy on the ground scrambles to his feet and puts some distance between himself and the imposing figure.

His friend, still retreating, calls over his shoulder, "No problem, dude. We're done here."

"Glad to hear it. Don't let me catch you here again. We don't want your kind around," Bowski warns.

With a gap forming between Bowski and the men, the short one musters some courage. "Yeah? Well, too bad. We go where we want. Besides, we've got friends here. They want us around."

Bowski takes several quick steps forward, prompting the men to pick up their pace. When Bowski comes to a halt, they hurl a series of colorful insults about his parentage over their shoulders before scurrying away. As it becomes clear they're leaving for good, Bowski turns to me.

"Sorry about them," he calls from across the street.

"They were simply annoying. They didn't actually *do* anything."

"Still." He steps off the curb and heads in my direction. Out of a now unneeded habit, he checks both directions before crossing the snow-covered street.

When he's on the same sidewalk as me, he gives me a smile, showing off white teeth illuminated by the light of the partial moon—impressively white, considering our circumstances. Without toothpaste or even running water, many people struggle with their dental hygiene. "I heard those two started showing up a few days ago. Glad I found them this time."

I dip my chin, causing my scarf to cover my mouth. "They've been here for a couple of days." My words come out muffled.

"Really? Did they bother you then too?"

With my head again held high, I say, "Yesterday. About the same. Cat calls . . . you know."

"Yeah. They shouldn't be doing that. May I walk you home?"

"No need. It's just up the block."

"You're Merissa the medic, right? I'm Ritchie Kasubowski. We met before."

"Yes. Merissa Weaver." I offer my gloved hand.

He gives it a shake with the perfect amount of firmness. I crane my neck to meet his eyes. My husband was tall, six foot two, but Bowski is well over that.

"Six-eight." He nods.

"Pardon?"

"You were wondering how tall I am, right? I'm six-eight."

"Oh. Yes . . . I guess you get asked that a lot."

"You have no idea. My favorite is, 'How's the weather up there?' or 'Do you play basketball?' A few others too."

"Must be annoying."

"I decided a long time ago not to let it bother me. You're new to the Black Hills, right? Came from Wyoming?"

"Montana. Thanks for shooing those guys away. I'll see you later." I walk away, leaving him standing there. I purposely avoid looking back. After passing the next house, I exhale sharply and watch my breath form a miniature cloud in the cold air.

It's the first official day of winter, December 21st, and I'm already eager for the season to be over. So far, it's been better than last winter, which had record-breaking cold and snowfall. Many people referred to it as a nuclear winter, given the detonation of bombs on both coasts and a high-altitude nuclear device resulting in an electromagnetic pulse. Ever since then, everything has been a struggle.

A struggle made worse in the past few months when my husband was killed and our home destroyed.

Well, not *our* home exactly. My mother-in-law's home. We started living with her after the EMP. When my husband and his older brother were killed while defending our neighborhood, Mother Pearl and I made an impulsive decision to head east to Rapid City, South Dakota, where Pearl's sister lives. My hand travels to my expanding waistline.

Suddenly, a voice startles me. "Well, well, pretty lady. Here you are again." I quickly sidestep as one of the two men from earlier emerge from beside an abandoned minivan.

He lets out a laugh. "Why are you so jumpy? We just want to get to know you." He motions to his friend. The shorter man steps into view, holding a two-foot piece of plastic pipe.

My breathing increases when I notice the gun in the hand of the taller one. He's not exactly aiming it at me, but it wouldn't take much for him to shift it in my direction.

Raising my left hand, I give a dismissive wave. "I'm not interested." Their eyes follow the movement of my arm, while my right hand subtly reaches for my semiauto 9-millimeter snugly tucked on my hip.

As my hand connects with the grip of my weapon, a voice booms out, "I thought I told you two to get out of here."

Both men spin around to face Bowski, his massive revolver drawn and pointed at them.

I continue to draw my gun, struggling with my winter gloves as they hinder my movement. I almost drop my weapon as I hurriedly seek cover behind the back quarter of the minivan. Kneeling by the deflated tire, I'm in an awkward position to observe the unfolding events, but I can still see the two troublemakers.

Time seems to slow as the man with the pipe hurls it in Bowski's direction, while the other guy raises the muzzle of his handgun. He lifts it only a few inches before Bowski's revolver barks.

The guy with the pipe collapses to the ground, curled up in a fetal position. The gun falls silent, and the man on the ground cries out, "Don't shoot! Don't shoot!"

"Merissa, are you okay?" Bowski asks.

"Y-yes. I'm good." I take a deep breath to calm my racing heart. "Does anyone need medical attention?"

As I peer around the minivan, Bowski comes into view. His gun is still trained on the man curled on the ground, who's now crying.

Bowski kicks the gun away from the guy he shot and shakes his head. "This one doesn't need treatment." He turns to the crying man. "Get to your feet. Keep your hands away from your holster or else you'll end up as dead as your druggie friend."

Within a few seconds, the man is unarmed and Bowski tells me I can come out. "This one isn't hurt. I think all he really needs is a change of underwear. And a trip to jail."

"No, man. I don't want to go to jail," the man pleads. "They don't treat people right in there."

Bowski grabs the man by the shirt collar and lifts him into the air so they are face to face. "And were you treating the lady right? I have a good idea of what you planned, and jail is too good for you. You deserve what your friend got."

The guy starts crying again, and his need for a change of underwear is confirmed as a wet spot appears on his pant leg. Bowski lowers the man to the ground.

"I'm sorry, man," the guy blubbers. "We were only having a little fun. We weren't going to hurt her. We thought, maybe— "

"You should stop talking now." Bowski shoves him backward, and the man hits hard on his bottom.

Bowski turns to me. "You got a radio?"

I peel off my small backpack. "I'm on call at the hospital tonight. I can contact the guard shack."

"Have them send a patroller to pick up this guy. Tell them to send Hugo too." Hugo, the mortician, is probably the busiest man in the Guard District of Rapid City.

After the guard on duty at the hospital confirms the situation is stable, he assures me he'll send the nearest patroller and get in touch with Hugo. As soon as he breaks off, Captain Williams asks if I'm okay.

"I'm not injured. Everything's fine, over," I reply.

"Did you subdue them on your own?" Williams inquires.

"Uh, no. Ritchie Kasubowski is here."

"Bowski," Ritchie corrects.

"Bowski," I repeat. "We're both fine, over."

There're several beats of silence before Williams says, "Would you mind coming in for a quick exam? Let's make sure all is well with your, uh, special project. Over."

I close my eyes and shake my head. I had only informed Captain Williams about my pregnancy a couple of days ago. It wasn't really a secret, but I didn't see the need to tell him earlier. Part of me feared he might discharge me from the med school program, or even dismiss me altogether and take away my position as a medic.

When I open my eyes, I find Bowski staring at me intently, and even the man on the ground is looking at me. "Yes, sir. I'll come in as soon as things are settled here. Over and out."

I purposely avoid Bowski's gaze. It's only a couple of minutes until the rumble of an engine sounds in the distance. The sheriff's department and the Citizen Patrollers—who are really part of the sheriff's department but go by a different name—have a couple of old ATVs and snowmobiles they use in their duties.

With gasoline long gone sour, these reworked machines now run on biodiesel. While the biodiesel is a huge help, it's produced in small batches and makes rationing necessary. The police and hospital use the precious fuel, but not the general public.

As the snowmobile comes to a stop, one of the Patrollers steps off. I recognize him as someone who has visited the hospital on several occasions. He nods at me before greeting Bowski with a handshake. "Should've known you'd be in the middle of this."

"You know me, always finding trouble."

"Hugo should be here shortly. Passed his wagon a couple of blocks back," the patroller informs us, shifting his attention to me. "You okay, ma'am?"

Is thirty-six old enough to be a ma'am?

"I'm fine, thank you," I reply, pulling my stocking hat lower on my head. I ask if they need me for anything else.

The patroller says he'd like to take my statement but suggests doing it at the hospital if I prefer. I agree and inform him I'll be working the day shift tomorrow. I give Bowski a quick smile and express my gratitude for his assistance.

"See you later, Merissa," he says, flashing his remarkably white teeth, his beard and mustache moving up and down with the motion.

I quickly turn and head to my house. I'll go into the hospital for a quick exam as Williams asked, but I need to let Mother Pearl know where I'm going first.

Williams may know about my "special project," but I have yet to share the news with my mother-in-law. I wanted to wait until I was sure the pregnancy was progressing well. The last thing I want is to get her hopes up or cause her unnecessary worry. Pregnancy and childbirth are challenging enough in today's world.

I shove down my fears, wishing it was the end of this long winter so I can hold my child—hold my *husband's* child.

Chapter 2

Katie

"Katie?" Kerry Hendricks peeks her head into the dentist's room where I'm organizing things after his monthly visit.

Usually, the traveling dentist would stay for the full week, Monday to Friday. However, since today is Wednesday and Christmas Eve, he finished early and is heading home to be with his wife and newborn baby boy. They had another son, but he died during the early days of the EMP due to some kind of accident.

I lean back from the cabinet and stretch my neck to look at her. "Yes?"

"Do you know a Bonnie Turner?"

"Bonnie Turner? I don't think so." I shrug. "But you know how it is. Is she asking for me?"

"She says you told her it would be okay if she came to the hospital instead of seeing her midwife." Kerry is wearing her heavy coat and boots. She retrieves a knit cap from her pocket and slips it on her head.

"Oh . . . I think I do know her. She was at the hospital, or her husband was, when Leo had his surgery. Can you take her to an exam room? Don't have her change. I want to talk with her first. She's a little . . . skittish. I'll be there shortly." I motion to her clothing. "Gathering wood?"

Kerry, who's officially on duty as a janitor today since the med school is on break until after Christmas, confirms she is.

I turn back to my work and quickly return the few things I have in my hands to the cabinet. As I secure the padlock, I consider how I wish Nettie Wolff were on duty today instead of Chastity Morrow. Although both are skilled doctors, Nettie has a way of putting apprehensive patients at ease, helping them understand that they're in the right place for proper treatment.

Chastity is competent, and her bedside manner is good, but she doesn't engage with the patients as much as Nettie does. Sometimes, I feel like her mind is elsewhere. Today, it's definitely elsewhere. Geoff

Landers, her current crush, is on duty, shadowing Jesse Talbot in his role as a medic.

Landers isn't thrilled with the assignment, believing he's above the role of a medic—too good for it, even. During the med school break, each student has been given several shifts, shadowing either a medic, a nurse, or a doctor. They even work as janitors at times.

Captain Williams wants to ensure they're familiar with all aspects of our hospital. With his foot healing well from his partial amputation, he's transitioned from a wheelchair to crutches while in the building and is back to taking regular shifts at the hospital and care facilities.

Having a med student shadow him during his shifts is not only for training purposes, but also as a precaution since he's not as agile as he used to be. When he makes his rounds at the facilities, his shadow pushes him in a wheelchair fitted with tiny skis on the front to help get through the snow and ice.

I check my watch. There's just over an hour left of the day shift. Depending on what's going on with her, Bonnie may see Chastity first, but Captain Williams will take over when he comes on duty at 1800 hours.

When I open the door to the exam room, Bonnie Turner spins around. From her position in the room, it appears she may have been pacing while waiting. "Hello. I'm happy to see you." I give her a smile.

She quickly lifts the edges of her lips before dropping them again. "Jack said I should come. I got off work early. They weren't happy about it, but . . . " She shrugs. "Will this take long?"

"What's going on?"

She points to her slightly protruding stomach. "I've been experiencing some pain, like menstrual cramps. I went to the midwife about it last night, but she . . . " Bonnie visibly swallows. "We didn't have anything she wanted in exchange, and I had already used all our ration chips for the week. Um, for Christmas."

My brow furrows. "The midwife charges?"

Bonnie raises her chin. "It's her livelihood."

"Her livelihood? She doesn't have a crew assignment? Doesn't she get her own ration chips?"

The pregnant woman's expression suggests she may have divulged too much. "I-I don't know. Not exactly."

I relax my shoulders and release a silent breath. "Tell me about the cramps."

She gives me a grateful look. "They come and go. I saw the midwife a few weeks ago, and she gave me some tea to help with morning sickness. I still have the sickness sometimes, and now the cramps. I'm almost out of the tea and am not sure what to do next."

"What kind of tea?"

"I brought the bag with me—what's left, anyway. I know when I used to go to the doctor, before all this, he always asked me about any meds I was taking." She slides a small backpack off and begins rummaging through it. After a few moments, she produces a small canvas bag. "I figured you might want to know too." She thrusts the bag in my direction.

I open the bag and take a sniff. It has a minty aroma, similar to the tea I often drink. There are other scents as well, perhaps ginger, and a few I can't quite identify. "When did you start taking this?"

"A couple weeks ago. The sickness was making it difficult to work, to eat, to do anything. The tea helps."

"Do you know what's in it?"

She shakes her head. "Not really. Peppermint, I think. Maybe rosemary."

"How much do you take?"

"I'm supposed to have a cup three or four times a day, but . . ." She drops her gaze. "Some days, when the nausea is really bad, I have more. I had to have Jack get me a refill last week. The midwife told him I shouldn't be out yet, but since I was, she went ahead and sold us another bag. I have to work. I need the tea to keep me from being too sick."

I motion toward one of the chairs as I move to the other. "Let's sit for a minute."

As we both take a seat, she squirms, stroking the sleeve of her jacket with one hand. I gather basic information from her, such as her full name, date of birth, and other pertinent details, including the date of her last menstrual cycle.

Like many in today's world of food rationing and weight loss, her periods had become irregular. She didn't even realize she was pregnant until she started feeling sick. "If I'd known it was okay to come here anytime and not just clinic days, I would've come. I got sick on a

Thursday and didn't want to wait until the next Tuesday when you had the clinic. Addison sees people every day."

"Addison?"

Her cheeks flush. "Um . . . she's the midwife. Not just a midwife. She practices various forms of medicine and offers different remedies." Her words rush out. She points at my clipboard. "Please don't write her name down, okay?"

My pen hovers above the paper. "Why not?"

"She doesn't want it to get around. She already has as many patients as she can handle. I was fortunate to be able to see her since we don't live right in her neighborhood. It was only because I had a friend who— " Bonnie slams her mouth shut.

Clearing my throat, I refrain from writing down Addison's name but silently repeat it to myself. "Did she give you anything else besides the tea?"

"I have a lotion. I brought it too." Bonnie reaches into the pack resting beside her leg and hands me a small baby food jar.

I unscrew the lid and inhale its strong, minty scent.

"I use it on my temples and under my nose. It helps with the nausea and tiredness. Addison said it'll help with stretch marks, too, but I don't have those yet. I try to use it sparingly so I'll have it when the stretch marks show up. It was . . . " She sighs. "It was pretty expensive."

While the hospital and other services operate as part of the reconstruction efforts without charge, I'm aware of the existence of an underground market that assigns value to certain items. The black market encompasses more than physical goods. As Bowski mentioned during our last conversation, we need to establish legitimate trade systems instead of relying on the hushed, unofficial transactions everyone pretends don't exist.

After replacing the jar's lid and inspecting it for any labels, I find "Form. 2B" written at the bottom, accompanied by what appears to be a shamrock symbol. "Do you know what's in it?"

Bonnie shrugs. "Mint, maybe?"

Smiling at her, I ask if she's taking anything else. When she says no, I ask her to describe her symptoms.

"Cramping, diarrhea, upset stomach, and general tiredness. I don't think I should feel this bad," she says, shaking her head. "Will I feel like this my entire pregnancy?"

I try to be reassuring but know she might. While I've never been pregnant, my sisters have. Angela, mom to now three-year-old Gavin, was sick and miserable throughout her entire pregnancy. First was the morning sickness, which lasted well into her sixth month. When that went away, the heartburn started and continued until Gavin was born.

I instruct Bonnie to change into a gown and tell her I'll return shortly with the doctor.

As I step into the hallway, I spot medic Jesse Talbot and Geoff Landers near the back door by Captain Williams's office. I head straight toward them. Jesse's going over something with Landers—something Geoff apparently doesn't feel is important, based on his body language. Either not important or, more likely, he thinks it's beneath him.

"Katie." Jesse nods at me. "Need help?"

"Is Stella Swenson shadowing as a nurse tonight?"

"Yep. She is."

"Good. I need her expertise. Our patient is taking some herbs given to her by a midwife in her area. She doesn't know exactly what's in them. I know a little about herbs and think maybe they might not be being used properly. Thought I'd check with Stella."

"Did you want to wait until Stella arrives? She took a radio. I could call her," Jesse suggests, pointing to the handheld walkie-talkie on his belt.

Geoff makes a noise of disgust and shakes his head. "Herbs not being used properly? Who cares? Most of them don't do a thing."

I tilt my head and raise an eyebrow. "The elderberry tincture?" I refrain from mentioning he was suspected of stealing the tincture for personal use, an incident that prompted us to lock up all herbal remedies.

A faint blush creeps up his neck before his ears change color. Taking a step toward me, he points an accusing finger. "Don't sass me, *nurse.*"

Jesse steps toward Landers. "As medics, our role is to assist the nurses and doctors. We work as a team." His voice remains calm but carries a hint of fierceness.

Landers rolls his eyes and steps closer to Jesse, their gazes locked in a confrontational standoff.

"What's going on?" Dr. Chastity Morrow calls from the break room's doorway. As she approaches us, I notice Kerry Hendricks emerging from the firewood room, her arms laden with logs. She glances in our direction but continues down the hallway toward the rooms.

Chastity places a hand on her hip. "Geoff?"

Uncertain about the situation and Geoff Landers's peculiar behavior, I respond, "We have a patient in exam room one. She's having a few difficulties and brought in some herbal remedies a midwife gave her."

"And? What does that have to do with these two?" She motions toward Jesse and Landers, who continue their intense standoff.

Jesse takes a step away from Landers and audibly exhales. "Sergeant Burnett— " he points at me, adhering to Captain Williams's insistence on using official titles " —suggested we check with Stella about the herbs she's using and the side effects they may cause."

I offer Jesse a grateful smile for succinctly summarizing our immediate concern.

Chastity snorts, echoing Landers's earlier reaction. "Stella and her voodoo herbs. I hope, once she gets a little more real medical training, she'll realize the absurdity of her *magic potions* and how desperately we need real medicine again."

Before I can respond, she waves a hand at me. "Oh, I know there's some benefit to them, but you all thinking they are a magic cure or somehow making people sick, is a problem. The sooner we can get back to relying on real medicine, the better."

Chastity turns to Jesse. "You need to stop your bullying."

Jesse's face registers shock. He opens his mouth to respond, but Chastity interrupts him. "I'm not going to listen to your excuses, Jesse Talbot. You act like you run this place. You're an orderly. That is all. We might give you the fancy title of medic, but all you're really good for is moving patients. Keep that in mind when you have a holier-than-thou attitude as your training the ones who'll be real doctors." She beams warmly at Landers.

The creaking door of Captain Williams's office grabs our attention. We all turn to look. Standing tall and proud, without crutches but wearing a walking boot, Captain Williams seems larger than life. No longer the injured man on the verge of death who had his foot partially amputated, he now stands as an officer in the South Dakota National Guard, a respected physician, and the person in charge of this hospital.

"What seems to be the problem?" A forced grin appears on his face, but his eyes remain hard. "Dr. Morrow? Mr. Landers?"

Chastity straightens her back and juts out her chin. "Nothing to worry about, sir." She motions to his foot. "Should you be standing? Let me help you to the chair."

"Or perhaps Mr. Talbot should assist me? Since, as you said, all he's good for is moving patients."

Chastity bites her lip. "I . . . " She smiles sweetly before raising her hands. It's no secret Captain Williams holds the medics in high regard, seeing them as much more than mere patient movers. "Perhaps I spoke without thinking."

"Perhaps you did. Let's get a few things straight. Every person associated with this hospital—whether doctor, nurse, medic, janitor, laundress, or cook—plays an important part. While we are, essentially, a military hospital and use our military ranks— " he motions to me and then himself " —the hierarchy isn't as pronounced as you, Dr. Morrow, made it sound."

"Yes, sir. I understand."

"And in addition, Mrs. Swenson and her voodoo herbs saved not only my life but countless others." Williams fixes Chastity with a look that visibly deflates her.

"We're years away from having a medical system like you're accustomed to. You may think it's a bunch of baloney, but there's true medicine in plants. Sergeant Burnett is correct in wanting to include Mrs. Swenson in her patient's treatment. Side effects from certain natural things can be as severe as prescription drugs. Am I making myself clear?"

He looks first to Chastity, who mumbles, "Yes, sir," before turning to Landers, who responds with a nonchalant shrug.

"Mr. Landers, is there something you don't understand?"

"Nope. I guess since you've decided it's your hospital and medical school, you can make the rules." Landers stares down Williams. "For now, at least."

My heart races more than it should over this entire exchange. And Landers's remark, delivered almost as a threat, intensifies the pounding.

"I see you've been talking with your uncle. If Melvin Cabal wants to take over this hospital, as well as the others operated under the guidance of the National Guard, I suppose that's going to be between him and the governor, considering we're acting under orders from the governor's office."

Williams gives Landers a wide smile. "In the meantime, this hospital will run in the manner I best see fit. The same goes for the medical school. Which, may I remind you, you are attending under probationary status. You may think you have me over a barrel, but that's only an illusion on your part."

The captain turns to me. "Make your call to Mrs. Swenson. See if she'd mind coming in a few minutes early. I'll see your patient shortly. Dr. Morrow, Mr. Landers, you can take off early. When you return for your shift tomorrow morning, I expect to see improvements in both of your attitudes."

Chapter 3

Merissa

"I'm delighted you could join us today, Merissa. Extending the festivities by celebrating Christmas Eve in addition to Christmas is truly wonderful. In today's world, we need all the reminders of the reasons behind our celebrations we can get. Did you enjoy Shawn's sermon?" Opal tilts her head while giving me a kind smile.

"I did. He's an excellent speaker." I don't mention how I'm completely surprised by her son's proficiency behind the pulpit. One on one, he's quiet and reserved. What I truly appreciate is how he transforms his sermons into conversations rather than traditional sermons.

I've never been a regular churchgoer, not really. My husband, Braedon, used to attend church regularly, and I'd accompany him on special occasions like Christmas.

After the EMP, he and I moved in with Mother Pearl. Her neighborhood started using the community center for church services. Somehow, I found myself going with Braedon most of the time. When he couldn't attend due to his work schedule, I'd go with Pearl or my sister-in-law Courtney.

The preacher, a kind man who contributed greatly to the community, often used what I considered to be religious jargon, without taking the time to explain the words and phrases. Braedon used to encourage me to read his Bible, but I kept postponing it. Sometimes, I wish I had thought of packing it when we left Livingston. Pearl has a Bible. I suppose I could ask her if I can read it.

"Are you sure you won't mind Pearl spending a few days here with us?"

I shake my head. "She'll enjoy it."

"Won't it make things harder for you? Your woodstove and food—well, don't worry about the food part. We'll send a care package home with you. You'll eat for days." Opal embraces me in a motherly hug.

Despite Pearl's standoffish nature, her sister Opal is the complete opposite.

The large shop used for the church service quickly transforms into a dining area. With most of the ranch's hired help in attendance, they've converted their large shop into a meeting hall. The presence of a woodstove makes it warm and comfortable.

Lunch is a delicious beef stew and cornbread. Owning a working cattle ranch has its advantages during the apocalypse. Opal and her husband, Kevin, have put in tremendous effort to keep the ranch operational. While they no longer sell cattle, they continue to provide food for the area. In exchange for beef and other crops, they have assigned workers.

Opal mentions it feels like a revolving door of people, as many are ill-equipped for the day-to-day labor required to sustain the ranch. However, they do have a dependable core crew residing on-site. She explains they'll need more people, especially for the crops, once the weather warms up.

Although they had a small garden before the attacks, primarily for family consumption, they plowed thirty acres for new crops after the cyberattack and the destruction of refineries—about a week before the EMP.

They already had several pastures with alfalfa, barley, and field corn, mainly for the cattle and as cash crops. The additional acreage was dedicated to fast-growing vegetables, legumes, and winter wheat.

Following the EMP, they manually plowed twenty more acres to expand their food crops. Opal has often mentioned how much more challenging everything has become without the machinery they relied on before.

Even butchering the cattle is a significant task that they handle on-site. They have an old tractor, unaffected by the EMP, that they use for transporting the carcasses.

Shawn mentioned how fortunate they are to have decent equipment, unlike the Native tribes who harvested and butchered buffalo using stone knives and clubs.

With a wistful expression, Opal mentioned that acquiring the skill of making flint knives could be useful, but Shawn dismissed the idea, stating they already have enough to do.

After lunch, I ask Opal if she minds if I use their gun range.

"Not at all. It's chilly out there. Make sure you bundle up," Opal says, looking directly at my stomach.

My cheeks flush. Although I haven't mentioned anything about the baby to her, I'm certain she knows. "I will. I'd like to run some dry-fire drills. After what happened the other day . . . " I shrug.

"It's a good idea. Pearl was nearly beside herself over that. Being able to defend yourself is important. Sounds like you did a fine job of it, but it's good Bowski was there too." She gives me a smile. "Want Shawn to join you? He's got some skills."

"It's not necessary."

"Did you need me?" Shawn magically appears over his mom's shoulder. "I heard about your troubles the other night. I'm glad you're okay."

"Merissa wants to use the range to run some dry-fire drills. Want to give her a hand?"

He agrees and says he'll be ready in five minutes. Although I would've been fine on my own, I'm okay with Shawn coming along. It isn't like he'll talk my ear off or anything.

Shawn doesn't find it peculiar I don't want to use live ammunition. When I first arrived at the ranch from Montana, they were training a few people, and live rounds were fired. However, like everything else, ammunition is limited. Shawn's dad, Kevin, has a reloading station, which helps, but he mentioned being low on primers. I'm not sure which cartridges it'll affect, but it's definitely something.

What I should really be doing is practicing archery and working with my horse, Brave. Mounted archery could be incredibly valuable in this post-apocalyptic world. Teaching others these skills would also be wise.

Walt Cox, a close friend who came with us from Montana, is also a mounted archer. Opal mentioned he has already been advising others on the archery aspect.

As if reading my thoughts, Shawn says, "Mr. Cox has been working with the horses. He said they're doing well. Rested up from the trip."

The journey from Livingston to Rapid City was long and arduous, especially for the horses, Mr. Cox, and a small group of others who traveled with us. Mother Pearl and I had it much easier, utilizing the private buses and other transports set up by enterprising individuals and communities. "I visited them when we first arrived today. They look good. Do you ride?"

He gives me a look like it's the dumbest question ever. "I grew up on the ranch. We've always had horses. The wagons were hobbies, something we did for parades and things."

"Pearl and I really appreciate you picking us up this morning. The wagon ride is certainly better than walking. How many wagons do you have?"

"Four wagons and a carriage. But only two teams. We're planning to train a team of oxen. If it goes well, we'll train more and maybe even use them for the community."

I smile at him and confess my love for horses while acknowledging my lack of knowledge about oxen.

After ensuring my gun is unloaded and showing Shawn, who visually and physically confirms the magazine is out and the chamber is empty, I return it to the holster and begin with a basic draw.

I struggle a bit with my heavy jacket getting in the way and feel awkward with the thin knit gloves, despite their limited protection. I make a few adjustments to my outside-the-waistband holster and try again. The slightly different positioning helps with the winter clothing. The gloves are still cumbersome but are better than the night of the attempted assault when a quick draw was necessary.

Shawn gestures toward my gloves. "Do those keep your hands warm?"

"Not much. They break the wind, but that's about all."

"I'll ask my mom. She might have something better, thin enough for shooting but not so slippery."

I purse my lips. Having less slippery gloves would be helpful. I practice a few more draws, focusing on gripping the weapon and establishing a solid foundation. Then I incorporate aligning the sights and creating an efficient path to my shooting eye.

Shawn observes as I repeat these basic movements a few more times. "Let me go find those gloves. I think they'll help." He trots off toward the house while I continue with my presentation drill.

Shawn is probably right about the gloves. The ones I'm wearing aren't suitable, and my fingers are already cold. In this weather, heavy ski gloves or mittens would be more appropriate, although shooting with such bulky gloves wouldn't work.

When Shawn returns, he hands me a pair of maroon gloves. They resemble driving gloves and have an indicator showing they can be used on now-defunct touchscreen devices. Although not thick, they're thermal lined and are considerably warmer than my current gloves.

"You could layer them," Shawn suggests, pointing to the knit gloves I dropped on the ground. "Keep those on and put the new ones on top."

Following his suggestion, I layer the gloves. They fit well, and my draw improves significantly, while my fingers feel warmer. I continue with several more draw practices and try different shooting stances. After about a half hour, I feel considerably more confident. I've also had enough of the cold.

Shawn compliments my progress, and when I remove the gloves, he tells me they're mine to keep. His mom made a bulk purchase of several pairs a few years ago.

It should seem strange Opal bought gloves in bulk, but somehow it seems fitting. When I return to the shop, I find that most of the group has already left. The tables and chairs have been put away, and a few people sit around the woodstove in folding camp chairs, engaged in casual conversation.

"Thanks for your help." I acknowledge Shawn with a nod as I head toward the main house, where I'm certain to find Pearl and Opal.

"No problem. I'll give you a ride back to town whenever you're ready."

Inside the sprawling farmhouse, Opal and Pearl are seated at the kitchen table. The wood cookstove, which used to be a decorative centerpiece, now emits ample heat.

Opal found the stove at an estate sale, envisioning it as the perfect addition to their planned dream home. While she had plans for a modern kitchen, she wanted to retain the farmhouse charm and knew the antique stove would be a perfect fit. Instead of merely showcasing it, they had it connected for practical use, although they hadn't utilized it until the EMP struck.

Being situated several miles from town, they relied on propane for their kitchen range. Just a few weeks before the successive attacks leading to the EMP, they had taken advantage of the summer season's discounted prices and filled their large tank. While they could still use the cooktop, the oven required electricity to function.

During the summer, they cooked outside and even baked in a dutch oven. But once winter arrived, they were grateful for the wood cookstove. It not only provides a convenient means of cooking and baking but also warms the spacious kitchen.

In addition to the wood cookstove, they have a masonry heater in the great room, which effectively heats the rest of the house. Opal refers to it as a "rocket mass heater," explaining it was designed to burn less wood and primarily heat people rather than the entire space.

Our own woodstove in the small house Mother Pearl and I occupy was homemade and follows a similar concept, with a large rock bench connected to the firebox. The rock bench heats up and keeps the space warm while offering a toasty place to sit. Pearl hates it and says it's an ugly eyesore that takes up too much space in our already too-small house. She may hate the way it looks, but at least we're warm.

As I unbutton my coat, Pearl's gaze narrows.

I follow her line of sight, which rests upon my stomach.

She gasps, her hands instinctively moving to cover her mouth. Opal smiles, while I press my lips tightly together and stifle a sigh.

I guess the cat's out of the bag now. Somehow, when I was fiddling with my holster, my clothing twisted and no longer conceals the evidence of my growing belly.

"Merissa?" Pearl's voice is softer and more compassionate than usual.

I sigh. "I–I've been waiting to tell you. I wanted to make sure . . . " I clear my throat.

"Did Braedon know?"

Tears threaten to fill my eyes as my nose tingles. "He knew. We'd only found out a short time before he passed. We wanted to wait until after everything was, uh, safe to share. To celebrate." I attempt a smile, although I'm certain it falls short.

Pearl slowly rises from her seat, abandoning her cane as she shuffles toward me. "I'm so glad. It's such a . . . a blessing, Merissa. I never thought . . . I'm going to be a grandma." She envelops me in an uncharacteristically tender hug.

Chapter 4

Merissa

"I don't really mind working on Christmas. Do you, Merissa?" Jacquie Haley asks.

"It's fine." I shrug, changing out of my street clothes and into hospital garb.

Today is an extra shift for me. Instead of working as a medic, I'm shadowing nurse Jacquie. Captain Williams offered me the day off, but since Pearl is staying at Opal's ranch, it makes sense to work. Besides, I need to learn as much as I can now. When the baby comes, I'll have to take several weeks off, which will put me behind the other med students.

After the altercation with those guys a few days ago, I returned to the hospital for an exam. Wanting to keep my pregnancy private, Captain Williams called his wife to assist. I was truly grateful for his consideration.

After the exam, Williams approached fellow medic Jesse Talbot to create a schedule that allows everyone a partner when traveling to and from work. This morning, Jesse and I walked together. Despite the violence issues in Rapid City since the EMP, the hospital area has remained relatively safe.

Given the predominantly female staff in nursing, it has been a recurring concern, and Jesse has made it a point to coordinate with other nurses on their shifts. Since Jesse and I rarely work the same shift as medics, we usually can't walk together.

The schedule will help, and Captain Williams plans to discuss the possibility of additional escorts with the National Guard or the deputies. The hospital has faced attacks before, possibly by the same individuals responsible for the attack on the festival in Monument District and the explosions at the ration centers, so we already have security guards.

A new guardhouse at the main entrance screens everyone seeking treatment, and there's also a concealed guard with a good view of the back door and part of the grounds. Additionally, a third sentry patrols the area.

Williams wants to explore the idea of having the sentry serve as an escort to and from work. It seems a bit excessive to me. I understand Jesse meeting people and walking with them, as long as it's not out of his way. But taking someone away from protecting the hospital? I'm not sure about that.

The memory of that night makes my stomach churn. While I wasn't initially scared when they catcalled me, everything changed when they jumped out from behind the minivan. If Bowski hadn't been there, could I have escaped? Would I have been able to draw my pistol in time to stop them?

I'd like to think I could; I've done it before. But now I feel slower, sluggish, and out of practice. Yesterday's training at the ranch was immensely helpful. Toward the end of the session, Shawn offered to let me live fire a few times, even offering to replace my 9-millimeter ammo. I declined, concerned about the proximity of the gunshots to my baby. Even at a distance from Bowski and his big revolver, I believe my baby reacted. He or she was quite active afterward.

After the wagon ride home, I continued practicing by setting up targets inside the house for dry-fire training. Pearl won't be home until tomorrow, giving me the privacy to keep practicing. I might suggest we maintain this makeshift gun range so she can train as well.

She's skilled with her sidearm, but she hasn't done drills since we left Livingston. Considering what happened the other night with those two guys, I downplayed my fear so she wouldn't worry. Now I'm thinking I should use the incident to encourage her to train.

The tricky part with Pearl is that I'll have a better response if I can make it seem like it was her idea. I'll have to think about how to twist things. Maybe I'll leave the targets up and let her inquire about them. If I downplay it, she might come to her own realization of why it's a good idea.

Of course, now that she knows about the baby, her focus will be on it. Preoccupied with the upcoming event, she might not even notice the targets.

Jacquie continues talking, recalling how quiet last Christmas was at the hospital due to a massive snowstorm. She ended up staying on-site for several days since it was easier than trying to go home. Today's weather is mild, with a slight chill and a few inches of snow on the ground, but nothing excessive. There's no reason why people in need can't reach us.

One interesting aspect of working in a hospital is we never know what kind of illness or injury will walk through the door. Working with such a lean staff adds to the excitement.

Each shift consists of a single doctor, a nurse, a medic, and a janitor. As a med student, I'm an addition to the team. There are other support staff, such as laundry and kitchen, but they only drop off and pick up instead of working on-site due to space constraints in this building.

I must say, considering what it is, it's not bad. The day shift can get a bit chaotic, especially when the doctor goes out for rounds at the nearby care centers. Captain Williams, with his recent foot problem and partial amputation, takes his wife and often Leo Burnett, who acts as his aide, with him on rounds. The other doctors go alone unless they have a med student shadowing them.

Williams suggested having the sentry, who wants to arrange walking escorts for us, accompany the two female doctors on their rounds. Honestly, the whole thing sounds a bit complicated. Those two men were the only troublemakers I saw. One of them is now dead, and the other is in jail on the other side of the city. The issue may have resolved itself.

"Which doc is on with us today?" I ask as we step into the hallway.

"Chastity Morrow. She's running late."

"Running late?"

"Well, technically she still has a couple more minutes," Jacquie says, pursing her lips and bobbing her head. "Nettie is fit to be tied. She said she's tired of Chastity sliding in at the last minute. She's going to ask Captain Williams to do something about it."

I gesture my understanding and begin to move away, but Jacquie isn't finished. "You know, they used to be friends. Chastity was one of the rotating docs—you've been here long enough to know about them?"

"Yes, Dr. Bollinger was here not long ago as a rotating doctor."

She laughs. "Yeah. That was part of the issue between Nettie and Chastity." Jacquie waves her hand. "Oh, I know I'm supposed to call them Dr. Wolff and Dr. Morrow. But before the med school started and Geoff Landers caused all sorts of issues, they were Doc Nettie and

Chastity. We were much more casual. Still respectful, but casual. Besides, those girls are almost half my age."

Jacquie is not only a wonderful nurse but also a nice lady. Although, I find her to be a bit too gossipy. Braedon would've laughed at me since he used to say it's normal for workmates to want to talk and share things, like water cooler chat.

Gossip wasn't much of a thing in my previous job as a wildfire crew engine captain with the Forest Service. Sure, we talked about our weekends or whatever, but it wasn't the same as being in this hospital. Even in the Coast Guard, I managed to avoid water cooler talk, and I liked it that way. Less chitchat is what I'd prefer now.

Jacquie isn't done yet. "Did you hear about the day Chastity and Nettie almost went to blows? I wasn't there, but Rand Hendricks was. He said it was something. As tiny as she is, Nettie could've taken her. I'm sure of it."

I'm not surprised janitor Rand Hendricks was the one who told Jacquie. He might be even more of a gossip than she is. Rand is quite different from his quiet and studious wife Kerry. Kerry is a med student I often work with. She started here as a janitor, too, and still takes those shifts in addition to her schoolwork. Being so busy probably keeps us from having time to buzz about other people.

"That was the end of their friendship. Now they barely even acknowledge each other. I tell you, though— " Jacquie's words are interrupted by the ring of the back doorbell. We both turn toward the door.

Dr. Morrow stomps her feet on the rug. Upon seeing us staring, she lifts her chin in acknowledgment.

"Speak of the devil," Jacquie mutters and shakes her head. "Do you know what to do to get started?"

"I do," I say.

"Make sure you check every time you hear one of the doors so you can be prepared. You'll take the patient first and gather their history, then I'll review your work. As long as it's not an emergency of some sort. Just take the easy stuff for now. A quiet Christmas Day, that's the hope."

A few hours into our shift, Jacquie's hope is holding up. We've had a few patients come in, but nothing major. I've finished taking a history from a man with a low-grade fever and a cough, which didn't seem too serious. Jacquie reviews my work and advises me to let Dr. Morrow know he's ready to be seen.

The doctor is in the break room with Geoff Landers. He showed up around half an hour ago, saying he wanted to spend Christmas with her. They huddled together, laughing like teenagers. They've been in the break room since.

I'll admit, they seem like an odd pair. She's in her early thirties, and he's a decade younger. Despite the troubles between Chastity and Nettie, Chastity has always been kind to me. She seems to be a good doctor; although, I know she's a physician assistant and not a medical doctor. Nettie, on the other hand, is a med student who has been serving as a physician for the past eighteen months. Trial by fire.

Nettie, Chastity, and nurse Katie Burnett are the reason Captain Williams wanted to start the med school. He admired how they performed under pressure, especially Katie, who had limited medical experience before the EMP.

Her previous town provided on-the-job training. I must admit, I had no idea she wasn't a trained nurse until someone told me. She seems to be almost on par with Jacquie, who has a four-year degree and twenty years of experience.

The only difference is Katie sometimes appears uncertain, especially when I first arrived. Lately, she's gained more confidence, and I believe Williams involving her in the med school has contributed to her newfound assurance.

I knock on the break room door. There's a giggle from the other side, followed by a muffled, "Just a minute."

A couple of minutes later, Chastity pokes her disheveled head out. While I genuinely wish Chastity and Geoff happiness, if that's what they want, I'm not sure this is the appropriate place for such public displays.

"Yes?"

"I have a gentleman in exam three. Low-grade fever and a cough. Said he started feeling bad yesterday, and it's hit him hard."

She lets out a sigh. "Fine. I'll be there shortly."

Shortly transforms into a half-hour wait. Meanwhile, I attend to another patient who exhibits similar symptoms, potentially more severe. Dr. Morrow completes the examination of the first patient while I assist. As we step into the hallway, we encounter Jesse and Geoff in a tense face-off.

Dr. Morrow's voice becomes shrill as she demands to know what's going on.

Geoff steps closer to the larger Jesse. "Ask him." He pokes a finger at Jesse's chest.

Jesse visibly bristles but remains rooted in place.

Chastity turns her attention to Jesse. "I won't tolerate any trouble from you today."

"I'm not the one causing trouble, Dr. Morrow. Your boyfriend here needs to be reminded— "

"Enough, Jesse." Chastity claps her hands. "Geoff is here to see me. *Me*. If I'm forced to work on Christmas Day, I can spend it with whomever I wish. And believe me— " she looks from Jesse to me and over my shoulder, where Jacquie is likely eavesdropping " —it's Geoff I want to be with. Not anyone else. Now back down, or I'll make sure Williams knows about this."

She grabs Geoff's hand and leads him toward the call room we use for long shifts; he glances over his shoulder with a smirk.

Once they've entered the room and firmly shut the door, Jesse shakes his head. "There's going to be trouble with those two."

Chapter 5

Katie

"Sergeant Burnett and, um— " He raises his gaze from his clipboard with names of those invited to the Camp Rapid Christmas festivities.

"Also, Sergeant Burnett." I offer the young private a smile.

He tilts his head slightly. "Do you work at the hospital?"

"We both do." I gesture toward Leo, choosing not to mention he's on leave from his assignment as a medic while his surgically repaired arm heals. With his involvement in the medical school and as Captain Williams's aide, he spends almost as much time there as I do.

The young man practically beams. "I'm Elliot Tillman. I sprained my ankle in the explosion at the ration center. You took care of me. You also helped with my dad when he was hit by shrapnel from the blast."

I nod, recognizing him as the person I was attending to when Deputy Shaw and Pennington County Sheriff Melvin Cabal arrived to see Captain Williams. Elliot had mentioned something to Deputy Shaw about applying for the Citizen Patrol, but it seems he chose to join the National Guard instead, or perhaps they chose him.

"How's the ankle?"

"No problems. Only hurt a few days."

"And your dad?" I remember tending to him and his subsequent discharge to a care facility.

"Good. He's been moved to one of the low-level care centers. He only needs a little help and is walking fine now. He's here today. They let me bring him as my guest. Which is great, considering I've only been in the Guard for two weeks."

"I thought you were trying to get into the Citizen Patrol?"

His face briefly darkens before his youthful smile returns. "This seemed a better option. Especially considering . . . well, anyway. I see Sergeant Burnett on the list twice. I'm only checking people in for another half hour, so maybe I'll see you inside." His grin broadens, and he allows us through.

Private Tillman is the fourth person to check our names off the list. The layers of security started with individuals of higher rank and more advanced age than young Elliot. At the second checkpoint, we even had to surrender our sidearms and receive a numbered card to reclaim them upon leaving.

Because of the ongoing threat from the individuals responsible for the assault on the festival and the attacks on our ration centers and hospitals, everyone stays on high alert. Leo, who has visited the base multiple times for various reasons, said he's never had to relinquish his weapon during previous visits.

As we step into the large building, Leo nudges me with his hip. "What are you thinking about?"

"Not much. Just . . . I like it here. I know we planned to stay in our house after we take our oath, but maybe . . . "

"They do have housing for married people." His eyes gleam as he nods.

Neither of us mentions one of the main reasons I'm suggesting moving onto the base is how uncomfortable I feel in our house—the same house where RJ Kittleson and Bryson Young held me hostage.

Although I was released unharmed, they both died there. Even with new furniture and a thorough cleaning, it still feels like a place of death. I think it affects my dog too. He's become much more skittish and whinier since the break-in.

We spot several familiar faces and stop to talk as we navigate through the room. Like Elliot Tillman's dad, many family members are present for the meal. The atmosphere is undeniably festive, further enhanced by the presence of a large, decorated Christmas tree in the corner.

Leo introduces me to a man he knows from his men's Bible study group. "You work at the hospital?" Duncan Robson asks while shaking my hand. When I tell him I do, he motions to a tall woman standing next to him. "This is my wife, Robyn. I think she's going to be visiting you soon." He wears a broad smile and a glimmer of excitement in his eyes.

The woman blushes. "I think . . . " She clears her throat and steps closer, speaking softly. "I may be pregnant. One of my friends said I could go to the hospital and not the local midwife?"

"Absolutely. We have clinic every Tuesday, but if you have any concerns on non-clinic days, we're available any time."

"Good." She bobs her head up and down. "I know the timing is terrible. We want children, but now . . . " She motions around the room. "I wish things were more stable."

Her husband and mine engage in their own conversation. I maintain a smile as she shares her excitement about having a baby but also expresses concerns about the timing. Robyn acknowledges the childbirth risks in today's circumstances.

My thoughts flash back to Bonnie, who's been struggling with morning sickness and feeling terrible. Stella provided her with a new herbal remedy, suggesting that the ones from the midwife were probably fine but not at the quantities Bonnie was using. Stella repeatedly emphasized the importance of precise dosage instructions and closer monitoring for Bonnie. Addison's casual distribution of potent herbs for profit unquestionably raises additional concerns.

When there's a pause in the conversation, I ask, "Do you live on base?"

"No. In a house nearby. Duncan was in the Guard before everything fell apart. We did live on base in the early days of the collapse, but with the influx of new recruits, space is limited."

"Oh?" My heart sinks a little upon hearing this. Leo gave me the impression there was ample housing available for married couples.

"Duncan says you're joining the Guard? You and your husband were part of the United Volunteers, right?"

I acknowledge we were part of the Volunteers and briefly discuss how we ended up here. I don't delve into the details of my initial doubts about joining the Guard but mention how much we love the Black Hills and the encouraging developments at the hospital and medical school. I focus on the positive aspects, avoiding any mention of workplace dramas involving Geoff Landers, Chastity Morrow, or others.

Robyn lowers her voice and leans in. "Did you hear about the troubles in Billings, Montana?"

I shake my head, curious about the issues she mentioned.

Leo gestures to the beverage table. "Want to get a drink? I'm parched."

I agree, feeling thirsty myself, and tell Robyn I'll see her soon. At the drink table, I take a deep breath, surprised by the aroma. "Hot apple cider? With cinnamon?"

Leo smiles. "They've been saving the cinnamon. I heard this is the last of it unless they find some in one of their salvage trips." Even at this stage of the apocalypse, the Guard still sends out teams, combining soldiers and assigned civilians, to recover useful items from houses, buildings, and warehouses.

"Sergeant Burnett." Lieutenant Paul nods at me, acknowledging my presence. Then he turns to Leo, "Burnett. Good to see you both. How's the cider?"

"Amazing, sir," I respond, while Leo expresses his gratitude for the invitation to the Christmas feast. I've always admired how Leo maintains a professional demeanor with Lieutenant Paul, even in social situations. He never refers to him by his first name, always using his rank or last name, even in our private conversations at home.

Paul remarks on the great turnout and the weather, noting people were willing to make the walk for a meal and socialize even in challenging conditions.

Lieutenant Paul asks Leo how the med school's going before asking me about my work schedule. I let him know I had a shift last night but am off today. He motions toward Leo's slinged arm. "When's the arm doc coming around again?"

"We're going to him. After the new year."

"I'm hoping he'll give a good report," Leo says as he rubs his broken arm. "Captain Williams checked it a few days ago and thinks it looks okay."

"Great." Paul acknowledges. "Once he releases you, we're ready to get you on our official roster." He turns toward me. "I know we planned on both of you taking your oath after the new year. We're waiting until Leo is cleared. You have the option of waiting with him if you'd like."

"Or I could go ahead as planned?" I glance at Leo, who gives me a smile and a single dip of his chin.

"Absolutely. Things won't change much for you. You'll still work at the hospital under Captain Williams as you do now under the Volunteer Unit. Um, well, the only remaining Volunteers in South Dakota as far as I know." Paul chuckles lightly. "The only new thing is putting in time for drills and if something comes up where we need a medic on a mission."

"You'd take me out as a medic?"

"You're already trained, right? With the Volunteers and before when you lived in Bakerville?"

I take a deep breath and nod. "When do you need my decision?"

"After Leo sees the bone doc?" he suggests. "Maybe we'll know more about his enlistment too?"

"We should know more then, sir," Leo adds. "What do you think, Katie?"

"Sure. Yes. I, uh . . . I think that sounds good, um, sir," I respond, my words stumbling slightly.

Paul lifts his chin. "Are you still having second thoughts?"

I shake my head. "No. It was difficult for me at first, knowing we'd be here for eight more years. But . . . " I glance around the room and gesture with my arm. "This is starting to feel like home. Rapid City. The Black Hills. It's amazing here. I'll still miss my family—I *do* miss my family."

My eyes well up with tears. If all went as planned, my sister Sarah got married last night. I now have a new brother-in-law and a new niece and nephew.

Paul points to a table against the wall. "Did you hear there's mail? I think you have an envelope."

My eyes widen in excitement. "Mail? How'd it get here? With winter, I mean."

"I believe it's a Christmas blessing," Paul responds with a smile. "I'll let you grab it. See you in the mess hall."

Leo and I quickly make our way to the table where the envelopes are kept. The soldier there observes the insignias on our jacket collars but notices we're not in the proper attire, wearing our Volunteer uniforms instead. She raises an eyebrow and asks if she can assist us.

Clearing my throat, I introduce myself. "I'm Sergeant Katie Burnett, United Volunteers. Lieutenant Paul said there might be an envelope for me?"

She lifts her chin. "Ah. I've heard about you." She lifts her chin toward Leo. "And you, too, if you're the other Sergeant Burnett with the Volunteers."

"Yes." Leo nods.

She turns to the boxes lined up on a table behind her, raising her voice slightly to be heard. "I didn't realize you'd be here today. Your envelopes are in the items to be delivered to the civilians tomorrow, though I did hear we're going to try to get them out today, after the main festivities. You know, like a Christmas gift? Let's see . . . here we go. One for Leo Burnett and three for Katie Burnett."

She turns with the envelopes in her hand—one a large manilla and the others white business sized. "Merry Christmas." She gives us a nod as she hands one of the white envelopes to Leo and the rest to me.

I hold the envelopes close to my chest, my heart pounding with excitement. Leo and I express our gratitude and quickly find a quiet corner.

In our semiprivate space, Leo pulls me close. "What an amazing Christmas gift. Letters from home. I never thought . . . " His voice catches. "Mine's from Jake. What about yours?"

"The big one is from Jake but probably has stuff from everyone. And there's one from Belinda and one from Kelley." Belinda and Kelley were my mentors at our small Bakerville clinic. They taught me everything I know about nursing and medicine.

"Do you want to open them now?" Leo asks.

I bite my lip and slowly shake my head. "Can we save them for home? What if I start crying? I wouldn't want that. You know, with this soon to be my new job. I can't have the other recruits see me crying."

"Right." Leo drops a kiss on my nose. "Can't have the sergeant in tears. Want to put everything in my pack? Then we'll go back to enjoying the party."

With the envelopes safely stowed away, Leo scans our surroundings before pulling me into another embrace. "Merry Christmas, Katie. I know this year hasn't been the easiest for us—leaving your family, the difficulties we faced as Volunteers when we arrived, and my own struggles with adjusting to this life. You know, me pretty much being a major jerk."

I can't help but giggle at his self-deprecating remark.

He takes a step back and looks into my eyes. "I'm truly sorry for being so difficult. I know you told Lieutenant Paul you're excited about joining the Guard."

I furrow my brow playfully. "Did I say excited?"

"Not exactly, but you implied it. You don't have to do it. I meant what I said before. We can fulfill our Volunteer obligation and go home."

I shake my head. "I may not have told him I was excited, but I do love our life here. We're doing something important . . . the hospital, the school."

"We can continue working at the hospital without joining the Guard. Finish our year and return to being civilians. Stay here, doing what we do, without any further commitment. Go home to Wyoming when it suits us."

"Is that what you want?"

He sighs. "It might be what I want, or it might be the only option I have. There's a chance my arm won't heal properly. If Bollinger doesn't clear me, I won't be able to join the Guard."

I knew this was a possibility, but I didn't realize it concerned Leo.

He quickly adds, "I don't want my ability to join the Guard to influence your decision. If you want to take the oath, I'm fully supportive. We shouldn't wait to see what happens with me. Your decision should be independent of mine." He nods several times to emphasize his point.

I rise on my toes and kiss him. "Thank you, Leo. It looks like people are moving to the other room—the mess hall? I'm starving. Let's save this discussion for another time. After we've read our letters from home and had a chance to pray over it."

"Sounds like a plan. Let's enjoy our Christmas feast."

Chapter 6

Katie

Major General Truss stands immobile at the front of the room, neither raising his hands nor making any gesture to grab attention. Nonetheless, the room falls silent within a minute.

His lips twitch and reveal a hint of a smile. He runs his fingers across his mustache and then his neatly groomed beard. Expressing gratitude for everyone's presence despite the weather, he offers a brief greeting to commence the Christmas dinner.

Sweeping his gaze across the room, he establishes eye contact with the assembled individuals. "Before we proceed, let's address the elephant in the room. Many of you have heard the rumors surrounding the events in Billings, Montana."

I glance at my husband. Robyn mentioned trouble in Billings, but Leo interrupted before she could give me the details.

Leo shrugs and shakes his head, indicating he hasn't heard anything either.

"Allow me to provide clarity amidst these rumors," General Truss continues. "It is indeed true there was an insurrection, or rather, an unsuccessful coup d'état."

A knot forms in my throat as I suppress the rising emotions. Billings is about an hour or so away from Bakerville, Wyoming, where my remaining family resides. Would the letter have information about this trouble?

Leo places his hand on my leg and leans closer. "I'm sure they're fine."

I give a quick nod and refocus on the general's words.

"We are currently gathering information, as the details of the incident are being transmitted through coded radio messages. You may have noticed the heightened security measures upon arriving for today's festivities. While we do not believe rebels have infiltrated our base, we are taking necessary precautions. Rest assured, if we discover any rebels among us, swift action will be taken."

His gaze once again scans the room. This time there's a hardness in his eyes, an edge. Relaxing his stance, he lowers his shoulders. "Now, let's get on with our Christmas celebration. Chaplain, will you offer a blessing for the food?"

Following the blessing, officers and their guests form a line on one side of the room, while enlisted personnel and their guests line up on the other. This gathering truly exemplifies a family event, with attendees of all ages, from infants to the elderly.

Leo and I join the enlisted line, walking behind his friend Duncan. Duncan's wife, Robyn, whispers about the troubling situation in Billings and wonders if the recent attacks we've experienced here might be linked to an insurrection attempt.

I shake my head. "I have no idea. I hope they catch whoever's doing it. Do we know exactly what happened in Billings?"

Duncan shrugs, and Leo shakes his head. "This is the first I've heard of it, but it does make sense with all the meetings and notes Williams has had lately. The general's announcement leaves me with more questions than answers." Leo rubs his recently repaired arm.

"Maybe now that it's out in the open, can you ask Captain Williams?" I suggest.

Leo tilts his head, contemplating the idea. "Maybe."

Glancing across the room, I spot Captain Williams seated at his table.

Upon reaching the serving line, I'm astonished by the abundance and variety of food. Witnessing the preparations of setting things up, the sight and aroma had already caused my stomach to rumble. The options on our side of the room, the enlisted section, appear no different from those in the officers' line; it's merely a logistical measure to expedite the process. Naturally, the number of enlisted personnel and their guests far surpasses that of the officers.

As the officers' line begins to slow down, I notice the general's aide redirecting people from the end of our line to the other side. A warm feeling washes over me.

I must admit, I hadn't been particularly enthused about joining the National Guard. Although South Dakota is geographically adjacent to Wyoming, my family resides on the western side of the state, east of Yellowstone National Park. The four-hundred-mile distance was insignificant when cars were operational, but now, with most travel occurring by bicycle, horseback, or on foot, the distance is almost insurmountable.

Gone are the long weekends spent visiting family. Nowadays, people only travel when absolutely necessary. Transportation itself presents a challenge, not to mention the risks posed by bandits and thieves. As much as I yearn to see my family, it won't happen any time soon.

The fact we're receiving mail today is truly surprising. I had assumed we wouldn't receive any letters until spring when travel becomes easier. My gaze drifts to our chairs and Leo's backpack, where the envelopes are safely tucked away. The letters will serve as a meaningful addition to the modest Christmas gift I managed to find for my husband.

As Leo and I settle back into our seats, a commotion erupts at the door. From my position, I can't see who's causing the disturbance, but a voice rings out, "Red Group, fall back to designated positions. Blue Group, standby."

Utensils clatter on tables, and chairs scrape as two dozen individuals swiftly exit the room. I recognize a few faces, including Duncan and Elliot. The general and his aide also join the departing group. One of the majors announces the base is under lockdown, instructing us to remain in the room.

The murmurs intensify throughout the room, mingling with the question in my own mind. "What's happening?"

Leo scoots his chair back and perches on the edge. Shaking his head, he replies, "Not sure."

Murmurs and quiet voices fill the room, but there is no hysteria or loud talk as we await further information. It doesn't take long, only about five minutes by my watch, before the general strides back in.

He raises his hands. "Thank you for your patience. All is well. Please resume your meal."

Despite his reassurance, it takes at least another ten minutes before the bulk of the people who left as part of Red Group and Blue Group return. Not everyone comes back, including Leo's friend Duncan.

I catch his wife's eye, and she shrugs, giving me a slight smile before taking a bite of her food. Across the table, a woman who was part of Red Group sits a few seats down. Her mother asks what happened.

The younger woman smiles lightly. "False alarm. This looks delicious. You shouldn't have waited for me. Your meal's cold."

"So is yours, dear. It's fine."

Like most others in the room, Leo and I also stopped eating when things fell apart. Even cold, the meal is still delicious. We were offered a variety of wild game, turkey, and beef roast. There are turnips, potatoes, and pumpkins, along with sautéed apples topped with cream for dessert. It's more food and a much richer meal than I've had in months.

I whisper to Leo, "Do you think they eat like this all the time?"

"They don't. They're on rations like us, except they don't use the ration chips. They're pretty much given what they need."

"Hmm. And us? Once we're sworn in and officially part of the National Guard, will we switch to their system? Even if we live off base?"

"It's different. Probably something like what Captain Williams has. He and his wife are given specialty ration chips redeemable on base at the commissary for nonfood goods and supplies. For food, they receive some stuff on base and other things off base. Honestly, I'm not exactly sure how it'll work for us."

I nod several times. "I heard there really isn't a lot of housing for married couples on base."

"Not a lot, but some. When it's closer to time, if you do decide you want to go through with the enlistment, we can weigh our options. I know staying in the house is hard for you."

Blinking several times, I try to control the emotions welling up inside me. "It is hard. Even with everything being fixed up and the new furniture, it still reminds me of how they died there." I don't mention the nightmares I still have from when they took me hostage. He knows. I've woken both of us up several times.

"We have options. We'll talk everything through and pray about it so we feel like we're following God's lead. I know . . . " His Adam's apple bobs a few times. "I know I was pretty awful about this. The way I kind of railroaded you into joining the Guard. I thought it was what was best for us, but I didn't take the time to give you all the details and make sure it was what you really wanted. And I certainly didn't take it to God. That's changing. We're going to take it slow, see what Dr. Bollinger says about my wrist, and then make the right decision for both of us. I love you, Katrina Burnett. I'm going to do right by you. By you and God."

I want to kiss him, to express how much I agree and appreciate his words. We've had a few rough months. His fall from the horse sent him into a depression, and during that time, he wasn't the Leo I knew, the man I loved and married. He's better now, despite the setback of his wrist not healing properly and needing surgery. We're starting to feel like a team again, and we're bringing God back into our lives and our marriage.

Since kissing isn't something we do in public, I touch his arm. "I ate so much. I'm almost looking forward to the walk home."

"It looks like things are wrapping up." He motions toward the people standing around the tables, engaged in conversation, slowly making their way toward the coats and winter gear. Although our time with the National Guard has been enjoyable, and we've felt welcomed as guests, I'm ready to go home. Ready to open our letters and enjoy the rest of our Christmas together.

Leo and I leave the room, exchanging words with people we know along the way. "Sergeant Burnett," Private Elliot Tillman greets me cheerfully before nodding at Leo. "This is my dad. Did you meet him when he was in your hospital?"

I turn to the older man, probably in his late forties but appearing much older. "I believe I did. How are you, Mr. Tillman?"

"Feeling much better. I'm in one of the care centers where we don't need much help. We call it a halfway house since we're halfway between broken and fixed. Get it? *Halfway* house." He chuckles at his own joke.

"Elliot here decided to join the National Guard." He rests a hand on his son's shoulder. "I'm proud of him."

"The sergeants are the two who are with the United Volunteers," Elliot says. "Remember me mentioning them?"

"I remember hearing about the controversy." Mr. Tillman raises his eyebrows. "Seems to me we can use all the help we can get. Sometimes, I don't know exactly what that governor of ours is thinking." He shakes his head. "Sure wouldn't get my vote—if we ever have elections again, that is."

"My dad used to be on the Rapid City Planning Commission. He met the governor a few times in that capacity."

I nod. "You're an architect, right?"

Mr. Tillman smiles. "I am. And if I remember correctly, you're an artist in addition to being a nurse. We discussed drawing, right?"

"Yes, we did. Have the doctors said when you'll be released to work again?"

He snorts. "Well, you know I'm no longer an architect, but rather on the water crew. It's still too physical for me. That's one reason Elliot joined the Guard, so we can live on base. I'll be able to do other work here, something within my abilities. He's in the dorms right now. But hopefully, when I'm well enough, they'll have something for us."

Leo and I spend a few more minutes with the Tillmans before excusing ourselves. We see Robyn Robson getting her coat on. I let Leo know I'm going to tell her goodbye.

She mentions Duncan is still working, so she's heading home. I ask if she wants to walk together, but she's already walking with another friend, who also lives off base, and whose husband was called to work. She hugs me goodbye and says she'll see me soon.

I turn back to Leo, who's now waiting with Captain Williams and his wife Alice.

"Well, Sergeants, did you get enough to eat?" Williams asks, leaning heavily on his crutches.

"Yes, sir." Leo nods. "It was fabulous."

"Indeed. They surely did put on a feast. Alice and I are ready to leave. Care to walk with us?"

"Thank you, sir," Leo and I say in unison.

Although the captain is adept at using crutches indoors, the ice and snow outside pose a challenge. His wife retrieves his outdoor wheelchair, equipped with tiny skis on the front. Leo offers to push, but I give him a look and point to his arm. His cheeks turn crimson as he nods.

Alice Williams chuckles, saying she's always wanted to push her husband around and finally has the chance.

Once outside the gates of Camp Rapid, Williams says, "I suspect you have questions about the trouble in Billings. It's a terrible thing, but something you should know about—something that could happen here."

Chapter 7

Katie

"Here, sir?" Leo gestures back toward the gates of Camp Rapid.

"Yes, here or at Ellsworth," Williams replies, tilting his chin eastward, indicating Ellsworth Air Force Base about fifteen miles away. "That's part of the trouble we had today."

"What did happen today?" I ask.

Williams shakes his head. "Today was a false alarm. A couple of men who'd had a little too much Christmas cheer decided to harass the guard."

I scrunch my face. "Injuries?"

Williams waves his gloved hand dismissively. "No, no. They were apprehended without incident. They're now in the holding area, sleeping it off—or at least that's what I've heard. Apparently, they're more into singing and carrying on rather than sleeping. But either way, they're in the holding room."

The holding room serves as our district's jail. I've been there before, not as a prisoner, but to identify individuals involved in a burglary ring. "So, there's no trouble?"

"Doesn't seem so. Just a couple of newcomers to the area that are causing a stir. Everyone's on edge due to the problems in Billings and the recent explosions. Of course, you both are well aware of those events. You've been in the thick of it."

I release a deep breath. Indeed, we have been in the thick of it. First, we were at the main hospital in the Monument District for Leo's arm examination. That evening, the community festival we attended was attacked, resulting in numerous casualties. A few days later, while picking up ration chips, the ration center exploded and claimed many lives.

Then, as Leo was recovering from wrist surgery and coming out of anesthesia, our hospital went into lockdown. While the attack on our facility was thwarted and the attackers killed, two other hospitals suffered damage along with deaths and injuries. We're aware of the local explosions, but we have no information about what's happening in Billings.

"I'll admit, I'm a little out of the loop, sir," Leo acknowledges. "Until today, Katie and I hadn't heard of any issues in Billings."

"Well, that's surprising. General Truss believed the news had spread among the civilians. His aide mentioned hearing talk from one of the food delivery personnel. Thought maybe Cabal might have said something, leading to the information getting out."

Melvin Cabal, the Sheriff of Pennington County, holds his position through appointment, having assumed it shortly after the EMP when the actual sheriff and undersheriff perished. Captain Williams has known Cabal for decades and doesn't seem to think much of him.

"Anyway," Williams continues, "some of the regular Army personnel, along with the new Volunteer Units stationed in Billings attempted to overthrow the leadership there. Their cover story was they didn't like the way things were being handled and felt people were being treated as slaves, had insufficient food, were overworked, and so on. I suspect there's some truth to that. They have much the same setup in Billings as we have here. Everyone's put on work crews, given rations, and expected to contribute. But they gained a lot of sympathy among the lower ranks and the Volunteers."

I don't appreciate Williams emphasizing the Volunteers' involvement in the insurrection.

Leo seems to share my sentiment. "Who led the insurrection? The Volunteers or the regular Army?"

"Neither. We believe the leader was a former government employee, possibly from the CIA or some other shadow agency. The rumors we're hearing . . . " Williams trails off and shakes his head. "The rumors are almost unbelievable. We only have basic information. It's all transmitted over secure radio channels, using a constantly changing code. So, some of what we think we're receiving may not even be accurate."

"That's quite challenging, sir," Leo says. "Is that the reason for increased security today?"

"Yes, precisely. We've done our best to vet our personnel, but we can't be entirely certain. And what better opportunity to strike at the National Guard than when so many are gathered together? Did you notice we were a bit shorthanded today?"

"Shorthanded?" I furrow my brow, causing my stocking cap to slip lower on my forehead. I remove it momentarily to readjust, immediately feeling the cold blast on my ears.

Williams nods. "We had designated survivors. It's part of our contingency plan in case our vetting and security measures fail."

I shake my head, unfamiliar with the identities of most individuals at Camp Rapid. Aside from a few enlisted guards at the hospital, my interactions are limited to Captain Williams and Lieutenant David Paul, Leo's friend who serves as our liaison to the Guard. He played a crucial role in assisting us in being accepted into the Guard, along with other members of the Volunteer Unit who opted to remain in the Black Hills.

There was a time when I wished Leo and I had stayed in the Volunteer Unit, left Rapid City, and fulfilled our one-year commitment elsewhere. If we had, Leo wouldn't have been on the horse when it spooked. We would've been stationed somewhere along the demarcation line, aiding refugees in finding safe homes and providing them with medical treatment.

However, now that our marriage has improved, I've come to appreciate our current situation. The hospital is a decent workplace, and teaching has had a positive impact on Leo's well-being, alleviating the depression caused by his injury and the enforced period of rest. Plus, we have our little dog, a true blessing stemming from an awful situation.

"Probably smart, sir," Leo agrees as we arrive at the corner where the Williamses live. "While I'd like to think something like what happened in Billings couldn't happen here, I think we all know anything can happen anywhere. Speaking of, has there been any news about the lead Katie passed on regarding the preacher and his followers?"

"The preacher that Bryson Young suggested may be responsible for the bombings? As far as I know, neither the preacher nor any of his followers have been found. Sheriff Cabal hasn't made any effort to locate them. The Guard has been preoccupied with the Billings situation and fortifying the base, but that'll likely change soon. You're absolutely right, Burnett. We're in a different world. However, I didn't tell you the most significant part about what happened in Billings. Brace yourself for this one."

Leo and I exchange a glance, anticipating what could be worse than an attempted coup. I know about things like this since something similar occurred in Bakerville last winter.

"What happened?" I ask.

"The CIA guy I was telling you about? He said this entire ordeal was orchestrated by a shadow government."

"The coup in Billings?"

"Not the coup . . . the attacks. From the plane crashes to the nukes—all an inside job."

My previously content stomach turns sour. An inside job? Could someone within our own government truly be responsible for putting us in this predicament? Leo had mentioned it before, one of his many conspiracy theories. But I never thought it could be real. But now, with Captain Williams also stating it, could it actually be true?

Leo shakes his head. "Sure, there were talks about conspiracy theories, but I don't think many people believed it to be true."

"Humph. You know what the difference is between a conspiracy theory and the truth?" Williams waggles his eyebrows. "About three months."

His wife chuckles and pats his shoulder. "Oh, Chris. You and your jokes."

I offer a polite laugh and Leo joins in. "Good one, sir."

Williams shifts his gaze toward me. "No shift tonight, Sergeant?"

"No, sir. Someone was kind enough to give me Christmas off to spend with my husband."

"You're welcome. I'm on duty at 1800, relieving Dr. Morrow. Seems I wasn't as kind to myself as I was to my staff. Alice doesn't mind, do you, dear?"

"It's not the first Christmas you've worked, and it likely won't be the last."

"Enjoy your evening, Sergeants. And Leo, let's meet tomorrow around 1500 hours. I want to go over the student evaluations you're working on so we can be ready when classes begin again on Monday. We've got a lot of ground to cover to get them all up to snuff for treating patients."

"Yes, sir. I'll see you tomorrow."

We wait as Alice Williams wheels her husband the short distance to their house. A ramp has been set up to assist her in reaching the front door. Once they're on the porch, she gives a slight wave to indicate everything is fine. I wave back before we continue our walk home.

All of us who work at the Guard District Hospital reside within a few blocks. It helps with personnel retrieval during emergencies, given the limited communication options. We do use handheld radios, but only those on call take them home since we have a limited number and limited charging capabilities. Since I'm off today and not on call, I don't have one.

However, tomorrow, I'll be on day shift from 0600 to 1800, followed by on-call duty from 1800 to 0600 the next day, until I resume my shift. During my on-call hours, I'll have the radio with me.

It's a decent schedule, but it can be challenging with our limited staff. While we all work hard, I'm grateful I'm not a janitor. They not only keep things clean and sanitary while tending to multiple woodstoves, but also assist the medics as orderlies and even help the nurses and doctors when needed.

As we approach the hospital, Leo points at the guard station. "It's empty?"

A sinking feeling washes over me. Since the recent attempted attack on our hospital, we always have a guard on duty. Where is the guard now?

Chapter 8

Katie

I scan the area, my gaze resting on the hospital entrance. Angry voices carry across the icy pavement. "Look."

Leo tilts his head and squints his eyes. "Is that Jesse and Landers?"

"Chastity too. And is Josiah Talbot with them? It's hard to tell with all the winter gear." While one man is bundled against the cold, the other three lack outerwear. Jesse and Chastity are even wearing thin scrubs, possibly with a few base layers underneath but clearly unprepared for this well-below-freezing weather. Geoff Landers appears slightly warmer, donning heavy twill painter's pants and a flannel shirt.

"It doesn't look good." Leo takes a decisive stride toward the hospital.

I reach out and grasp his arm. "Be careful."

He nods and continues forward.

I scurry behind him, my significantly shorter legs requiring almost two steps for every one of his.

As we approach the group, Leo calls out, "Hey, guys. What's up?"

Landers shoots Leo a glance. "None of your business, Burnett. Move along."

"Jesse. Josiah." Leo greets the Talbot brothers. Jesse, standing rigidly with clenched fists a few feet in front of Landers, relaxes his shoulders.

"Hey, Leo." Though he addresses Leo, Jesse keeps his eyes fixed on Landers.

Leo turns to Chastity. "Dr. Morrow, you seem cold."

With her hand resting on Landers's shoulder, she gives Leo a dirty look as she shivers.

Leo takes a step closer to the group. "Everything okay?"

"Not sure," Josiah replies. "Seems there's a little issue."

"Humph," Chastity scoffs. "I should let Geoff settle it. He can handle an old man like Jesse any day."

Jesse tenses his back, his fists opening and closing.

Chastity removes her hand from Landers's shoulder and points at me. "Why don't you run off and tell Captain Williams? Collect your brownie points like a good little soldier."

Her words strike me like a slap across the face. I fight back my emotions. "Dr. Morrow, have I done something wrong? Have I offended you in some way?"

"Your goody-two-shoes act is utterly offensive. I'm starting to think Eugene Newsome was right about you. Your skills are mediocre at best, but you've managed to deceive Williams and Nettie. Not that it's a great accomplishment. Neither of them are particularly intelligent nor perceptive. It's obvious— "

"Chastity," Landers interjects in a low warning tone.

Chastity waves him off. "It's not like it's a big secret. Besides, it makes sense. As soon as— "

"Are you planning a coup, like they did in Billings?" Josiah interrupts.

"A coup? Hardly." She leans back on her heels. "Do you honestly think it's wise to have the military in control of our hospitals? Apart from Williams, there are only three or four doctors in all the districts who are current or former military. The rest of us are civilians. *Civilians.* Why should we be under their control?"

"Because the governor said so, that's why." Josiah dismisses her with a wave of his hand. "Look, you three need to get it together. Geoff, you're not even on shift, are you? Go home."

"You don't get to tell him what to do." Chastity steps forward. "He's visiting *me*. If I have to work on Christmas instead of getting the day off— " she glares at me " —I can have anyone here I want."

"Not if they're causing trouble." Josiah shakes his head. "Remember, the Citizen Patrol and the National Guard are responsible for maintaining hospital security, both inside and out." He jabs a finger in Landers's direction. "If someone on the inside is causing trouble, they're out."

"You don't need to fight my battles, little brother." Jesse places a hand on Josiah's shoulder.

Landers snorts. "It's not like you can fight your own. Weren't we supposed to step outside and settle this like men?"

"Is that why your girlfriend followed you out?"

Landers lunges at Jesse, who deftly sidesteps him, causing Landers to slip on the slick ice. He lets out a yelp.

Chastity rushes to his side. "Now look what you've done! You're . . . you're fired, Jesse Talbot! Clear out your locker and leave."

Jesse's face turns crimson, while Josiah bursts into laughter. "Fired? That's rich. Did we not just discuss this hospital is under the purview of the National Guard? I'm pretty sure you're not part of the hierarchy, which means you don't have the power to fire anyone. But you know who does? *Captain Williams.* Katie isn't the one who'll report this situation to the captain. It'll be detailed in my report. Deputy Shaw will ensure the captain is aware. They won't let it slide."

Landers awkwardly rises to his feet. His hand fumbles toward his sidearm.

Josiah changes his stance. His rifle, which is slung across his front, subtly shifts into the ready position. In a nearly trance-like state, my own hand instinctively moves toward the grip of my concealed carry pistol.

"Easy there, sport." Josiah raises his chin at Landers. "Let's not do something that can't be undone."

"Geoff," Chastity squeals.

Landers spreads his hands out to his sides. "I wasn't . . . " He shakes his head and appears remorseful, but then he straightens and lifts his chin defiantly. "You all think you're so special, so smart. Soon, you'll see you aren't as smart as you think."

Chastity places a hand on his arm. "Let's go back inside and have our Christmas snack." She shoots Jesse a look. "Stay out of my way, Talbot."

As they walk away, Landers almost slips on a patch of ice but manages to regain his footing at the last minute. We remain silent until the door closes and the ringing of the entry bell fades.

"What was that all about, bro?" Josiah asks Jesse.

Jesse clicks his tongue. "I have no idea. I mean, it wasn't really anything. He made a snide remark, nothing new. I warned him to stop, and the next thing I knew, he mentioned taking it outside. I dismissed him, but he kept pushing." Jesse lets out a hollow laugh. "I guess I forgot my manners for a minute and thought I'd teach him a quick lesson."

"Well, the days of 'stepping outside' to settle things are over. Especially with someone like Landers. It's clear he won't fight fair," Josiah remarks.

I let out a noisy breath. "I can't believe he reached for his gun."

"Humph. He may have gone for it, but his skills aren't where they should be," Leo says. "He needs some draw training."

I snicker. "I guess he didn't have a mom who repeatedly said, 'Practice your draw or don't carry.'" A bittersweet feeling washes over me as my mom's voice fills my mind.

She used to say this phrase, not only after the EMP plunged us into an apocalyptic world but even before, when she first started carrying concealed. My mom and Jake would spend time at the range every week, combining draw practice with target practice. After the EMP, weapons practice became an almost daily part of our lives. We didn't engage in a lot of live firing, but we did dry-fire practice, draw practice, and drills.

"Well, I'm glad he's weak on the draw, at least for our purposes tonight," Josiah says, before turning to Leo and me. "How was the shindig?"

Leo lifts a shoulder, while I answer, "It was fun. Everyone was great."

"Heard you had a little excitement."

Leo chuckles. "News sure travels fast around here." He looks at me. "About some things."

"The radio, man." Josiah motions to his shirt collar. "They put us on alert."

"What do you know about Billings, Montana?" Leo asks.

Josiah clears his throat. "Um . . . what do *you* know about Billings?"

"There was some kind of attempted coup? The general was vague, but he made it sound like we should've already heard something. We're out of the loop. Captain Williams told us a bit more, but it's still rather confusing."

Josiah nods as Jesse asks, "A coup in Billings? I'm out of the loop too."

"We were briefed, but not until after the National Guard did their own sweep."

"Sweep?" I ask.

"Personnel check. Not too easy in today's world without computers, and who knows how accurate it really was. But they seem confident. Not confident enough they didn't have us on backup though." He motions to Leo's hip. "They let you keep your gun for the party?"

"Nope. Had to check them."

"Yep. Heard they'd be doing that."

"What else did you hear?" Jesse asks with a shiver.

Josiah tilts his head. "The thing in Billings involved regular military, an Army major, Volunteers, and some other people. The orchestrators were tried and executed for treason. Most of them, anyway. There were a few deals made, lives spared in exchange for information. Rumor is, it's not only Billings. It's widespread. They even masterminded the original attacks, along with the nuclear strikes."

The sick feeling I experienced earlier when Williams mentioned the inside job returns.

Jesse pales. "Rumor?"

"Well . . . " Josiah lifts a shoulder. "I didn't hear the radio broadcasts or read the transcripts. Shaw tells us what he thinks we need to know. He said there's a report stating someone involved in the coup was bragging about these actions being necessary to clean up the country. But that guy ended up dead, so he couldn't be interrogated. It's officially all hearsay from the person he told. Shaw said it sounds legitimate, though. The guy was some kind of superspy, and he shared the information with other spies, thinking they might be part of a different operating cell within the coup."

My brow crinkles. Although Captain Williams mentioned the orchestrator was affiliated with the CIA or something, he didn't mention other spies in Billings. The whole thing sounds a little strange, especially when considering some of the people back home in Bakerville, less than a hundred miles from Billings.

We didn't know until after the EMP, but one of my mom's close friends, Doris, used to work for the government. She'd joke about her government job before the world fell apart, saying things like if she told you what she really did, she'd have to kill you. Then she'd laugh and claim she was merely a paper pusher. It turns out the "have to kill you" joke was closer to reality than we thought.

We discovered exactly how willing she was to kill when a group of refugees arrived in our town. Doris recognized one of the women and pulled out her pistol. It turned out both women had worked together on a failed spy mission. It was a tense few minutes until we sorted out why the woman, Kimba Hoffmann, along with her husband and their children, happened to show up in Bakerville.

The Hoffmanns insisted it was mere coincidence. They didn't know Doris lived there, and they were not on any mission. They claimed to be retired from official operations and had their own consulting firm in Denver before the attacks forced them out of the city. They were only briefly stopping in Bakerville on their way to Bozeman, Montana, to seek refuge with some friends.

Eventually, Doris came to trust the Hoffmanns. More than trust. They became like family. The Hoffmanns spent most of the winter in our town, leaving for Montana last March as spring approached. Could they be involved in the insurrection?

"So . . . are you guys good here?" Leo asks.

Jesse sighs. "I'm feeling a little foolish for egging Landers on. Chastity was right about me being the old man."

The way Jesse says it makes me smile. Although he is older than Leo and me, he's only in his midthirties. As a former military member, he has kept himself in shape. I'm certain that in hand-to-hand combat, he'd defeat Landers any day.

Landers is young, only twenty, and conceited. He was a first-year student at Black Hills State University in nearby Spearfish, majoring in biology before everything fell apart. He claimed he intended to pursue a premed path.

After the collapse, he joined many different work crews but couldn't find a good fit. That's pretty common; many people switch from one crew to another. Most of the crews involve manual labor, something most of us weren't accustomed to in our previous world.

Now, survival requires hard work. Leo and I have it relatively easy with being part of the medical team. We don't have to chop our own firewood or carry our own water. While we do cook most of our meals on the woodstove in our house, we also receive more precooked meals than most people.

When the opportunity to undergo medical training with Williams's new school arose, Landers jumped at the chance. I don't entirely blame him. Williams initially had a low opinion of Landers and rejected him as a student. However, something happened—I'm not exactly sure what—causing the captain to change his mind.

Williams's original instincts were correct. Landers is not a good fit. Although he seems to possess some skills and has a basic understanding of the theoretical knowledge, he doesn't strike me as doctor material. Initially, he didn't impress Chastity either . . . at least not until the day Leo and I caught them making out on her front porch. Since then, they've formed a strange pair.

The entire situation saddens me, especially because I thought Chastity and I were friends. She has only been at our hospital for a few weeks but has been incredibly kind and has gone out of her way to help me learn.

"You have about three hours left on your shift, right? Think things will be okay?" Leo drops a hand on Jesse's shoulder.

"Yeah, man. It'll be fine. I'll stay out of their way, like Chastity said. Maybe it'll stay quiet today and I won't even see them."

"Shh." Leo shakes his head. "Now you've jinxed it. Get ready for the patients."

We all laugh at the likely truth. It rarely fails. When someone mentions the day being calm or quiet, everything falls apart shortly afterward.

Leo and I say our goodbyes, telling Jesse to go inside and warm up by one of the woodstoves and to keep his head down. He lifts a hand before entering the front door. We walk back to the guard shack with Josiah, who continues to talk about what a troublemaker Landers is.

When we reach the shack, the men shake hands. "Nice seeing you," Josiah says. "I wasn't joking about including this in the report. Your names will be mentioned."

"Figured," Leo agrees. "Something needs to be done about Landers. I've suggested several times we drop him from the program. Williams keeps giving him another chance. As far as I'm concerned, he's run out of opportunities."

Chapter 9

Katie

Leo and I walk silently the rest of the way home. When we reach our front door, I can hear our little dog on the other side of it, his tail thumping on the hardwood floor.

Until the break-in by Kittleson and Young, we used to keep Geronimo contained in the laundry room while we worked or were away. He was so upset when the men broke in, he managed to somehow destroy the hollow-core door and escape. With a new door in place, we tried putting him in the laundry room again, but he hates it and whines any time he even gets near it.

Geronimo, who we usually call Gerry, now gets free run of the house or stays with the neighbor while we're gone. Captain Williams, himself a dog lover, has even let Gerry go to med school with Leo, setting him up in an unused room.

After entering our house and tending to Gerry's needs, I add small pieces of wood to the dying embers in the woodstove. We try to keep the fire burning continuously, not only to ward off the cold but also because it's easier to rekindle a fire than to start a new one.

Matches are scarce, so we rely on flint for ignition. We conserve paper as much as possible, opting to recycle it rather than using it for tinder. In the fall, we collected dried grass, leaves, and small twigs, but building a fire from scratch remains a challenge. As a lick of flame shoots up in the woodstove, I can't help but smile.

"Just a few more minutes, and it'll start giving off heat. Want a cup of tea?" I ask Leo.

Kneeling next to Gerry, Leo rubs the dog's chin. "I'm still stuffed from the meal. Too full for tea, even. I think I'll go change, and then maybe we can read the letters?"

"I can hardly wait. Ever since Lieutenant Paul told us about them, I've been nearly giddy. Part of me wants to savor the anticipation a little longer, but the rest of me . . . " I raise my hands in surrender. "I'm going to change too."

It takes about fifteen minutes for both of us to get dressed comfortably, and the fire finally emits a comforting warmth. Although there were still coals, the fire had dwindled enough to create a chill in the room. I pull a blanket over my legs as I sink into the plush couch—a recent addition to our home after our previous one was destroyed during the break-in.

The large manila envelope and three smaller envelopes sit on the coffee table, accompanied by the letter opener we took from our desk. Leo leans forward and asks, "Mind if I open the big one?"

"Sure, go ahead. It's from Jake. I'm guessing he did what he did last time and included all the family letters in one envelope. It's strange he sent you a separate one." I motion toward the business-sized white envelope on the table.

"I thought so too." Leo slides the opener under the flap of the large envelope and begins extracting its contents.

I gasp as I see what he pulls out. "What's that?"

Leo picks up the small plastic bag. "Seeds? There's another one still in the envelope." He places the second bag on the table before delving back into the envelope. "Um, two more."

I grab one of the baggies and read Jake's neat handwriting. "Beet seeds, for planting or sprouting in a mason jar." I let out a laugh. "Jake is the best. Sending us food from afar. What do the others say?"

"This one is broccoli, the other mustard." Leo makes a face. "Mustard?"

"I've had mustard seed sprouts before. They're good, but a bit . . . well, mustardy."

Leo chuckles. "I guess they would be."

I smile. "But they'll provide us with essential nutrients—greens. You know I've been talking about sprouting the seeds Jake gave us when we left Bakerville. I haven't had the chance. Our underperforming indoor garden already takes up too much of my free time."

"Show me what to do. I'll take the lead on the sprouts."

"Really? That'd be great. I have two lids Jake gave me. I know I have at least one quart-size mason jar. Maybe we can find a second." I deflate slightly. "Were jars some of the things we lost in the explosion at the ration center?"

Leo shakes his head. "I'm not sure. I'll ask around and see if I can find a second one. Just a regular jar?"

"Wide mouth to fit the lid. Or we can put a piece of cloth over the top and use a rubber band. It needs to be some sort of strainer. I copied the directions from my mom's survival binder. I have it with the lids. It's easy."

"All right, then. I'll do it." Leo sets the seeds aside. "There are letters from each of your sisters, folded but without envelopes. And one from Malcolm too." He raises his eyebrows mischievously at the mention of my little brother's name. "Several papers from Jake as well." He gestures toward the stack of papers held together by a paperclip. The top page is filled with Jake's handwriting. "Where should we start?"

"Belinda's? Mind if we read hers first?" Belinda Bosco is the reason I became a nurse. In the early days of the attacks, she took me under her wing and taught me what I needed to know to be part of the Bakerville medical team. Belinda, a surgical nurse practitioner, quickly took on the role of a doctor alongside an actual physician and various other trained people, including a chiropractor and a veterinarian. We were fortunate to have such knowledgeable individuals in our small town.

Leo, who had training as an EMT, suggested I join the medical team. I understand why Belinda initially had reservations, and I don't blame her. If I were in her position, I wouldn't have wanted me either. Yet, here I am, thanks to her. Captain Williams often uses me as an example when teaching laypeople about medicine.

True to her nature, Belinda devotes a portion of her letter to medical matters. She acknowledges receiving the letter I sent weeks ago and expresses her admiration for how thoroughly I considered the treatment options. She offers a few suggestions of her own and provides me with new scenarios and assignments.

Toward the end of the letter, she shares personal anecdotes about her son TJ and their life at the ski resort. Just like last year, the town of Bakerville moved out of the basin and relocated to a small privately owned ski resort and dude ranch. Belinda mentions there's considerably less snow this year, and with the military stationed along the highway outside Bakerville, they feel much safer.

She sent this letter through Jake when a group he was part of went down to the basin for a goose hunt, hoping to pass it on to the military unit. Belinda acknowledges it may be spring before I read her letter and can respond. She assures me she'll continue writing and sending letters whenever it's possible to dispatch someone with mail.

"She sounds good." Leo dips his chin. "Strong."

"She always does. Even with the troubles she's had, she's a survivor, a fighter. Next up . . . Kelley?"

I reach for the envelope from our town's other nurse practitioner, Kelley Hudson. While Belinda specializes in surgery, Kelley's a psych nurse. Her letter is more personal, containing a surprising note about her daughter Sylvia and Dax Cameron getting married. There was no grand ceremony; they tied the knot after a Sunday worship service, right before a regular lunch.

"Good for them," Leo comments. "They're a nice match." He gets up from the couch. "I think I'll put some water on. Even though I'm still full, a cup of tea sounds good. You got a new blend, right?"

"A Christmas blend. Stella gave it to me as a gift. She said it's a specialty mix to help keep us well over the dark days of winter. It has rose hips and peppermint . . . and something else I can't remember. I haven't tried it yet, but it smells delicious."

I place Kelley's letter on the table and rise to my feet. Gerry promptly follows suit and stretches. "You've got the right idea, pup." I raise my arms above my head and stand on my toes. "I feel like I need a good workout to help my food digest."

"We're not used to eating so much at once. And to think, that would've been an average meal—a regular Tuesday night supper— before the apocalypse."

"Things have certainly changed."

I add more wood to the fire and fill the kettle, moving it to a hot spot. Leo puts the loose tea in our reusable muslin teabags and places them in mugs. With the mugs on the coffee table and the kettle warming up, he suggests reading another letter while we wait.

"How about Malcolm's? I'm sure it's short." My almost twelve-year-old brother isn't a fan of writing.

Leo picks up the single sheet of paper, which has a couple of short paragraphs on one side and a sketch on the other. "It is short. He drew you a picture."

"Is it . . . is it me? Strumming a guitar?"

Leo chuckles. "Maybe? You want me to read this one?"

I wave my hand for him to proceed. Malcolm talks about their activities, such as archery practice and his guitar lessons. It turns out the drawing isn't of me, although there is some resemblance. It's actually of a new girl in the community that's teaching Malcolm to play guitar. Malcolm mentions they're even working on a special homecoming song for when Leo and I return to Bakerville. Although the letter is short, it brings tears to my eyes.

With the kettle whistling, I use a potholder to grab it and fill our mugs. While it cools, I take out my sister Calley's letter. She writes several paragraphs about baby Mollie and how quickly she's growing.

She then discusses her job in the radio room where she monitors transmissions over the Amateur Radio system while living on the mountain for the winter. It's the perfect job as it allows her to have Mollie with her.

Calley mentions hearing a lot of information coming out of the Western Wastelands, the areas declared uninhabitable by the president. These areas include all of California and most of Oregon and Washington. We've been trying to stay informed since Jake's brother and his family lived in Northern California when the bombs hit. My grandparents haven't stopped praying for their younger son's safety.

Calley states some people are still living in the destroyed areas and refuse to leave. There's a broadcaster who insists the country is being lied to. According to him, the bombs were smaller than reported, the damage not as severe, and there's no valid reason for drawing the demarcation line where it is. He claims there are nefarious reasons behind it. Calley mentions people don't really take him seriously, and other radio operators even talk over him when he starts his rants.

I look up from the letter. "What do you think about that?"

"Hard to say. I'm sure there are plenty of people who aren't happy about being forced out." Leo lets out a chuckle. "Seems like it's conspiracy day today. What'd Williams say? Give it three months?"

I shake my head. "Why lie about it?"

"Which part?"

"I mean the president. He must know what's happening in the Wastelands, right? Otherwise, why would he force people to move out? It doesn't make much sense."

Leo shakes his head. "I don't know. Like I said, maybe the guy is simply upset about having to leave. Does she mention how she heard this broadcast? If he's in California, would she hear him directly in the mountains of western Wyoming?"

"I don't think so. Do you want me to read that section again?"

"Would you mind?"

"*There's a broadcaster who insists we're being lied to, that there's no reason for the president to declare all of California uninhabitable, unless he has some hidden agenda. I don't think anyone takes him seriously, but it does lead to some lively conversations. I can barely keep up with my notes when things get going.*" I look up from the letter. "What do you think?"

"Hard telling. She does make it sound like she's hearing the California guy and several others. I don't know. We certainly never heard anyone in California last winter."

"Yeah, but sometimes what we were told was very limited." We both remember the tight grip on our little community. Everything changed when Bakerville experienced its own attempted coup d'état. After that, the blackout on news was lifted. Bakerville, Billings—what other places have had an attempted overthrow?

"What are you thinking?"

I wave the letter. "I wish Calley was clearer on this. Should I keep reading?"

"You know Calley. She loves telling the stories but does it in her own way."

I shrug before returning to the letter. Most of the remaining content revolves around neighborhood happenings. I'm not saying Calley gossips, but she likes to keep track of what's going on in the community. I think that's one reason she was assigned to the radio room. She has a knack for hearing and remembering things. While Calley does sometimes add her own spin to information, everything in the radio room is recorded as it comes in, ensuring it remains unbiased. Most likely, anyway.

As I reach for my sister Angela's letter, there's a loud knock on the door. "Leo? Katie? Are you home?"

I jump to my feet and look at Leo. "Is that Jesse?"

Leo's already on his feet. "Must be trouble at the hospital."

Leo, Gerry, and I all reach the door simultaneously. Leo checks the peephole, confirming it's Jesse, before yanking it open. "What happened?"

"Trouble at the base. They're reporting mass casualties. We're calling everyone in."

"We'll be there."

Jesse nods before spinning around. "It sounds like a bad one," he calls over his shoulder. "Best hurry."

My heart races, pounding in my ears. Trouble at the base—Camp Rapid—where not long ago we were enjoying our Christmas feast. Leo is already moving toward the bedroom to change back into his regular clothing. It only takes us a few minutes to get dressed again. As I tie my boots, I ask, "What about Gerry? We could be there awhile. You think the Harringtons will take him?"

"Good idea. Let's see if they can."

Less than fifteen minutes have passed since Jesse knocked on our door, and we're already on our way to the hospital. Our next-door neighbors, the Harringtons, are kind enough to keep Gerry. Oscar Harrington, a member of the Citizen Patrol and part of our police force, has already left. His wife mentioned hearing about an explosion.

Chapter 10

Merissa

"Where do you want me?"

"Well, Merissa . . . " Jacquie Haley purses her lips. "Let's see. I'll take care of triage—out there." She gestures toward the front of the building.

Seated on the bench by the back door, which serves as a mudroom, Jacquie laces her snow boots. She's already donned multiple layers of street clothes over her scrubs. "No sense in both of us being cold. Captain Williams will be here any time, and Jesse will round up as many of our staff as possible. If he finds Katie Burnett— "

"He'll find her. Jesse said they were heading home after stopping here earlier." I refrain from mentioning the reason for their stop, which was the near brawl between Geoff Landers and Jesse Talbot.

I can't fathom what got into those two. Jesse's suggestion to settle it outside like men was almost comical. Geoff, who's smaller in stature, grew pale. It was only because of Chastity's insane urging that Geoff didn't back down. She was practically gleeful, and she even warned Jesse that he'd regret it.

Truth be told, in an actual fight, Chastity would probably fare better against Jesse than Geoff ever could. She's a tough woman. Or at least she used to be. Lately, with Geoff by her side, she has been acting rather strange.

"I'll suggest to the captain that Katie run the inside show and act as a treatment coordinator," Jacquie says as she stands. "Where's Chastity?"

"She went to the guard station to ensure they were aware of the situation and how to direct the injured." We offered to go to Camp Rapid, to bring our makeshift ambulances and assist in gathering their wounded. However, they assured us they would do what they could from their end and deliver them to us.

We simply need to be prepared for an influx. We should expect numerous casualties, in the double digits, with the first wave of injured. The base will keep those who are least injured and fatalities on-site. "Chastity told Rand to get bundled up too. She wants him to help at the guard station."

"What will he be doing?"

I respond with a shrug. "She said she had an idea to prevent the craziness we had when the ration center exploded."

"Do you think it's the same group responsible for the other explosions? It has to be, right?"

The lock on the back door wiggles, then the door swings open.

"Captain Williams," Jacquie and I say simultaneously. I nod, and she waves her hand. Jacquie adds, "Hello, Mrs. Williams," as the elegant woman pushes the specially adapted wheelchair into the building. I step aside to give them ample space.

"What do we know?" the captain asks as he pushes himself from the wheelchair.

Jacquie gives a brief overview of the details the National Guard relayed about the explosion. Then she says she'll take triage outside and label people using the number method. She asks about having Katie as a treatment coordinator.

"That sounds like a solid plan. When Leo arrives, I want him with me. Alice, will you also stay and assist? I could use your help in surgery."

"Certainly." Mrs. Williams takes off the hood of her jacket, unveiling a chic wool beret, which added an extra layer of defense against the temperature.

"Where's Dr. Morrow?" Williams asks as he reaches for the crutches he uses while in the hospital. Seeing his need, his wife steps forward and grabs one crutch, followed by the other.

"She's making sure the guard house knows what to do." Jacquie grabs her coat. "I'd best get out there. They should be here any minute." She hurries down the hallway, stopping at the nurse's desk and grabbing something I can't quite make out. As she slips it into her pocket, I realize it's a marking pen. The iconic ink will be used to indicate the course of treatment.

Jacquie has a job I wouldn't envy. She'll have mere minutes to decide whether a person can be saved—or, more accurately, whether we have the resources to save them.

Eighteen months into the apocalypse, our hospital is far from capable of achieving the miracles it once did, with its unlimited antibiotics, supplies, and staff.

"Where do you want me, Captain?"

He asks about the whereabouts of other staff members. I inform him several off-duty personnel have already arrived, including Dr. Wolff. People are getting dressed and preparing. I don't mention Geoff has been here for most of the day, nor do I say anything about the altercation between him and Jesse.

Captain Williams gives me a nod. "I want you to float, wherever people need you." He glances at my stomach, which seems larger than usual today.

I don't know if it's because my body relaxed once Pearl found out about the baby or for some other reason, but I suddenly appear enormous. I'm sure, based on the glances I've received today, Jacquie and Jesse both noticed my increased girth. Not Chastity, though. She's been in her own little world.

"Be careful with transferring patients," Williams cautions.

I nod as the front doorbell rings. Chastity shivers as she steps into the entryway. She dashed out in such a hurry she didn't bother with a jacket. Earlier today, during Geoff and Jesse's altercation, she wasn't appropriately dressed for the outdoors either. Apparently, hypothermia isn't a concern for her.

Rather than approaching us, she shouts down the hallway informing us the first truckload of wounded has passed the guard house. "I'll be right back out." She motions to the break room.

As she disappears inside the break room, Dr. Wolff and several others emerge from it. There's a moment of chaos as Williams instructs Wolff on where to position everyone. He mentions he needs a moment to change and that he'll handle any surgeries with his wife, Leo, and one of the other nurses assisting.

Kerry Hendricks will also be in the surgical suite, overseeing the recovery room. Nettie Wolff will address all nonsurgical matters and prepare patients for Williams. Chastity will duplicate Nettie's efforts.

As the majority of us scatter, Dr. Wolff requests a moment to speak with Captain Williams. Glancing back, I'm almost certain I see her mouth the name "Chastity Morrow."

"They're here!" one of the staff members exclaims, prompting everyone to rush toward the front door. It'll be only a minute or two until Jacquie has the first person triaged and brought inside. Anticipating the initial minutes to be chaotic as everyone figures out their tasks, I hold back.

I'm near the break room door when it swings open. Geoff glances toward the back door, then the front. He runs his hand through his hair, his gaze meeting mine as he smirks and strides toward the entrance.

Chastity follows behind him, her short hair disheveled and her eyes wide. What's going on with her?

She signals for me to join her. I take a step closer, and she lets out a cough, barely covering her mouth with her elbow.

"Are you okay?" I ask, taking a step back.

She waves her arm—the same one she used to muffle her cough. I swear I can see germs floating through the air. The two sick individuals from last night spread enough despite our infection control practices. We don't need one of our doctors falling ill as well.

"Sorry. It's cold outside. I wanted to make sure you know what happened earlier wasn't a big deal. There's no need to involve Williams. Josiah Talbot mentioned including it in his report, but with everything that's happening— " She waves both arms this time. "No one's going to care about a little spat between grown men." She lets out a heavy sniff.

I study her face. Her eyes are red and wild. I can't tell if she's sick or if something else is going on. "Do you need a few minutes to get yourself together?"

"What? No, I'm fine. Like I said, it's cold. Stay out of my business. That's all I'm saying." She sidesteps me as Captain Williams's office door opens, followed by the thumping of his crutches as he moves down the hallway. The front doorbell rings, and our first patient is brought in. Chastity calls out to Williams, volunteering to attend to the first patient.

"Dr. Morrow?" I reach for her sleeve—the one she didn't cough on.

She narrows her eyes. "What?"

"Are you sure you're not sick? Perhaps you should wear a mask."

She jerks her arm away. "I'm perfectly fine. I don't need a medic questioning my abilities."

I contemplate informing her I'm not inquiring about her abilities but rather her health. The last thing we need is for her to spread any illness to the injured individuals.

As two more wounded patients are brought in, she gives me a sharp glare and hurries away.

I cringe when I see her attending to the first patient without even pausing at the bottle of hand sanitizer on the nurse's desk.

When Nettie Wolff rushes by, she asks if I'm okay.

"Yes, Doctor."

Unlike Chastity Morrow, Dr. Wolff takes the time to sanitize as she instructs one of the staff members to bring the next patient to exam room two.

I mimic her actions and quickly clean my hands. As I rub them together, I concentrate on the motion, trying to drown out the screams and cries of the injured as they're brought in.

"You're our floater." Dr. Wolff nods. "Do what you can to help. If you see Leo, be sure to send him to the captain. He'll need him. And . . . " She lets out a sigh. "Keep an eye on Dr. Morrow. She seems a little . . . off."

My gaze shifts to Chastity, who's assessing a patient. "Take her to surgery. Captain Williams's team will do all the pre-op and everything," she commands.

Chastity looks better already. Strong and confident as she moves to the next patient. Dr. Wolff quicksteps to the entryway where the inside triage is happening. She signals for me to join her.

Whispering close to my ear, she asks, "Are you familiar with the numbering system? Make sure all the patients marked with a three are lined up along the hallway for now. Keep them comfortable."

She turns to a young man with a black "3" written across his forehead. "Merissa's going to get you moved away from this door. It'll be warmer and more comfortable until we can see you." She offers him a smile.

"Sure, Doc. I don't feel too bad. Not much pain."

With the young man on a board stretcher, I motion to Jesse. I hadn't even realized he had returned from his search for additional personnel. He grabs the arm of an unfamiliar man, likely connected to the hospital or one of the care centers in some way.

"What's the plan?" Jesse asks.

"Line the right side of the hallway. Group the patients marked with a three together. The doctors are currently attending to the urgent cases." I attempt to offer a reassuring smile to the man on the stretcher. Although the number three on his forehead indicates his injuries are too severe to survive, I attempt to convey that his condition is not as critical as others. It's a lie, but what else can I do?

Jesse points to the man with him. "He'll assist with transferring people. We already have the tables set up." He motions with his chin toward the specially constructed tables designed for this purpose. The tables act as board beds to hold the stretchers. "The gurneys are outside. Once the tables and gurneys are full, we'll need to put the stretchers on the floor."

"You think we'll have that many wounded?"

He gives me an almost haunted look. "That many and more. I spoke with the driver that delivered the first of the wounded. It's bad, really bad. We'll transfer people off the stretchers and onto the treatment tables. They'll need the stretchers back with this number of wounded." Jesse looks in the direction of two women scurrying toward us.

I hesitate a moment as the men move into position next to the treatment table. The women communicate effectively with each other and the stretcher-bearers, moving the injured young man from the board stretcher to the table.

Sensing the situation is under control, I hurry back to the front, where the next patient is already waiting. Taking a deep breath, I once again focus on my task and block out the chaos surrounding me.

Chapter 11

Katie

As Leo and I fast walk to the hospital, I ask, "Do you think it's the same people? The preacher's group?"

"Could be. Of course, we don't know the preacher is behind any of the explosions," Leo answers.

Josiah Talbot signals us to approach the guard station, his face revealing the gravity of the situation. "It's bad. There are already a dozen here. More on the way." While he speaks, a pickup truck in the driveway revs its engine and begins to move.

Leo and I quickly step aside, recognizing the driver as someone from the day's festivities; his hands grip the wheel with tension.

Leo gestures toward a small group of people near the medical school. "What's happening over there?"

Josiah snorts. "Family. Chastity said to keep them out. She sent Rand Hendricks to monitor them. It's freezing out here, and naturally, they're worried. I'm not sure they'll be content staying there much longer. Rand might need some assistance, but I don't know who. Right now, it's all hands on deck."

"Why are they not allowed inside?"

Josiah throws up his hands. "Ask *Dr.* Morrow."

The scene at the hospital entrance is nothing short of chaos. Nurse Jacquie Haley is outside handling triage.

In the early days of the district hospital, they employed a color-coded triage system, assigning different colored markers to each injured individual. Red meant immediate treatment, yellow and green could wait, and black signified the deceased or those beyond saving.

When they ran out of green markers, they resorted to a number system, with one indicating immediate attention, two for patients who could wait until all the ones were taken care of, and three to provide comfort without life-saving measures.

Jacquie directs us inside. My role is to act as the treatment officer, overseeing the wounded and ensuring the smooth functioning of triage while offering solace to the dying. While I know it's an important job, it's also incredibly difficult. I fight back my emotions and stiffen my spine as I prepare for the hours ahead.

"Captain Williams is already in surgery. He wants Leo with him." Jacquie informs us. "It's going to be a long night. They're only sending us the most severe cases for now. They're holding back on sending everyone."

Leo reaches for my hand and gives it a reassuring squeeze. "Be careful."

I respond with a vacant nod. Inside the building, a sea of bloody individuals greets me. Makeshift treatment tables line the hallway, while boards serve as improvised stretchers directly on the floor. At first glance, every forehead displays the number three.

Part of my responsibility is to monitor the patients continually and ensure the assigned numbers given by Jacquie remain appropriate. Someone's condition may initially suggest a three, but circumstances can change rapidly.

However, it becomes evident this won't be the case for most of these individuals. For now, my task primarily revolves around keeping them comfortable and documenting the deceased.

Armed with a clipboard, I begin moving among the patients, checking their dog tags for names and recording their injury status along with any obvious issues. Several have suffered mangled limbs and shrapnel injuries along with severe burns from the explosion. These wounds appear even more severe than those we encountered a few weeks ago following the attack on our ration center.

In that blast, the explosion razed the building, taking the lives of almost everyone inside. Those outside the building were mostly spared unless they were near the front of the line. A significant portion of those individuals experienced profound agony before death mercifully claimed them.

Chastity walks down the hall, causing my heart to quicken its pace. I worry about another confrontation with her. She looks worn out, her red eyes and disheveled hair conveying her exhaustion. With this emergency being in the early stages, I wonder about her appearance.

"Williams is already in surgery," she says. "All the exam rooms are filled. These— " She shakes her head. "You know what to do?"

"I do," I reply.

She gives me a grave look. "The next load will be here shortly. I'll be in exam room two. Find me if there's any . . . " She tilts her head. She doesn't need to finish her sentence . . . *if there's any we can save.*

"Yes, Doctor."

With everyone else attending to patients who have a chance of survival, I survey the remaining men and women in the hallway. My gaze falls on one of the gurneys, and I close my eyes as I recognize the young man lying there: Elliot Tillman. I approach his side and take a quick assessment.

He's dirty and bedraggled, but no glaring injuries are evident. Nevertheless, a number three adorns his forehead as he stares blankly at the ceiling, tears silently streaming down his face and pooling in his ears.

I adjust my stance and fake a serene expression. "Hey, Elliot."

He turns his head slightly, seeming not to recognize me at first, but then a faint smile graces his lip. "Hi, Sergeant Burnett. It's a good thing you left early. My dad went back to his place too. I'm glad. Do you think . . . will someone tell him I'm here?"

"I'm sure they will. A lot of people are helping at Camp Rapid. They'll reach out to the families."

Elliot swallows. "Could you make sure he knows I was asking about him?"

I rest my hand on his arm. "He'll know. Just relax now. Do you have much pain?"

He grimaces. "It's kind of strange. I know I should, but nothing really hurts. It all feels kind of far away."

I straighten my shoulders and drop a hand on his arm. His lack of pain is good for his comfort, but it also suggests the severity of his injuries. It reminds me of my mother.

A few weeks before her passing, she suffered a fall that left her paralyzed from the shoulders down. Similar to Elliot, we lacked the necessary medical supplies to do more than keep her comfortable.

Unlike Elliot, my mother was already ill before her fall, as cancer had ravaged her body, inflicting intense pain. Her paralysis came as a relief. Nonetheless, losing her was devastating—one of the most challenging experiences I've ever faced. The silver lining lay in my mom not dying alone. We were all there, surrounding her with love.

"Let me see if I can send someone to find your dad. Give me a few minutes."

Almost on cue, one of the med students enters through the door. He spots me and rushes over. "Jacquie said to ask where you need me."

"Okay, great." I motion for him to follow me. Once we find a quiet corner, as far away as possible, I speak in a hushed voice. "Did you notice the numbers on their foreheads?"

He nods shakily.

"Do you know what they mean?"

"No life-saving measures. Keep them comfortable," he replies.

"If you were facing death, would you prefer to be alone in a hallway while your spouse or parent was waiting outside in the cold, or have a loved one holding your hand?"

He pulls out a pen from his pocket. "I'll find the family. Give me the names." He writes Elliot's name on his hand.

"You should find some paper. There will be too many names for your hand."

"I'll use my arm. Save the paper. It's a big group out there. Thirty, maybe forty."

I glance down the crowded hallway. "Bring two per person, okay?"

Although Josiah mentioned Chastity assigned Rand Hendricks to keep the families away, it's possible she did so under Captain Williams's orders. I should consult with the captain about allowing people inside, but with him currently in surgery . . .

I let out a sigh. I'll address it later. "Hurry back. I'll have more names for you soon."

I return to Elliot. "Someone's looking for your dad. I can't make any promises, but I'll keep you updated."

I move to the next stretcher and kneel beside a woman who appears unresponsive. I check her pulse—it's faint but present. I proceed to examine her dog tags. Like most others, they're hand-forged, indicating she wasn't part of the National Guard before our world fell apart. I jot down her name and date of birth before moving to the next person. I've assessed three individuals when the front doorbell chimes.

The next wave of injured has arrived. I direct the soldiers on where to place the stretchers. There are three more patients with a number three on their foreheads and one with a number one, signaling the need for immediate treatment. The doorbell rings again, and Merissa Weaver emerges from an examination room.

"With the way that bell keeps ringing, I thought you might need a hand." She quickly surveys the new patients. "We're almost finished in exam one."

Kneeling beside the woman marked with a number one, I notice Merissa's slightly awkward movements. Her protruding stomach hinders her mobility. It seems she has begun to show, with her barely noticeable baby bump now prominently visible.

Catching my gaze, she clicks her tongue. "I know. There's no hiding it now."

"Your mother-in-law?"

"Ecstatic. I'll fill you in later." Merissa turns to the young woman. "Hey there, I'm going to get a few supplies and get an IV started."

The woman mumbles something about hating needles.

"I'll be gentle, I promise," Merissa reassures her with a smile.

While Merissa fetches the necessary supplies, I record the names of our new patients. Another truck arrives, bringing in several more individuals—two on stretchers and four able to walk, each marked with a number two on their foreheads.

Pennington County Sheriff's Deputy Broderick Shaw carries one of the stretchers. "Katie." He acknowledges with a nod. "How many so far?"

I glance at my sheet. "Eighteen. I still need to record a few down the hall. That'll make twenty-two."

He closes his eyes and shakes his head. "And there's at least that many going straight to Hugo." Hugo is our undertaker.

I nod in acknowledgment. "Are more on their way here?"

"Minor injuries only. They'll be monitored on the base until we give the word to transport them. We need to keep things a little less chaotic here."

At that moment, the front doorbell rings, drawing our attention. The med student returns with Mr. Tillman. "Excuse me, Deputy." I take a deep breath and brace myself for the news I'm about to deliver.

Chapter 12

Katie

"Hi, Mr. Tillman. I'm Katie. We met earlier today, remember?"

The man's face reflects a mixture of agony and distress. "Um, yes. Where's my boy?"

I place my hand on his forearm. "May I speak with you for a moment?"

His eyes search my face, further revealing his emotions. Tears well up as he lowers his shoulder and lifts his chin. His voice cracks when he finally speaks. "Is he dead?"

Motioning him away from the others, I speak quietly. "He's alive, but there's nothing we can do for him. I had someone come to get you so you can stay with him. Okay?"

He nods.

"Mr. Tillman. Do you understand what I'm saying?"

"You're telling me my boy is going to die, and this is the last time I'll talk to him."

"Yes, sir. That's what I'm telling you. He told me he isn't in any pain. Please give me one moment and I'll take you to him."

I give the med student three more names and send him off before escorting Mr. Tillman to his son.

"Hey, Dad." Elliot gives a weak smile.

Mr. Tillman gathers his emotions. "Hello, son." His voice cracks on the word *son*.

Granting them the privacy they need, I leave to retrieve a pile of nonwhite sheets from the linen closet. I drape a sheet over each person, concealing the worst of their wounds.

While awaiting the arrival of additional family members, I make my way to the patients I haven't added to my list yet. Two have already passed, and I note their times of death on my paper. I wish I could've been there to hold their hands as they passed.

A couple of hours go by as I move from patient to patient, doing what I can to keep them comfortable. The med student continues to assist in locating family members and monitoring the injured. We arrange chairs for families to sit next to their loved ones, while those on ground-level stretchers sit on the floor alongside them atop a pillow or blanket.

Three more patients have succumbed to their injuries, with two passing away in the presence of their loved ones. Despite the large number of patients and their families, the hospital remains surprisingly quiet.

The surgical suite has had two patients, both still in the recovery room, and Williams is working on a third. Chastity and Nettie have remained in the exam rooms, leaving the other nurses and medics to bring patients to them. Surprisingly, it's all gone rather smoothly.

As I kneel next to a chair, checking the vitals of one of our less injured patients, Chastity strides down the hallway and makes a beeline for me.

"What's the meaning of this?" she calls out, still a few feet away.

"Uh-oh," my patient mutters.

I swallow and stand. "Doctor?"

She motions down the hallway. "Why are all these people here?"

I take in a deep breath and straighten my shoulders. "Perhaps we can discuss this somewhere else?"

Chastity narrows her eyes. "We'll discuss it right now." Her voice carries throughout the waiting area, drawing everyone's attention to us.

Deputy Shaw takes a step toward us. "Doctor, may I see you outside? Katie, please join us."

"I'll take over here," Merissa says.

We step outside and are greeted by a blast of cold air. I shed my heavy winter coat and boots upon arrival but hadn't changed into scrubs, thinking I may need to help with bringing in patients. I'm thankful for the turtleneck, jeans, and long underwear I'm wearing.

Before the door is fully shut, Chastity grips my arm tight enough to make me yelp. "You had no business bringing people in here. I ordered Rand to keep them away. You do not have the authority to override my order."

Standing at my full five-foot-four height, I meet her gaze. "Denying people the presence of their loved ones as they pass is a cruel act. If you made the choice to let them die alone, you're the one at fault, not me."

Her slap lands forcefully, spinning my head to the side. I gasp for breath.

"Hey!" Shaw grabs Chastity's arm. "That's enough."

"How dare you!" Chastity spews, showering me with her words and saliva. She manages to free herself from Shaw's grip.

Shaw orders her to calm down, but she responds by hurling a string of colorful insults at him, me, my husband, and seemingly everyone I've ever known. Her furious tirade attracts the attention of several soldiers and deputies milling around outside, and they gather near us.

Shaw reaches for her again. "I said that's enough."

Chastity wrenches her arm away from him and points a bony finger in my direction. "You better believe this isn't over. I'm taking this straight to Captain Williams. You'll be scrubbing bedpans at a care center by tomorrow."

"Like you threatened Jesse earlier?" Josiah Talbot asks from the sidelines.

Shaw tilts his head, emitting a resounding crack. "I'm starting to see a pattern here, Chastity," he says in a low, calm voice. "I read the earlier report."

Chastity faces him squarely. "That's Dr. Morrow to you. This hospital is not under your control, so you butt out."

He takes a step closer. "The hospital is within my jurisdiction, and I *witnessed* you assault someone. If we still had a jail, I'd probably be hauling you off to it."

I close my eyes. The jail at Camp Rapid served not only the National Guard but also the sheriff's department. It was ground zero, the site of the explosion.

The prevailing theory is the intoxicated men who had harassed the guards during our Christmas dinner had smuggled in explosives— suicide bombers. The question of why they weren't searched before being placed in the holding room remains. Unfortunately, only one of the people who escorted them to the room survived. Captain Williams operated on him, and he's currently in recovery.

The extent of the damage raises questions about the number of explosives used. The blast devastated the entire building, which housed the holding cells and the adjacent recreation room utilized by the enlisted. Most of the casualties were my age or younger—new recruits who had been unwinding after the dinner feast.

Discovering the identities of these men will be the next task. Were they connected to the group responsible for planting bombs at the Monument District festival, as well as our ration centers and hospitals? Those attacks claimed over a thousand lives.

Or is this incident related to what occurred in Billings, Montana? Could it be a precursor to an attempted coup in Rapid City? Somehow, that doesn't feel right. If someone intended to stage a coup, wouldn't they target the general and those directly beneath him? Why destroy the jail and an enlisted area?

"Sergeant Burnett?"

"Um, yes?" I turn to face Shaw.

"What do you want to do? Press charges?"

In these times, there are no courts or anything of the sort. Something as trivial as a slap—though my face still stings from it—is almost laughable considering the world we live in.

"No. No, of course not."

Chastity snorts. "Of course not," she mocks in my voice. "Poor little Katie. Always playing the victim, aren't you?"

Shaw shakes his head. "Quit while you can, *Chastity*."

She narrows her eyes. "I'm reporting all of this to Captain Williams, including how you're siding with an insubordinate. We'll see who ends up needing to quit." With a single finger wag in my direction, she pivots on her heel and strides away.

Once she disappears inside, Shaw asks if I'm all right.

I shrug and shake my head. "I knew I'd face repercussions. After all, I made a decision outside my area of expertise. But I didn't expect . . . " I raise my hand to my stinging cheek. "I need to get back to my patients."

"I'll walk you in," he says, then motions for the others to resume their duties.

Chapter 13

Katie

The hospital's interior is eerily quiet, with a few hushed conversations and occasional cries. As Shaw and I enter, the people near the entrance door stare at us. Some of them are uncomfortable and avert their eyes, and one man shakes his head.

After finishing with her patient, Merissa hurries over. "Are you okay?"

I swallow down my emotions and nod. "I'll manage."

"You should go wash up. Maybe put a wet cloth on your face."

"You saw?"

"Yeah, it was quite a show. You should've smacked her back." Merissa quirks an eyebrow.

Shaw snorts. "She should've. What happened between you two? I thought you were friends?"

I shake my head. "I thought we were too. I don't know what I did."

"I don't think you did anything," Merissa says. "She's different now, not only with you but with all of us. I noticed it when the orthopedic surgeon was here during your husband's surgery. Now that she's with Landers, she's really something."

"Have you seen Leo?" I ask. "Does he . . . does he know what happened?"

"I don't think he's left the surgical suite since Williams called him in there hours ago. But it shouldn't be much longer. We took in the last patient while you were outside. Everyone else . . . " She tilts her head and grimaces. In a soft voice, she says, "We lost another one while you were outside."

I let out a sigh. "Who?"

She gives me the name of a young woman. My gaze falls on her stretcher, where a man sits on the floor, holding her hand.

"I'm going to wash up."

"I'll walk with you." Shaw gestures toward the hallway leading to the bathrooms.

I lift my eyebrows.

"Chastity seems a little . . . unhinged. She's probably already told Geoff Landers what happened. I'd hate to see them both confront you. I'll wait by the door."

I'm shocked when I look in the mirror. My left cheek is beet red, bearing the obvious outline of a hand. There's a small scratch near my temple from her fingernail grazing me. I press the floor pedal a few times, and tepid water starts flowing from the faucet.

I splash my face, disregarding the sting from the water on my cut. As I lean over the sink, tears begin to flow. I stop pumping the pedal and rest my elbows on the counter.

I truly don't understand what caused Chastity to turn on me like this. We were friends when she first started working here, even during her rotation before she was permanently assigned. I think Merissa is right; it started when the surgeon who operated on Leo's arm was here. Both Chastity and Nettie have a history with Dr. Bollinger, some torrid love triangle.

His visit is when things started changing between Chastity and me. Not just with me, as Merissa mentioned, but with others too. Chastity and Nettie used to be housemates, sharing a small three-bedroom house with another woman from one of the care centers. After their big blow-up here at the hospital, Chastity moved out and settled in Dr. Eugene Newsome's old house.

Newsome's former house, the scene of two murders and a suicide, was where Leo and I first saw Chastity with Landers. We walked by and witnessed them making out on the front porch. Landers has been a problem since he got involved with the hospital. He comes across as a know-it-all but doesn't actually know as much as he thinks.

I don't know for sure, but I heard Landers moved in with Chastity, at least unofficially. He stays at her place more often than at the studio apartment above a garage where he officially lives. I honestly don't understand why Chastity has changed so much. She's a skilled doctor, even excellent, but her interpersonal skills have suddenly deteriorated.

I remove the bobby pins and hair band holding my curly mane in place. Running my fingers through my hair to separate the strands, I let out a sigh. Could there be something medically wrong with her? Maybe something stress-related? We're all on edge every day.

Sadly, today's events are fairly common. It's been over eighteen months since everything fell apart. Is Chastity cracking under the pressure? Is her relationship with Landers accelerating her decline?

I'll discuss it with Nettie and see what she thinks. Of course, since I disobeyed Chastity's orders to keep families out of the hospital, Nettie might not be interested in my thoughts. Both she and Williams are likely to side with Chastity. A nurse shouldn't override a doctor's orders, even if they seem inhumane.

While the hierarchy here isn't terrible, there is a pecking order. Nurses are below doctors. Other nurses tell me it's always this way and they simply accept it. They also say our hospital isn't nearly as bad as other places.

I put my hair back into a ponytail at the base of my neck and wrap it in a bun. I secure it with the flimsy bobby pins, which aren't really enough to hold my hair tightly, but they'll have to do. I've heard someone is crocheting snoods, which might be a better option for my hair, especially since I only have three hair bands and a few bobby pins left.

"Katie?" Leo's firm knock on the door interrupts my thoughts.

I take a quick glance in the mirror. There's no hiding the damage to my face. I unlock the door and invite him in.

His mouth tightens. "I heard what happened. Does it hurt?"

"Not much," I lie. It stings like crazy.

"Williams knows. He wants to see you in his office."

"Is he angry?"

"Very. This isn't going to be ignored."

"I understand. I thought it was the right thing to do. I kept thinking about my mom and— "

"He's not angry at you. He's angry at Chastity. Landers too. Seems it was his idea to keep the families outside, to make them wait in the cold. I think Williams sees some logic in it, but he would've preferred to make the call himself. He also would've opened up the med school for the families. And he definitely would've done what you did and allowed someone to be with their dying loved ones."

My sigh seems to start at my toes. "Still . . . I should've asked someone, but they were so busy. Did Williams not know the families were outside?"

"He had no idea. He came in through the back door, as usual. Chastity didn't say anything. He's been in the surgical suite since shortly after he arrived. It's like a bubble in there."

I glance in the mirror again, then straighten my shoulders. "Are you going to his office with me?"

"Nope. I have my own orders. Shaw will be with you, along with Chastity and Landers."

"Great. This should be fun." I reach for the door handle, but Leo puts his hand on my arm and urges me into a hug.

He whispers, "I'm proud of you. You showed real initiative by bringing in the families. You knew there would be trouble, yet you did it anyway."

"Guess I'm developing a backbone, huh?"

"You definitely are. I know things haven't been easy. Your mom's passing, moving here and adjusting to a new environment, and me falling and being a major jerk." He scrunches his face and shrugs. "It's taken a toll. But you're strong. A fighter. You know how to do the right thing."

"I don't, not really. I'm just leaning on the Lord, wanting Him to guide me. To guide *us*."

Leo's expression falters. "That's what we both need to do—now more than ever. These losses are huge. I, um . . . " He pauses as tears well in his eyes. "Did you hear Duncan is among the dead?"

"Duncan? Your friend from the Bible study group? Robyn's husband, the one we were sitting with at dinner?"

Leo's face tenses and his eyes moisten as he gives a weak nod.

"They don't live on base. He was still there?"

"Seems so. He was one of the men assigned as a jailer."

"Oh no. Robyn . . . she's expecting a baby."

He nods again and turns to the door. He holds it open for me to exit first. Chastity and Landers stand at the end of the hallway, near Captain Williams's office door. Their heads are close together, and both studiously avoid looking in our direction.

Deputy Shaw is still leaning against the wall, in pretty much the same place he was when I entered the bathroom. "Better?"

I dip my chin. "I'm fine."

"You ready for this?" he asks.

"Where's Williams?"

"In his office. He wanted everyone to wait out here until you were ready. We're all supposed to go in together. He didn't want to get one-sided information."

"Okay, great."

Leo drops his hand on my shoulder. "You'll be fine. Remember that new backbone, and use it."

We're still about a dozen feet away when Landers shoots me a dirty look and sharply knocks on the office door. Williams's voice booms through the wall, ordering us to enter.

Chapter 14

Katie

My heart pounds, and my mouth feels dry. I wish I had taken the time to get a drink of water before entering Williams's office. Although Leo assured me the captain isn't angry with me, I can't be sure. Disobeying a doctor's order is strongly discouraged.

Williams sits behind his desk. He gestures to the chairs scattered around the room. "Pull them over."

After arranging the chairs and seating ourselves, he leans back. "Imagine my surprise— "

"This simply can't continue," Chastity interrupts. "Katie Burnett— "

"Don't speak another word, Dr. Morrow. Sit there quietly. You will have a chance to speak, but only after I'm finished."

"But, sir— "

"Was I not clear?"

She slams her mouth shut and stares straight ahead, sitting rigidly. Like Chastity, I'm perched on the edge of my seat, my body tense. Shaw, too, seems to be sitting almost at attention.

Landers is the odd one out, slouching and looking untidy as he sprawls in his seat. He rests his legs in front of him, his back only halfway touching the chair. In many ways, he displays his youthful disposition. Despite being only a few years younger than me, he often lacks maturity.

"As I was saying," Captain Williams continues, "imagine my surprise to discover one of my doctors and one of my nurses engaged in a fight in the driveway during a catastrophe."

Embarrassment flushes my cheeks as his gaze bores into me. He shifts his gaze to Landers. "And you can imagine my double surprise when I learned this was the second such incident today, involving many of the same people. I received a written report from Shaw's deputy— "

"You received a falsified report from Josiah Talbot." Landers waves his hand dismissively. "He took his brother's side."

"Interrupt me again and you're removed from the medical program."

"I'd like to see you try," Landers sneers.

Williams straightens slightly, his face impassive. "You and your uncle may think you have me over a barrel, but you're mistaken." He glances at Shaw before returning his penetrating gaze to Landers. "Your uncle will not be successful in his quest to take over the hospital. Deputy Shaw, can you report?"

Shaw turns toward Landers. "Around 1600 hours today, shortly before the explosion at Camp Rapid, I received a directive from the Office of the Governor. Any efforts to overturn the current reconstruction system will be considered an attempted coup d'état."

Coup d'état? That seems to be the word of the day. Chastity and Landers expressed concerns earlier about the military controlling the hospitals—concerns originating from Landers's uncle Melvin Cabal, acting Pennington County Sheriff. Did he intend to violently seize control of the hospitals? How would such a thing even work?

A flash of concern crosses Landers's face, but he quickly recovers and shrugs. "So? What's that have to do with me?"

Captain Williams steeples his hands below his chin. "Very little. I allowed you to be part of the medical school as a concession to your uncle. The original agreement was I would let you in, and he'd cease his attempts to change the current operations. Successful operations, I might add. As you well know, this didn't happen. Instead, he used you as a spy."

Landers scoffs. "Don't flatter yourself. You're not doing anything worthy of reporting. You think this place is something special? It's not." He points at me. "You choose useless and weak people to try, and then pretend they're prodigies? Ha. Ask Chastity."

With her gaze fixed on her toes, Chastity barely shakes her head.

"What?" Landers asks. "Suddenly nothing to say? You think this whole thing is as much of a sham as I do. You've said it yourself, turning untalented individuals into doctors and nurses is a waste of time."

"Is that true, Dr. Morrow?" Williams asks, his tone biting.

Still not looking up, Chastity whispers, "It was just talk, sir. Blowing off steam at the end of a long day."

"So, you don't believe our medical school is a waste of time?" Although he directs the question at Chastity, his eyes remain on Landers.

Landers smirks. "She believes it. Especially because my uncle promised her this hospital once you're gone."

"You don't say?" Williams's face breaks into a wide grin. "Well, why wait, Chastity? If you're interested in taking over, I'll give you the reins today."

"That won't be necessary," Chastity mutters.

Williams maintains his gaze on Chastity, her head still down. He sighs before turning back to Landers. "Well, Mr. Landers, it seems your attempt to take over has failed. Remember, your spot in this med school is probationary. One wrong move, and you'll be dismissed."

"Dismissed? I'm not one of your soldiers. I'm here voluntarily. Correction—I *was* here. I quit."

Chastity's head shoots up. "No, Geoff." She reaches for him. "That's exactly what he wants."

"And he's getting it." Landers turns to Williams. "I'm glad to be done with this. Your school's going to fail anyway. You selected a witch doctor and a janitor to be doctors." He points to me. "You have people who don't know shinola as teachers. Then you harass people," he accuses, pointing his finger at himself. "People with genuine talent, whom you make it impossible to succeed. It's all part of a deliberate scheme. But rest assured, it'll come to an end soon enough."

Surprisingly composed, Williams gestures toward the door. "Thank you for your opinion, Mr. Landers. Please empty your locker on your way out."

Coming out of her near stupor, Chastity stands. "If he goes, I go."

Williams lets out a weary sigh, while Shaw shakes his head.

"I mean it," Chastity says, placing a hand on her hip.

With a smirk plastered on his face, Landers reaches out his hand. "Let's go, baby."

Chastity swallows. "Is this what you want, Chris?"

Williams runs a hand through his thinning hair. "You do what you've got to do, Chastity. You're an excellent physician, an asset to our hospital. These things of late, they're unusual. Out of character for you." His eyes shift toward Landers, who still holds his hand out for Chastity to take.

Landers drops his arm to his side. "Decide what you want." He turns and storms out of the room, deliberately slamming the door behind him.

Chastity slumps her shoulders. "I won't stay here if I'm not wanted."

"Things need to change. You can't keep berating and assaulting people," Williams says.

She lifts her head and nods wearily. "I understand." Her voice is barely audible.

"What do you want to do?"

Chastity slowly returns to her chair. "Tell me what you need from me."

Captain Williams nods. "End it with Landers. He's bad news. And whatever . . . " Williams clears his throat. "Whatever recreational activities you've been engaging in, they need to stop."

Chastity's face turns red as she bites her lip. "Yes, sir."

I furrow my brow and glance at Shaw. He gives a subtle nod. Whatever Williams is referring to, Shaw seems to be aware of it.

"Katie?"

My eyes dart to the captain, who rarely calls me by my first name.

"Will you be able to continue working with Dr. Morrow?"

"Um, yes, of course. I, uh . . . " I take a deep breath and mentally straighten my posture. I look at Chastity, who's staring at the floor. "I'm truly sorry I disobeyed your orders."

"They weren't mine. It was Geoff's idea. I-I went along with it." She still doesn't look up. "Bringing the families in was the right thing to do. I can see that now."

"Bringing them in via a controlled manner was the right choice." Williams nods. "Setting up a secondary location wasn't a terrible idea. But leaving them out in the freezing temperatures . . . " He shakes his head.

"Rand opened up the med school for them and got the woodstoves going. We still have a long night ahead of us, so we need to ensure people are as comfortable as possible. Leo's moving the injured from stretchers on the ground to beds when appropriate." Williams looks at Shaw. "Do we have a count of the deceased?"

"Approximately eighteen who didn't leave the base. Katie?"

I retrieve the folded paper from my pocket, the one where I jotted down backup numbers after recording them on the official clipboard. "Sixteen deceased, fourteen being kept comfortable, and twenty-two undergoing treatment. There are still at least two dozen with minor injuries at the base, waiting for our approval to transport. Um . . . these numbers might have changed. It's been about twenty minutes since my last count."

Williams shakes his head. "Did the governor send us additional troops?"

"They should be at the base already," Shaw responds. "The ones who took the orders to Sheriff Cabal were to come directly here once they ensured there would be no repercussions from the situation."

"Repercussions?" Chastity and I repeat simultaneously.

"There was a concern he may not take the orders in the spirit they were intended—to keep our efforts united."

"But he did?" Chastity asks. "He understands the governor wants us all to work together to survive?"

Williams adjusts in his chair, causing it to squeak. "You seem to be changing your stance, Dr. Morrow. Just a few minutes ago, you appeared to support Sheriff Cabal's actions."

"I'm sorry, sir. Sometimes . . . sometimes it's hard to know what the best course of action is." She coughs and quickly covers her mouth with her elbow. "Sorry. This day is catching up with me." She lets out a weary sigh.

Chastity looks exhausted. I'm sure we all do, but she appears especially disheveled. Her short hair is sticking up in various places, and she has dark circles under her eyes.

"How long has it been?" Shaw asks.

At first, no one responds. I'm not sure whom he's addressing or what he means. After several seconds, Chastity releases a sigh. "Since this afternoon." She clears her throat. "After the incident with Jesse Talbot."

Williams slams his hands on the table. "You treated patients while you were high?"

Chapter 15

Katie

The room falls into complete silence, save for the soft sob emanating from Chastity. I wish I'd had the chance to slip away before this bombshell was dropped. Chastity Morrow has confessed she was under the influence of drugs when the first wave of explosion patients arrived.

Chastity gulps, and her voice trembles. "I thought it'd be a quiet day. We'd had the trouble with Jesse and . . . and we needed a release."

Cutting to the chase, Shaw asks, "Do you have an addiction?"

"Of course not," she whispers, barely audible. "It was just . . . fun. A way to unwind, you know?" She lifts her red-rimmed eyes to meet Williams's.

He drops his chin and lets out a sigh. "I can't have you in my hospital. Not until you're well."

"I'll stop. I can quit. I'm not addicted."

"How long have you been using?" Shaw asks.

"A few weeks, since Geoff and I started . . . " She touches her ear to her shoulder. "Not long."

Williams rubs his fingers across his forehead. "That's several weeks, right?"

She exhales sharply. "The first time was after we did your surgery."

"Were you— "

"No." She shakes her head rapidly. "No. *After.* Never until that night. I was upset, thinking you might not make it. Maybe Nettie and I didn't know enough. I mean, you're the doctor. I'm a PA, and she's a med student."

"You've both been functioning as doctors since the EMP."

"Well, yes. But it's just . . . I was feeling bad. Geoff showed up at my house with a bottle of homemade wine he'd gotten from . . . " She looks at Shaw.

"On the black market?" he suggests.

"Yeah. The wine was fine, but I was still a mess. He said he had something stronger."

"Ploy?"

She sighs. "Yeah, I guess. But it goes by several names. I thought it was plain old weed at first . . . marijuana. But it hit me so hard. Geoff later told me it was synthetic. There may have been some marijuana mixed in, but it had other things too."

"Yet you continued using it, knowing what it was."

She lowers her gaze. "I kept using it."

"If it's the drug we're seeing, it's highly addictive—and deadly."

I raise my hand.

Williams waves his arm. "Go ahead."

"The one we were briefed about?"

"The same one." Shaw nods. Chastity looks as if she wishes she could disappear. "What'd you tell them, Chris?"

"What we discussed. How you found a few deceased individuals and suspected it was due to the drug." He directs his attention to Chastity. "You may have dodged a bullet, Dr. Morrow."

Her voice is soft. "I know."

"What can we do to help you?"

"I'll be fine. I told you— "

"Alice and I have extra space. Why don't you stay with us a few days?"

"No." Her response is harsh. She clears her throat. "No, thank you. It's not necessary. Shaw may believe it's highly addictive, but it isn't a problem for me." Her smile resembles more of a grimace. "I'm fine. Truly."

Williams exhales. "You have tomorrow off?"

"The next two days."

Williams looks at Shaw, who shakes his head. The captain gives Chastity a disapproving look. "I have little choice but to trust you can sober up on your own. When you return to work, I expect an update. I'll rearrange the schedule so you always have a shadow."

"That's not— "

"It is necessary. We'll probably have a med student do it, but possibly a medic or nurse. We'll have an extra on every shift. I can't trust you right now, Chastity. Until you earn my trust again, we'll all pay the price with extra work."

"Will you announce this?" She looks from Williams to Shaw and finally to me.

Williams answers, "I haven't fully decided how we'll handle this. While I don't intend to embarrass you, I do intend to protect our patients and our hospital." He motions toward me. "And our staff."

I know Williams is trying to help me, but pointing out how Chastity slapped me now feels unpleasant. Finding out she's using some sort of synthetic drug explains her recent behavior and even the slap. Despite my desire to stand up for myself, I can't help but feel sympathy for Chastity. I give her a weak smile.

She responds with a sheepish shake of her head, and the tears start again. I pull a handkerchief from my pocket. She mutters her thanks before using it. Several awkward minutes pass as we all avoid looking at her.

I ask if they need me for anything else or if I can go back out. Williams tells me to go ahead and get the numbers caught up. He'll be out shortly for an updated report, and then we can discuss Camp Rapid sending over the remaining wounded.

I leave the room and spend a few moments composing myself, taking several deep breaths as I observe the situation around me. The hall still has makeshift tables and gurneys along one side of the wall. Family members sit in chairs next to their loved ones. All the stretchers have been moved, creating more space and better physical comfort for the injured and visitors.

I reach for the bottle of heavy-duty alcohol-based sanitizer, made for us by a distillery in the Black Hills, and give my hands a generous squirt. Rubbing in the cleanser is almost therapeutic. I square my shoulders and make my way down the hall, starting with the first gurney—Private Emily Williamson.

Her boyfriend, who's also in the Guard, is by her side. He was working in the kitchen when the explosion happened, and she was in the rec room. While we marked her as a three, she may still have a chance if she regains consciousness.

While unlikely, it's possible her head wound isn't as severe as we believe. Without x-rays, CT scans, and MRIs, we diagnose as best we can. Other than her head, there's little physically wrong with her.

The boyfriend tells me there's been no change; she hasn't moved, and her breathing seems to have slowed down.

"Keep talking to her. Hold her hand. Let her know you're here." I give him a small smile and make a new note on the info sheet. I need to connect with Merissa and get the official record, but this will suffice for now.

I visit each of the injured and their families along the way as I move toward the front entrance where I last saw Merissa. While everyone injured has been marked as receiving no excessive measures, some, like Elliot Tillman, who likely severed his spinal column, are alert and oriented. Others are unconscious, like Emily.

Everyone has someone by their side. Some are praying, and some are talking quietly. There's even a couple laughing softly as they reminisce. The injured who are awake and aware likely know they're going to die and there's nothing we can do to prevent their death.

Merissa sees me and waves the clipboard in my direction before lifting a finger to signal me to wait a minute.

When Merissa and I finally connect, she quietly asks how I'm feeling while she stares at my cheek.

"Does it still look bad?"

"It's not good." Her mouth tilts into a slight smile. "I saw Landers storm out of here."

I pull my lips into a tight line. "Yeah. It got pretty crazy in there. Did you keep the report up to date?"

"It should be accurate. We've kept Rand in the loop, too, so he can send over family as they arrive." She passes the clipboard to me.

Merissa steps closer and lowers her voice. "Leo's in exam room three. Dr. Wolff took one of the triaged people in there. She thought, maybe . . . " She tilts her head. "His dad's sitting over there, waiting for news."

My eyes follow Merissa's line of sight to Elliot Tillman's dad. "Really?"

She shrugs. "Maybe. Dr. Wolff did a pinprick exam, and he responded. So . . . " She waves her hand. "Unfortunately, he's the only one she felt needed a more in-depth exam. Are the other doctors almost done?"

"Not sure. They were still talking when I left. The captain asked me to check the records and find out if we're ready to receive the rest of the wounded."

Merissa nods. "I think we're close."

"I'll talk with Mr. Tillman, and then I'll do a quick run-through to see exactly where we're at."

"We lost two more. All the deceased have been moved to patient room A. We've been holding off on calling Hugo. We're letting the families stay with them for now while Hugo does what he needs to at the base. I can't even imagine . . . " She shakes her head.

I briefly rest my hand on her forearm, and then step away.

Mr. Tillman stands when he sees me heading in his direction. "Sergeant?"

I offer a smile. "I don't have any news. I just wanted to check on you and see if you need anything while you wait."

"They told me not to get my hopes up."

"It's hard not to have hope. I know Dr. Wolff will do everything possible. She's extremely skilled. She worked with a neurosurgeon before starting at this hospital." I don't mention that Nettie was a med student *shadowing* the neurosurgeon, not actually practicing medicine.

"If he's paralyzed, there's not much they can do for him, right?"

"It depends on the injury. Without x-rays, we don't know the exact location of the paralysis. We can only gauge it based on his physical symptoms—where he has sensations and his ability to move. Let's see what Dr. Wolff determines from the exam."

"Thank you, Sergeant."

"Can I get you anything? Are you comfortable?"

"Comfortable enough. I'm not used to so much activity in one day. We walked from the care center to the base and then back again. When I heard about the explosion, I walked here. Didn't even check out of my halfway house." He gives me a wry smile. "They're probably wondering where I am."

"We can call them on the radio and let them know you're here."

"Would you? That'd be helpful."

I assure him I will, then make sure he's sitting again and is as comfortable as can be expected. I head to the desk with the radio base. One of the medics also carries a handheld radio in case we can't hear the base.

"Jesse, can you let the care center know that Mr. Tillman is here?"

"I will. Also, Hugo should be here within fifteen minutes to begin taking care of our deceased. Once we have a little more space available, the next wave of injured will be sent over from Camp Rapid."

Reluctantly, I knock on Williams's office door to let him know Hugo is on his way. He'll need to approve each transfer. Chastity and Shaw are still with him. She keeps her eyes on the ground when I poke my head in. Williams says he'll be ready.

Deputy Shaw asks if he's needed for anything, and when Williams tells him no, he steps out of the room. "You okay?" Shaw asks once we've closed the door.

I give a nod. "Better. I didn't realize— " I wave a hand toward the closed door. "About Chastity."

"I don't think anyone knew until recently. I only put it together this afternoon when Josiah told me about the trouble with Jesse and Landers. Did he leave?"

"Landers? I think so, that's what I heard."

"I'm going to check with my sentries. We're giving him a no-trespass order so he can't come to the hospital or the med school. If it were up to me, we'd run him out of town." Shaw stalks out the back door of the building.

It takes me the whole fifteen minutes, during which Hugo is expected to arrive, to catch up on my records. As I stop and talk with each family of the deceased, I let them know about the mortuary wagon arriving. Due to our urban location, most people will have their loved ones buried in the community cemeteries established since the EMP. One woman says she'll have her husband buried at a friend's place outside of town.

The front doorbell sounds and draws my attention. Hugo has arrived, accompanied by several people to assist him.

Chapter 16

Katie

With my clipboard in hand, I swiftly approach Hugo, Bowski, and the others. "Thank you for coming," I say, instantly feeling foolish. "I mean . . . " I shake my head.

"What happened to you?" Bowski gestures toward my face.

I instinctively touch my cheek. "Oh, uh . . . just a misunderstanding." I turn to Hugo and give him instructions. I've already prepared a card for each deceased person and have placed them on their stretchers. The cards contain basic information, with assistance from those who knew the deceased and the ones without family being based on their dog tags and injuries.

"Let me grab Captain Williams. He'll need to sign off on each card before you take them," I say.

Captain Williams is still in his office. He instructs Chastity to go to the on-call room and get some rest. Despite her insistence on going home, he advises her to take a break for now, reassuring her of a possible need for her later. As she follows us out of the office, she keeps her head down until she reaches the sleeping room.

Williams assigns me the task of leading as he makes his way to the first stretcher. The person lying there is alone without any family present. I relay the information I've gathered, and the captain shakes his head. "I've met this man. He was part of the Guard before the EMP."

I nod, noting the neat and tidy dog tag indicating his pre-EMP status.

Williams lets out a sigh and signs the card. "His wife died in a car crash on the day of the cyberattack. The traffic lights stopped working, and she got caught up in the chaos." Williams stands at attention, holding his crutches to the side. "Thank you for your service, Sergeant."

After he finishes signing, I signal Hugo. Williams and I continue down the row, with the captain offering his condolences to the families of the deceased soldiers, even though they aren't under his direct command. He acknowledges their bravery for serving their country and community.

When we finish attending to the deceased, there are still two gurneys in the hallway. Private Emily Williamson lies on one; her boyfriend's in a chair by her side. The other gurney is occupied by a man whose family has yet to arrive.

"Do we know if his family is in the med school?" Williams asks.

"Not yet, sir. They've done well at keeping up. Rand has an updated list and is sending people over as they arrive."

"Let's make sure we stay on it. Do we have an estimated time of arrival for the next wave of injured?"

"We're waiting for your approval to have them sent over. All are said to be in stable condition," I reply.

"Where's Dr. Wolff?"

"She and Leo are in exam room three. There was a patient who may have had an improvement."

"A level three patient?"

I lift my shoulders. "He seemed to be paralyzed. Nettie was doing rounds, and he showed some signs of feeling. I heard this secondhand."

"Let's go find out. Afterward, we can give the green light to send in the next batch of patients."

I knock lightly on the door of the exam room. Nettie invites us in, and I hold the door open for Captain Williams to enter first.

She gives him a slight smile. "Private Elliot Tillman has sensation in his legs. I'm not sure exactly what we're dealing with, but the examination is . . . " She looks to the young man and gives him a nod. "It's hopeful."

Leo stands nearby while a nurse adjusts the IV bag pole at Elliot's head.

"We've started him on IV fluids," Nettie continues, "and inserted a catheter. My suggestion is we allow him to rest and then reevaluate in about twelve hours."

"All right. Let's find a room for Private Tillman." Captain Williams spends a few more minutes talking to Elliot. When the captain learns Elliot's dad is in the waiting area, he asks me to update him and then take him into the room once his son is moved. He also instructs me to have Jesse notify Camp Rapid to begin sending the next wave in fifteen minutes.

It's a busy time as we get Elliot moved and clean all the rooms. Hugo and his crew are removing the last of the deceased when the radio alerts us that the truck has left with the next batch of injured.

The busyness of the day continues as the next wave of injured arrives. We've moved through about half of the expected wounded when Chastity comes out of the sleeping room. She still looks ragged, but after cleaning up in the bathroom, she's at least somewhat presentable.

My cheek is still red from her slap, and she cringes when she sees me.

With our hospital overflowing, we place the least injured patients that still require monitoring in the med school. Rand Hendricks efficiently warmed up the building by firing up all of the woodstoves. Beds are scarce, but we've salvaged many folding cots for our use.

Leo, Jacquie, and one of the med students take charge of the med school patients, using our handheld radios to stay in touch. Nettie will go back and forth between the buildings.

In addition to the wounded from Camp Rapid, we've had two people come in with the flu, both brought in by family when they became almost delirious with fever. They're in a private room in the med school to avoid infecting the injured.

About an hour after sunrise, the day after Christmas, I finally feel like things are slowing down. We've lost four more patients, including Private Emily Williamson, since Hugo and his team removed the initial deceased. He has sent Bowski and another man to retrieve the additional bodies.

"How's everyone holding up?" Bowski asks as he and I approach the first person. Captain Williams has already signed off on the death cards, so they're ready to go.

"Tired. You guys?"

"Yeah. Tired. Did you hear the news out of the California Wasteland?" Bowski asks.

"What news?"

"There was a radio report yesterday. Amateur radio. They said they're getting aid from China."

I crinkle my brow. "What kind of aid?"

"Supply drops. Air drops." He gestures as if something is falling. "They're parachuting things in. Food and supplies. There were papers with them that said, 'Merry Christmas from your friends in China.'"

"Just supplies?"

"That was it. Supplies."

"Hmm. I think I saw a movie or TV show about something like that."

"Yup. And I don't think it ended well. Supplies today, and who knows what tomorrow will bring."

"I'm sure they can use the stuff. Especially if they're giving them food. I thought China had their own troubles. Aren't they supposed to be taking over Thailand or somewhere?"

He snorts. "They were probably done with that a long time ago. Besides, what official news do we get? The president doesn't talk about anything happening anywhere but here. We barely get any info about home. Just do this, do that. Who knows what China, Russia, North Korea—any of the big players are up to."

"That's true. And really, food. They need it."

"No doubt. Makes me wonder what their long-term plan is, though."

I lift my shoulders. "I got a letter from my sister. She said there's a guy on the radio who . . . " I look around to see if anyone is near us. I take a step closer and lower my voice. "She said that he's saying there's no reason to evacuate everyone."

"That's Five O'clock Charlie."

"What?"

"That's what he calls himself. He broadcasts at five in the morning and five at night his time."

"Is his name Charlie?"

"Maybe? It's the name he uses. Said he got it from an old television show."

"Is he the same one who mentioned the Chinese supplies?"

"He's one of them. Several people reported it."

"How many people still have working radios?"

"There are quite a few. Some people had hardened radios. Others had backup parts or managed to salvage parts. Communications are improving. I've even . . . " Bowski's jaw clenches, and he inhales noisily. "I've sent a few messages myself, trying to find my wife and daughter. The town they were last in, though . . . there's no one on the radio around there. At least I haven't found anyone yet."

"I'm sorry."

"Yeah. Leo said you have family in California too?"

"My stepdad's brother and his wife. I'm not close to them, but I've met them a few times on vacations. He has two daughters slightly younger than me."

"Have they tried calling them on the radio?"

"Not to my knowledge. Things weren't working well when we left Bakerville. I don't know much about the current situation." I don't mention the fact that I still have several letters at home to read from the packet of mail we received yesterday.

Yesterday.

It feels like a lot longer since we were enjoying our Christmas feast with the National Guard, laughing and talking with people, some of whom are now deceased. A wave of sadness washes over me as I think of Duncan's new widow, Robyn.

Once Bowski and his helper finish, I make my rounds again and update our patient records. Now that we've slowed down and are gaining control over our wounded, we'll catch up on the records by creating an individual file for each person.

Each treatment room has a stack of papers with the patient's name and relevant information. Although commercially produced paper is scarce, we salvaged a good amount for our use, along with file folders. I start organizing everything to begin the paperwork.

"Need a hand?" Merissa asks.

"I barely know where to start. I guess maybe the recovery room? Do you want to gather everything up from exam room one?"

"Yep. Paperwork is always a great way to pass the time."

"Are you on your scheduled shift now?"

"I am. You're on night shift tonight, right? Are you going home for some sleep?"

"As soon as I organize some of this. Then I'll check with Captain Williams. He's on tonight as well."

"He's in his office. His wife brought food over—for all of us. She said he's going to eat before resting on his cot."

My stomach rumbles at the thought of food. I haven't had anything except a few sips of water since we arrived here yesterday afternoon.

"Where's the food?"

"Over at the med school. They still have their break room empty; ours is full of patients. The hospital kitchen also brought some. Not only for the patients but extra for us too."

"Okay. Great. I'll gather all the records from the room and go over there after I check in with Dr. Wolff." Normally, I would check with all the doctors on call, but right now, I'm not sure I want to see Chastity. "Have you eaten?"

"I have. Oh, I almost forgot. I spent Christmas Eve day with Opal. She asked me to invite you and Leo to join everyone on New Year's Day. She said to bring your little dog too."

I let out a laugh. "My little dog isn't so little now. He's growing fast."

"Opal said to bring him. There'll be a church service followed by brunch. You're on night shift that day, right?"

I lift my shoulders. "Maybe? It's very kind of her to invite us. I'll check the schedule. Are you going?"

"I'm planning on it. It's nice to go to the ranch. Quiet. Sometimes, I think Mother Pearl would prefer if we stayed there instead of me taking the job at the hospital and attending school."

"Does she want to move to the ranch?"

"We talked about it. She's going to stay with me. I, uh . . . she knows about the baby now." Merissa lets out a soft laugh. "It's hard to hide. She's excited and can't wait to help with him or her. Pearl knows being part of the school and hospital are good for me. It's good for her too. Did you hear she's been assigned to a work crew?"

I furrow my brow, trying to picture what kind of crew the elderly woman may have been added to. The few elderlies who've survived to this point of the apocalypse, especially those who are medically frail, are given work to do from home. While Pearl isn't in terrible shape, she does use a cane, and there are concerns about her mobility.

"Yep, it's true." Merissa smiles. "She's going to help at the daycare down the street from us. Pearl's not exactly warm and fuzzy, but she insists it'll be good training for when the baby arrives."

"That's great! How many children are there?"

"Quite a few, but not many babies right now. Of course, my baby will go there. And it's so close to here, I'll be able to visit during breaks. School breaks, anyway. Probably not during regular shifts. I'll have to figure out the nursing and everything. Captain Williams said it'll work out."

"I thought he told Leo you'd be able to bring the baby with you?"

"He did? He didn't say anything to me. I'll have to ask." She glances at her stomach. "Later. When it's closer to time. Anyway, Opal will send a wagon to pick us up for the New Year's celebration."

"It sounds good. Great, even. We've been trying to attend church service together. Leo goes to his men's Bible study and has gone to the base service a few times." My face falters as I shake my head. "I don't even know how many people Leo knows from there who died today. At least one."

She rests her hand on my shoulder. "I'm new to God and His ways. Church wasn't something I thought I needed until after the EMP. Even then, I wasn't too sure. When we were still in Livingston, when my husband was alive, we used to pray and read the Bible. I still take comfort in praying. There are a lot of new widows and widowers today. Sons and daughters, fathers and mothers who've lost loved ones. I'm not sure what we can do to help them, but I'm praying God will guide us."

My eyes sting with tears from Merissa's simple words. I whisper a soft, "Amen."

Chapter 17

Merissa

"How many is that?" Kerry Hendricks asks as we clean the exam room.

"Eight tonight—so far. We're only halfway through our shift."

"And five yesterday?"

I shrug. "Sounds right. We've been seeing a few every day since right before Christmas."

"I hope it's not like last year. A virus went through around this same time, and about a dozen people died. Most of them went unnoticed until later. They didn't seek treatment, simply stayed home and died."

"I heard there have been issues with people wanting to come to the hospital. Maybe that's changing?"

"We're trying to spread the word that people can come here. Stella played a significant role in making that happen. She's been urging other herbalists to encourage their patients to seek help at our hospital. It seems to be working. Alternatively, people might be starting to remember how life used to be and regain trust in our hospital." Kerry shrugs.

"Why didn't they trust it before?"

"I think it was a misunderstanding more than anything. When they first started putting it together, it was the captain and Doc Nettie—I mean, *Dr. Wolff*." She flares her eyes.

Even though Geoff Landers is no longer part of the med school, we still use proper titles. There was some discussion among the rest of us suggesting maybe, with Landers gone, we could be less formal. His lack of respect for everyone was the main reason we maintained formality. Captain Williams made it clear we should still refer to everyone correctly.

I don't mind being called Mrs. Weaver, but part of me wishes I could use my former Coast Guard rank, Petty Officer Second Class.

Petty Officer Weaver would fit in better with Captain Williams and the two Sergeant Burnetts.

Deputy Shaw, whose dad was also in the Coast Guard, inquired about my specialty. When I mentioned being a Damage Controlman, which just happened to be the same MOS as his dad, he was practically ecstatic. He even affectionately calls me DC2 for Damage Controlman Second Class. Or maybe they could call me "boss" like my wildfire crew did, which would undoubtedly raise a few eyebrows.

Jesse has mentioned he'd prefer being called Sergeant Talbot and is considering joining the National Guard. After his time in the Army, the Guard makes sense. I'm mildly surprised he hasn't done it already. If my circumstances were different, I'd probably join too. As if reading my mind, my baby gives me a solid kick in the ribs. My hand automatically goes to my stomach.

Kerry points to my stomach. "You okay?"

Now that Pearl knows about the baby, and my stomach looks like I've got a watermelon under my shirt, my pregnancy is no longer a secret. "He's just kicking. Nothing new."

She lets out a sigh. "Rand and I were trying for a baby . . . before all of this. It was month after month of disappointment. We had an appointment scheduled with a fertility doctor. Then the EMP hit, and . . . " Kerry lifts her shoulders. "I think we'll start trying again, once things are better. I can't imagine being pregnant right now." A look of embarrassment crosses her face. "I mean, I'm happy for you, but— "

I raise my hand. "Believe me, I understand. It's scary."

Kerry drops her shoulders and seems to relax. "I didn't even realize you were pregnant until the explosion at Camp Rapid. You hid it well."

I chuckle. "Not anymore."

We complete the room cleaning, and Kerry ushers in a patient from the waiting area. Today, I'm working as a medic while Kerry shadows a nurse. It's the final shift of my four-day run, and exhaustion has set in.

We've been inundated with sick people, and with it being New Year's Eve, there's potential for heightened craziness. I hope by the time my shift ends at 1800 hours, the chaos will remain at a minimum. The overnight shift might have a tough time, though.

Losing Geoff from our med school program and hospital rotations hasn't proven to be a significant loss. Despite his presence as a warm body, it turns out he didn't contribute much.

Dr. Morrow has been moping around since his departure and is currently on probation. The events surrounding her altercation with Katie remain unclear, but the fallout is evident. Now, she constantly has a shadow accompanying her during shifts, often a med student or a nurse from a care center.

During my first shift shadowing Dr. Morrow, I experienced an awkward and uncomfortable twelve hours. She barely spoke to me. Acting as her shadow, Captain Williams's orders are for us to accompany her everywhere except the bathroom. It's definitely an excessive amount of togetherness for my liking.

Rumors about why Dr. Morrow requires a shadow are rampant. Some believe Geoff threatened her, necessitating a safety precaution. Others speculate she made a mistake with a patient, and the shadowing ensures it won't happen again. Another theory suggests she has a drinking problem, even with the nationwide alcohol ban in place. The return of prohibition hasn't curbed the availability of black-market booze.

The drug trade continues to thrive alongside the alcohol trade. Following reports of a new synthetic drug before Christmas, we're now witnessing potential overdoses in the hospital. So far, no deaths have occurred on-site, but two additional deaths have been discovered elsewhere and are suspected to be overdose-related.

The drug called Ploy isn't the sole problem; homemade moonshine is equally dangerous. With the rising number of overdoses, persistent violence, and ongoing sickness, the establishment of the med school proves to be a valuable decision.

It amuses me mildly to think someone like me could become a doctor someday. While I took a few college courses, I never considered myself studious. As a Damage Controlman in the Coast Guard, I received basic first aid and medical training. I took extra medical classes, which proved beneficial after leaving the Coast Guard and joining the Forest Service.

However, becoming a doctor wasn't on my radar, especially at the age of thirty-six. Pursuing a twelve-year education seems unreasonable. Yet, Captain Williams's advanced course offers a promising alternative. He intends to train me as a fully qualified Doctor of the Apocalypse within two or three years.

Geoff once asked what would happen to us when the lights come back on and our world returns to normal. Although I occasionally ponder a return to normalcy, I doubt it'll occur any time soon.

While we're making progress toward recovery, particularly here in the Black Hills where we're considered leaders in the reconstruction efforts, it won't be as simple as flipping a switch.

Furthermore, after living here for several months, I suspect much of the talk about the Black Hills leading is mere propaganda. Whether perpetuated by the president or the South Dakota governor, things aren't nearly as advanced as the reports suggest.

The same applies to Billings, Montana. During our brief stay there, Mother Pearl and I found it to be no different from any other place; it was essentially a third-world country.

Now, with the information about the attempted coup d'état in Billings, I'm increasingly skeptical of the information we're being fed. With more rumors circulating, from the series of attacks to the nuclear bombs, the more it all sounds like an inside job.

However we ended up in this situation, we must keep moving forward. The only way out is through.

The radio on my hip emits a high-pitched squeal, snapping me out of my contemplation. "Rover One to hospital base, come in."

I take a deep breath and bring the walkie-talkie to my mouth. Rover One refers to law enforcement, either one of the deputies or the Citizen Patrol. It's sometimes challenging to distinguish between them without seeing them in person due to their similar uniforms.

"This is base. Go ahead, Rover One. Over."

"We need your medic. We have transportation and will arrive in five minutes. Be armored."

"Understood. Five minutes to arrival. Medic will be at the guard station, fully armored. Base out."

Dr. Wolff nods upon hearing the radio transmission. "You're good to go?"

"Yes, of course." It's standard operating procedure for me, as the medic, to accompany the police or soldiers upon their request. I slip into the closet housing our tactical gear. Five minutes isn't much time to put on the multiple layers I need.

I grab body armor and a Kevlar helmet before rushing to the break room where my locker is located. I pull my heavy cargo trousers over my scrubs and put on a sweatshirt. I slip the armor on, leaving one side of the Velcro undone for a buddy to check later.

Then, I hasten to the backdoor, where my boots, coat, and other winter gear are stored. I quickly lace up my boots, leaving my coat unfastened and winter gloves in my pocket, but manage to put on my beanie and helmet. With my personal emergency gear hanging from one shoulder in a daypack and the hospital gear in a large duffle bag, I'm ready to go.

As I step out of the front door, I'm sure I've exceeded the five-minute mark. I hurry to the guard station, located two hundred yards away. Despite the cold, I find myself out of breath and perspiring when I finally reach it.

Josiah Talbot is on duty at the guard station and nods at me. "Want to step in here and do up your boots?"

I reply with a breathless nod as he makes space for me to use the lone straight-back chair. I manage to tie both boots and zip up my coat before Josiah alerts me to the approaching truck. By the time they arrive, I have my boots laced, coat zipped, and gloves on.

Deputy Shaw emerges from the passenger's side of the old white pickup, adorned with a hand-painted gold star lined in black on each door. "DC2." He nods at me. "Take the front seat. I'll ride in the back and brief the team."

"Yes, sir."

I recognize the driver, identified by the red band around his arm as a member of the Citizen Patrol. The sheriff's deputies still wear official county or city uniforms, albeit worn and threadbare.

After the EMP, the city police department dissolved, and the remaining employees were absorbed into the county sheriff's department, along with a few highway patrol officers. Although they collaborate with the sheriff's department, the highway patrol operates independently under the direction of the governor.

The whole arrangement can be confusing. Initially, the sheriff's department hired deputies to replace those who were either killed or had to prioritize their families. However, something went wrong in a different district, and the recruitment of official deputies was halted. That's when the Citizen Patrol was established.

Instead of traditional deputy uniforms, they wear plain clothes with a red armband indicating their status. Some people have drawn parallels between the red armbands and a past fascist group, usually those who have had negative encounters with the law.

The driver offers me a tight smile and a nod. "Weaver, right?"

"Right. And your name?"

"Oscar Harrington."

As soon as he mentions his name, I remember him as the one who lost his father last fall and was severely injured himself a few weeks later while trying to apprehend his father's killers.

The assailants were part of a burglary ring involved in the black market. They targeted individuals based on what they brought in for trade. They'd follow them home and conduct reconnaissance to determine their work schedules. Then, they would break in and steal valuables while the victims were away. Unfortunately, they weren't always accurate in predicting their targets' schedules.

On the night of the break-in, both Oscar and his dad were supposed to be at work but had a last-minute schedule change. Tragically, Oscar's father was killed during the robbery.

The burglars had been a mere nuisance up to that point, but they became public enemy number one after they took the life of a law enforcement officer. In November, the culprits were captured but managed to escape during their transfer to the main jail.

A violent confrontation ensued, resulting in the deaths of two law enforcement officers and all but three escapees. Eventually, all the escapees were accounted for, with two of them breaking into Katie Burnett's house to seek medical treatment. None of them survived.

Rumors circulated about the escape being an inside job, with someone from law enforcement aiding them. I must admit, it wouldn't surprise me.

"What's the situation?" I ask.

"Some kind of standoff. One of our team members is pinned down after attempting to intervene in a domestic dispute."

My lips tighten, and my stomach churns at the mention of a domestic dispute. During my early days as a hospital medic, I underwent training alongside the officers, and they emphasized the dangers of such situations.

The trainer, previously employed by the Rapid City Police Department, stressed how domestic violence perpetrators could turn on a dime, harming not only their loved ones but also the responding officers, often displaying little remorse. I suppress a sigh as Oscar takes a sharp right turn.

Chapter 18

Merissa

As we make the turn, the tail end of the truck hits a slick spot and fishtails. Oscar expertly regains control. I glance out the back window, peering through the fully stocked gun rack, to ensure everyone in the bed of the truck is okay.

Despite a few inches of snow on the ground, this winter is somewhat normal compared to the previous one. The temperature fluctuates, sometimes snowing and turning cold, then warming up above freezing with a few days of sunshine. We're currently in a warming trend, with single-digit nighttime temperatures and relatively balmy midthirties during the daytime. If not for the biting wind, it'd be T-shirt weather.

Thanks to the warming cycles, vehicles have been operable this winter, unlike last year when the Black Hills, Livingston, and every other place I've heard of were buried under record-breaking snowfall. The deep snow, combined with the absence of above-freezing days and a shortage of snowplows, made it difficult for the pickup trucks and other vehicles to move.

The snow hindered many things, including some of the violence we're witnessing this winter. Most people hunkered down and focused on survival, but not everyone made it. Many froze to death, others fell ill, and some chose to end their own lives in this new world.

Around April, when the weather began to transition from perpetual winter to something resembling spring, they established detailed workforces and ration systems, officially dividing the city into manageable districts.

The project had been in progress since before the snow, with the establishment of various satellite hospitals and infrastructure. The division of the city and the work and ration framework received numerous accolades for the reconstruction efforts.

Another factor contributing to the praise is the underground research facility in nearby Lead, South Dakota. While I'm uncertain about the specifics of their research, there's a rumor their scientific equipment survived the EMP due to the depth of the facility. Now it's being used to help the Black Hills and the entire country recover. A knock on the truck's cab interrupts my thoughts.

Oscar slows to a stop and rolls down his window. "Right here, boss?"

"We're a few blocks out, so we'll use this as our staging area and walk the rest of the way."

Assuming it's safe from the ongoing situation, we all unload. Glancing around, I realize I'm unfamiliar with the area. It's not surprising since I mainly travel between my small house and the hospital. If my memory of the city map is correct, we're east toward the Main Street District.

"McKay." Deputy Shaw points to a man around my age. "You're with Medic Weaver." He turns to me. "Switch your radio to the operations channel if you haven't already."

I nod and comply, as he proceeds to assign stations to the other four men and two women. Oscar is part of the assault team, so he hands the truck key to McKay.

As everyone completes their final gear check, McKay offers to inspect my setup. He ensures my body armor is properly placed, and I do the same for him. After the others depart, McKay and I retreat to the cab of the truck to escape the wind, maintaining a comfortable silence.

Within a few minutes, gunfire erupts in the distance. McKay shakes his head. "Too soon. They didn't have time to get into position."

The voice on the radio confirms McKay's suspicions. "He's on the run. Repeat, he's on the run. I'm hit and lost sight of him."

Chewing the inside of my mouth, I shake my head. My trainer was right about domestic disputes often turning bad. "What do we do?"

"We wait here until Shaw either calls us or magically appears. Are you armed?" He removes his semiautomatic pistol from his hip and places it within easy reach on the dashboard.

I retrieve my own weapon and position it on the seat next to my leg.

He responds with a curt nod. "We have the rifle and shotgun too. You know how to work them?"

Giving him a nod of my own, I confirm I do.

The gunfire subsides, and the radio falls silent as seconds tick by. I open my mouth to inquire about leaving the truck when there's a knock on my window. Startled, I turn my head and find myself face to face with the muzzle of a gun.

"Hands up!" shouts the masked man outside.

McKay lets out a groan and mutters something about his own stupidity.

My stomach sinks as I place my hands on the dashboard.

The man raises his other hand, and before I can fully comprehend the situation, he hits the window.

McKay yells at me to get down as he swiftly reaches for his pistol on the dashboard. I lower my head into my lap as the gunshot reverberates in the confined space, causing my ears to ring and startling my unborn baby.

The man outside returns fire while shouting something I can't discern.

McKay makes a gurgling noise as the assailant fires again. With my head still down, I grip the handle of my pistol, trying to maintain focus. After the second shot, the man's obscenities fade away.

I remain as still as possible, keeping my pistol under the open window. I glance toward McKay. His blood-soaked hands clutch his neck.

I take a deep breath and use the radio to inform Shaw and his team we've been attacked and McKay is injured. I suspect the assailant has left, but I'm uncertain. Shaw instructs me to keep my head down and assures me help is on the way.

"Hold on, McKay," I say, even though it's evident his wound is fatal. "They're on their way. We'll . . . " I shake my head.

His eyes close, and his hands fall away from his neck.

I slump my shoulders. "Sorry, McKay." Biting my cheek, I realize I don't even know his first name. While I appreciated his lack of chitchat earlier, part of me wishes I had asked about him. Is he married? Does he have children? Did he know God?

My eyes widen. That's not something I'd typically consider. I barely know God myself, so why am I wondering if this stranger who died next to me did?

"Weaver, come in."

"I'm here, over."

"We have eyes on the truck. You appear to be alone. We're going to approach. Do not shoot. Repeat, do not shoot."

"Copy that."

Within seconds, an officer orders me to open the door and step out. I place my pistol on the truck floor and cautiously open the door, ensuring my hands remain visible. Oscar Harrington comes into view from the truck's tailgate. "McKay?"

I shake my head.

"Clear," Harrington shouts. Three more team members emerge from their concealed positions. I tilt my head, silently asking if I can lower my hands.

"Go." Harrington nods.

I move to the driver's side and reach through the shattered window to confirm McKay's condition.

Deputy Shaw joins me. "We lost him?"

"He was shot in the neck. There wasn't . . . " I shake my head. "Sorry."

Shaw lets out a weary sigh. "Did you see the shooter?"

"Not really. He was wearing a ski mask. Is he your assailant?"

"Did you see his clothes?"

I close my eyes and recall the scene. The muzzle at the window. The black ski mask. A hooded sweater in a burned yellow shade. "Black ski mask and a dark yellow sweater." I gesture to my own hoodie. "That's all I saw."

Shaw's expression hardens. "Sounds like our guy. Patitucci is injured. They're bringing him to you, along with the assailant's girlfriend. She was beaten."

He turns to Oscar Harrington. "Let's move McKay to the truck bed, then follow the blood trail and locate the suspect. We'll wait until Patitucci is stable so Weaver can drive him to the hospital." He turns back to me. "Do you need someone with you?"

"I'll manage." I don't mention I'm not entirely familiar with the area. Although I'm unfamiliar with this neighborhood, I paid attention during the drive here and am confident I can find my way back.

"Uh, Shaw?" Oscar Harrington steps forward. "He attacked our vehicle once . . . " Oscar raises his hands.

Shaw's mouth tightens into a grim line. "Send Holce to ride shotgun."

A minute or two later, a trio of Patrollers, one supported by the others, comes into view. Following closely behind is a woman, clutching her arm to her side with visible blood on her face. Patitucci's wound isn't life-threatening but requires more medical attention than I can provide in the field. The woman may have a broken bone in her arm and requires a few stitches on her face.

Holce turns out to be one of the women in the group. She rides in the truck bed with McKay's remains, while Patitucci and the assailant's girlfriend ride in the cab with me. Most of the glass in the side windows were shattered by the gunshots.

After Holce pointed it out, I discovered a small piece of glass had nicked my cheek. It was nothing more than a scratch, and I didn't bother with an adhesive bandage since supplies are limited. I simply wiped it with a damp cloth and called it good. I'll have Dr. Wolff or one of the nurses check it later.

The return journey to the hospital is uneventful, and I manage to navigate without any wrong turns. By the time I finish my report and wrap up with everyone involved in my day, the overnight shift has already taken over.

"What happened?" Katie Burnett asks, gesturing toward my cheek.

"I had a medic call. There was an incident. One of the Patrollers was killed."

Her eyes widen, and her mouth forms an *O*. "You're okay?"

I shrug. "I'm uninjured. It was . . . " I sigh. "Are you still heading out to the ranch tomorrow?"

She gives me a long look. "We're looking forward to it. It'll be nice to have a day off—a peaceful day."

Chapter 19

Katie

"Hello, Opal!" I wave and call out as the wagon approaches. "I didn't expect you to be the one to pick us up."

"Good morning, Katie and Leo." She gives us both a wide smile. "Are ya kidding? I love drivin' the wagon. Mind riding in the back? Pearl will want to sit on the bench."

"No problem."

"Look at your little dog. He's finally living up to his name. Hello, Geronimo."

Gerry wags his tail and gives her a doggy grin, then promptly trips over his large paws as he steps toward the wagon. One of the horses reacts to Gerry's sudden movement, causing both my dog and my husband to move in the opposite direction.

"That was close," Leo mutters.

Opal chuckles. "See you're still not a fan, Leo. Don't worry. They can't hurt you none while you're in the wagon . . . as long as I don't try and run 'em." She laughs again.

I lift Gerry and set him on the wagon. Leo motions for me to go ahead. Even with his arm in a sling, getting into the wagon is easy for him and his long legs. It's more challenging for me, but I manage.

Pillows, cushions, and blankets are arranged along the bed of the wagon. Gerry wastes no time finding a spot, spinning around to get comfortable. I nestle in next to him, and he puts his head on my lap, allowing me to cover us both with the blanket. He lets out a contented sigh.

I lean back against the front of the wagon, close enough to Opal for conversation if needed. Like Gerry, I let out my own contented sigh. A day away is exactly what I need. I even managed to get two hours of sleep after finishing my shift this morning at 0600 before Opal picked us up. With the entire day off, I'm almost ecstatic. Leo reaches for my hand, indicating we're ready.

With an "ayup," Opal gets the horses moving, and we pick up Merissa and her mother-in-law Pearl at their house down the block.

Merissa rides in the back with us. She pulls a blanket up to her chin. "I thought you were going to bring your dog?"

Leo laughs and gestures toward the lump under the blanket as I pull it back to show her. Gerry lifts his head, then readjusts his position.

"Aww! He's adorable."

"He knows it too." I cover us both with the blanket again. It's cold today, a departure from the warm and comfortable winter days we've experienced recently. A fresh layer of snow has graced the landscape overnight, painting everything in a pristine and picturesque manner— a fitting start to the new year.

As Gerry snuggles closer to me, I can't help but wonder what this year holds in store. My prayers are for peace and a return to normalcy; although, I must admit that I no longer grasp the concept of "normal." People talk about a new normal, but considering how things have changed, that phrase seems inadequate.

I let out a slow breath and try to calm my thoughts amidst the chaos of uncertainty. Today's church service is precisely what I need—a chance to connect with others, especially Opal, whose calming presence always steadies my jumbled mind. I swallow my emotions and manage a smile for Merissa.

Returning the smile, she nods. "Did you see the report on Elliot Tillman?"

"I read it and talked with him for a bit last night. His dad showed up too. They're going to try to move him to one of the care centers today, maybe tomorrow."

"He does seem to be doing well," Merissa says, "even though he still doesn't have much feeling below the waist. Sometimes he responds to sensations, other times he doesn't."

"Right now, it's a waiting game." I pet Gerry as I speak. "Captain Williams thinks the spinal cord may simply be swollen. If that's the case, he could recover almost fully."

"Yeah. I'm sure once med school starts up again, we'll be studying paralysis." She turns to Leo with an expectant look.

"No doubt." He nods.

Although Leo has also been looking forward to going to Opal's today to be with other believers, part of his brain is elsewhere. It's been a difficult week with the memorial for the dead. With winter in full force and the ground frozen, the burials won't happen until spring.

In addition to Duncan Robson, Leo knew four others who were killed—three from his Bible study group and one from his visits to the base. The search for the people behind the explosions continues.

While we initially believed the bombing on the base was by the same people responsible for the other explosions, there's some concern the two events are unrelated. The original detonations involved explosive devices left behind while the perpetrators escaped. These were suicide bombers. There's still concern about how the men were able to get the explosives into the jail with them.

Whether it's the same group, part of the military attempting insurrection as in Billings, or a new force, we're paying attention. It's possible the men who caused the explosion are behind it all. They're now dead, so we might not have anything to worry about. However, it's unlikely. More likely, those men were pawns in a bigger plan.

Unfortunately, with many of our service men and women killed, we can't increase sentries and guards to help protect our vulnerable locations. Even the hospital, which had three guards since the attack on the ration building, is down to two.

They're keeping two in place—one in the front and one in the back—since we experienced a failed attack a few weeks ago. While the attack on our hospital failed, two other district hospitals suffered damage and casualties.

The sheriff's office and Citizen Patrol also take sentry shifts. But now they're short-staffed, too, after one of the Patrollers died and another was injured yesterday when Merissa went out on a call with them. The injured patroller will recover, but it'll be several weeks before he can work again.

"So, tomorrow?" Merissa asks. "We're still on?"

"We're on, but we'll take it easy." I motion toward her expanding stomach. A few days ago, Nettie and I discussed starting basic hand-to-hand combat training. Before the EMP, Leo and I took classes in Krav Maga, an Israeli martial art and an efficient form of self-defense.

After moving to Bakerville, our community received martial arts training as part of our survival resources. I've needed to use these skills on more than one occasion. Before Leo broke his arms, we regularly practiced to maintain our skills.

With all the recent violence in Rapid City, Nettie asked if I'd teach her a few moves. We were practicing during our lunch break the other day when Stella Swenson asked to join. She told a few others, and now we're forming casual classes.

Merissa, who's also trained in self-defense, will help lead the classes along with Kerry Hendricks, who gained basic fighting skills during her time in the Army. Captain Williams even offered us a room in the med school building to use, and Lieutenant David Paul said he might find us a few floor mats.

Merissa leans toward me. "What's going on with Chastity?"

"Uh . . . " I lift my hands slightly without removing them from under the blanket. The motion causes Gerry to move closer to my leg. I quickly drop my hands and pat his head.

"Mm-hmm. I'll admit, I was surprised nothing more came of her slapping you. I thought maybe she'd be fired right alongside Geoff Landers. Did you hear he left? Moved to Deadwood or somewhere."

"Good," Leo mutters. Although we both heard he left, neither of us is confident he'll stay gone. The guy is trouble.

"Yeah. It's crazy about the sheriff and his attempt to take over the hospitals." Merissa shakes her head. "What's the purpose? I guess corruption isn't dead, even in the apocalypse."

"Especially not in the apocalypse." Leo shakes his head. "It seems to be running rampant. Although I do think some good will come out of the trouble with Melvin Cabal and his quest for power. I saw Bowski yesterday, and he said there's a rumor the governor is going to change the ration process, trying to somehow integrate it with the black market. Bowski didn't have many details, but he's been called to a meeting about it."

"Really?" Merissa asks, a soft smile flittering across her face.

"In Pierre?" I ask, wondering why this is the first I've heard about this.

"No, they're meeting in Wall. Wall Drug is being used as a conference hall. I don't even think the governor is in Pierre now. The Office of the Governor has been on the move . . . hiding out, sort of like we think the president is doing."

Since we first started hearing radio announcements from the United States president last February, it's been almost like a game trying to figure out where he is. The rumor is he moves around a lot, staying hidden as best as possible. After the senators and representatives were assassinated in the early days of the attacks, it became necessary. The governors of each state are supposedly doing something similar, as well as the remaining members of Congress.

Not that it significantly impacts our day-to-day lives. Although the South Dakota governor still appears to be actively leading, most states aren't in the same position. We've heard the Montana governor hasn't been seen or heard from since before the EMP. The Wyoming governor made a solitary radio announcement, and that's about it.

Perhaps it's a good thing this governor wants to meet with Bowski, although part of me wonders if it could be some kind of trap, maybe an attempt to completely eradicate the black market rather than bringing it into legal channels.

"When's the meeting?"

"Not sure. They said they'd let him know. Depends on weather and other factors."

I give a nod.

"About Chastity?" Merissa asks.

Sighing, I shake my head. "I don't know much more than what Captain Williams said. She's having a rough time and needs assistance while on her shifts."

I must admit, I was mildly surprised Williams didn't openly disclose her drug use, especially considering the briefing we received about the drug problem afflicting Rapid City and the surrounding area. Deputy Shaw confided in me his disagreement with Williams's decision but deferred to him since he's in charge of the hospital.

The ride to Opal's farm is brief and passes quickly as Merissa and I engage in conversation. I attempt to ask her how she's holding up after yesterday's events, particularly the death of McKay. She dismisses my concern with a wave of her hand and changes the subject by asking about Gerry.

Occasionally, Opal or Pearl chime in for a chat, but for the most part, the two sisters enjoy their own lively conversation and laughter.

As we turn onto Opal's lengthy driveway, Merissa raises her chin. "It's nice to see them like this. Mother Pearl needs to laugh more."

"How's her job at the daycare going?"

"It seems fine. She's only gone once so far. She's with the babies, so they aren't too rowdy. Nonetheless, it takes a toll on her. I know she wants to contribute, and I admire her for that. But at her age, they have easier tasks and rations for a reason."

When Opal brings the wagon to a halt, several individuals emerge from the house, barn, and other structures. I'm assisted down from the wagon, and Gerry is showered with attention by a young girl around six years old.

It's a whirlwind as we meet people, with names and faces blending together. I spot Opal's son Shawn, one of the few familiar faces, and offer him a wave. He nods in return.

Bowski is standing beside Shawn. I had no idea he'd be here today. A blush spreads across Merissa's cheeks, and she acknowledges him with a subtle wave. My gaze lingers on her for a few moments, and I consider her reaction. Leo takes the initiative to step forward and greet the men.

"All right, all right," Opal interjects, motioning everyone back. "Give them some room. You all act like you've never seen people before. Goodness." She turns to Merissa and me. "Don't worry. We're all excited to have the celebration. Katie, have you met my husband, Kevin?" She gestures with her thumb toward the man standing beside her, one of the few who hasn't introduced himself.

He resembles a slightly older and shorter version of Shawn, with his hair pulled back into a ponytail at the nape of his neck. His hair might even be longer than mine—I wonder where he finds hair bands.

"Welcome." He nods at me. "Merissa, good to see you. You're looking well."

Merissa tightens her coat around her midsection. "I'm feeling well, thanks."

"Shall we all head inside where it's warm? I believe everyone's here, and we can start the service."

I motion to Gerry.

Opal crouches down beside him. "Bring him along. He can listen to the Word of the Lord with the rest of us. I'm sure some of our dogs will join as well." She motions toward two large dogs sitting at the outskirts of the gathering.

Another person holds a small, fluffy dog in their arms. The person lifts the dog's paw and makes it wave at us. The simple action, so commonplace in years gone by but rarely witnessed in today's world, almost brings tears to my eyes.

Chapter 20

Katie

Kevin guides us toward the spacious barn, which feels more like a garage with its cement floor and roaring woodstove. As we enter through a small door, he points out a bathroom on the right. The back of the garage is equipped with large overhead doors, all three shut tight to keep the cold at bay.

Folding and camp chairs have been arranged in front of a lectern near the warm fire, while a freestanding coatrack stands nearby. Leo hangs up his coat, but I choose to keep mine on. Despite the room feeling warm, I'm still chilly from the wagon ride.

Shawn, whom I've always considered to be a quiet person due to his infrequent speech, steps to the front. He appears nervous as he walks, but once he reaches the handcrafted pulpit, a transformation takes place before our eyes. His shoulders relax, and a smile spreads across his bearded face. With a calm demeanor, he surveys the room. "Thank you all for joining us today. We are especially grateful for our guests."

He nods toward us before turning his attention to another group, welcoming them as friends and neighbors. I wonder if they're the same neighbors I had heard about—the ones training their dogs for sentry duty.

While dogs can be highly beneficial and have historically been put to work, Opal said these dogs have been trained with a tendency toward aggression. She recognized the value of training dogs—using their own dogs on the ranch to assist with cattle and as watchdogs—but she disagreed with the intensity of the neighbor's training methods.

I glance down at Gerry, who sits calmly by my feet. His eyes fixate on one of Opal's large dogs resting at the end of the row. The big dog flicks its tail a few times before lying down and resting its chin on its front paws.

"Shall we stand?" Shawn asks. Once we're on our feet, he leads us in singing "Rock of Ages." The initial softness of the song gradually gains momentum as everyone becomes more comfortable. Following the song, Shawn leads us in prayer, and then we sing two more songs I'm not familiar with.

Shawn's preaching is amazing. His voice is clear, resonating throughout the spacious building. He preaches from the book of Micah. While I'm not well-acquainted with this book, I'm deeply moved by his reading as I follow along in my own Bible.

The room falls into complete silence when he recites the words, "And what does the Lord require of you? To act justly and to love mercy and to walk humbly with your God."

"I know I haven't always acted justly. I certainly did not love mercy, and I was not always humble."

"You've got that right," a woman, whom I believe was introduced as Shawn's sister and Opal's older daughter, interjects.

Shawn points at her and winks. "She knows too many of my secrets. You know who else knows my secrets? God."

Shawn continues with his sermon, delving into other verses that not only highlight what God observes but also emphasize His love for us and remind us of what the Lord requires from us.

My gaze shifts to the back of Bowski's head, reminding me of a conversation we had a few weeks ago. Bowski spoke of how he made it a point to help the people of Rapid City in the hope God would see his actions and ensure the well-being of his wife and child, wherever they may be. Bowski claimed he was not performing these acts for his salvation, but rather to exhibit the fruit of his salvation. Although I'm not entirely convinced he's fulfilling God's expectations, his methods are very human.

My mind drifts to the letters we received from home. Although the letters didn't contain any significant news, it was heartening to hear from home and learn about everyone's activities.

The letters were dated in November, and Sarah's letter was brimming with plans for her Christmas wedding. Angela extensively discussed the family's endeavors and the jobs everyone has taken on to keep the community running smoothly throughout the winter.

This year, she has been assigned to work in the greenhouses, which amuses her since she has never had a green thumb and struggled to keep houseplants alive. Sarah is once again in charge of the sewing and mending crew, primarily comprised of the few remaining elderly individuals who wish to contribute.

Jake's letter, despite appearing to be several pages long and held together with a paper clip, was actually only one page front and back. The remaining papers were items he had sent from my mom's filing cabinet, thinking they might be useful to us as we join the National Guard.

In my letter, I had communicated how Lieutenant Paul mentioned if we could provide proof of our college education, there might be a chance for us to be commissioned as officers. Jake sent copies of my transcripts, which my mom had retained. Surprisingly, she also had a copy of a graduation announcement about Leo. It seems she wanted to know precisely who I was dating and conducted a thorough internet search in the weeks prior to the attacks.

According to Jake, my mom had several copies of various findings, including the list from K-State of individuals who received their spring degrees. It sounds like something my mom would do.

We're still uncertain if these documents will have any impact on our status within the National Guard. With the recent deaths and funerals, we're waiting for a more appropriate time to present them to Captain Williams or Lieutenant Paul and see what they say.

After gathering all the prayer requests, Shawn offers a prayer and leads us in a final song. "Again, thank you for joining us today. We'll take a few minutes to transform from church service to dining hall."

Considering Leo's one-armed condition, he does his best to help rearrange things. Mostly, he keeps Gerry out of the way while I follow Opal into the house to assist with the final food preparations. With most of the cooking already completed in advance, it's only a few minutes before we bring the food out to the waiting tables. The meal is delightful but not extravagant, just simple and delicious home cooking.

One of the dishes is a delectable beef stew accompanied by amazing biscuits. Opal informs me the biscuits are made from wheat they grew and processed on their own land. Although they thought they had a decent harvest, their supply is already running low, and they won't have enough wheat to last until the next harvest.

Corn and barley, which they have cultivated in the past for livestock feed, produced better than the wheat. Nonetheless, they're satisfied with their initial attempt at becoming farmers instead of solely ranchers. Winter wheat seeds have already been sown, and they hope for a bountiful harvest to come in late May or sometime in June. Opal is optimistic about the harvest's yield.

I'm at the dessert table when the door flies open. "We've got trouble!" a man yells. Chairs clatter across the cement floor as everyone gets to their feet. I rush back to Leo's side.

Kevin Maher calls out, "What's wrong?"

"Something's happening at the fence line. Hayward's dogs are going crazy. Earl and Hobbins have gone to check. They sent me to get reinforcements."

Opal shakes her head. "They might have cornered a deer again. You know what happened the last time."

"We'd better check," Kevin says before calling out several names. They all grab their coats and quickly head out.

"Please, go ahead and finish your meal," Opal says. "They'll set up a perimeter. The cowbells will sound if we're under attack. You all know to go to the office next to the bathroom?"

People nod and agree they do, while the other guests shake their heads. Merissa leans over and tells us the room next to the bathroom has been reinforced. The children and elderly will go in there while the rest of us take up guard positions.

Even though Opal encourages people to eat, no one does. She strides toward us. "I'm sure all will be fine. Those dogs often overreact to things. But just in case, you have your med kits?"

I gesture to my backpack hanging off my chair. Leo's is on the floor. Merissa points to her kit on the floor before saying, "I think we're set with med kits. Plus, you have one, too, right?"

Opal gives a single nod. "The infirmary is well stocked. Like I said, it's probably nothing."

Many long minutes pass, about fifteen according to my watch, until Shawn comes through the door. "We've got injured. They're being taken to the infirmary."

Leo, Merissa, and I grab our coats and bags and follow Shawn. Pearl and her friend Walt, who came east with them from Montana, offer to watch Gerry for us. Opal says she'll be right behind us.

Outside, several men I've yet to meet, along with Kevin, Bowski, and some of the others from the church service, are standing around.

Off to the side, another group of men and three dogs are present. All the dogs have blood on them in various places, including their snouts.

Did they cause the injuries, or were they injured too? They seem fine and are sitting attentively. I avert my eyes from the dogs back toward Shawn. As we near a building, Merissa touches Shawn's arm. "What are we dealing with?"

"The dogs." He motions back toward the groups of men and three dogs. "Hayward thought his ranch was under attack. He sent out the dogs. One of the men inside—a boy, really—says they were passing through, trespassing but not doing anything bad. He's got some bad bites. The other man is worse. The third man . . . " Shawn shakes his head. "He didn't make it. He died on the way here."

"Three dogs took down three men?" I ask.

Shawn tilts his head. "Yeah. Three unarmed men. A rarity in today's world, but we didn't find any weapons on them. The one talking said they'd been robbed a few days ago. They were trying to find someplace safe and heard Rapid City had food in exchange for work."

Leo sighs. "Let's see what we have." As we take a step forward, there's a shout from the gathered crowd. I turn to see what's happening just in time to witness the punches starting to fly. The shouting escalates, and it's a full-on brawl. The three dogs remain off to the side, hair raised and teeth bared, but unmoving.

I head toward the fight, but Leo puts his hand on my arm. "Stay here."

"You all knock it off!" Opal yells, then starts ringing a cowbell. The clanging jolts some of the fighters out of action.

A few men from inside the garage join Opal. They step forward and start pulling people apart while she keeps ringing the bell. It takes a full minute before the ruckus subsides. There are still shouts and threats of violence, but the physical altercation is over. Kevin, who was part of the fight, sends his wife a sheepish look. His nose is bloody, and there's a cut on his chin.

Leo groans. "Looks like we'll be doing some bandaging."

"You all better watch yourselves," an older man points to Kevin.

"Take your dogs and go home, Hayward." Kevin points toward a house in the distance. "Your dogs killed an innocent man. The sheriff is going to hear about this."

"My dogs protected my property. Your property too. They did what I've trained them to do."

I glance at the dogs again. My heart aches at the things they've been trained for. It proves the saying I've heard: there are no bad dogs, only bad owners. Does Hayward using his dogs as killing machines make him a bad owner? In the world we used to live in, there'd be no doubt. But now, the lines are blurred. Survival is survival. We've all done things we've hated doing to preserve our lives and the lives of loved ones.

The neighbor whistles, and his dogs take off. Some of his men look pretty banged up and are limping as they walk. I ask Leo if we should check them, but Shawn says Hayward's wife will take care of them.

Leo asks Merissa and me if we can take care of the men in the infirmary, and he'll do a quick triage of the others, sending anyone who needs care to us.

"Be careful," I say, motioning to his arm.

Inside the small shed, which has been turned into an infirmary, there are two twin-sized beds. There's a man on each. Merissa and I each choose one. My guy is unconscious and has a makeshift tourniquet around his arm. The arm below the device is a mangled mess.

My stomach churns at the sight. While the tourniquet is not a professional job, it seems to be holding. I take my own tourniquet out of my bag and put it in place above the bandanna, leaving what was already there intact. I mark the time on the one I apply, subtracting twenty minutes to account for the original.

I turn to Merissa. "My guy needs the hospital. There's a tourniquet in place."

"Yep. He needs a doctor too." She gives the young man, who's talking and coherent, a slight smile before turning to Shawn. "Is the hospital in your district available?"

"It still isn't at full capacity since the explosion. I'll get the wagon. We'll go to your hospital."

A few minutes later, the injured men are loaded into the wagon. Pearl says she'll stay at the ranch for now. Opal says she'll take care of the brawlers since there aren't any serious injuries. They'll keep the dead man until arrangements can be made. Merissa's patient thanks Opal.

"How old are you?" Opal asks.
The boy mutters something indistinct.
"Pardon?" Opal says.
He clears his throat. "I'm sixteen."
Merissa and I both let out a sigh at the plight of the boy.

Chapter 21

Merissa

When we reach the hospital, the place is hopping. "Merissa." Jacquie Haley gives me a nod. "What do you have?"

"Dog attack," I say. "Katie's patient is critical. Mine is stable."

She turns to Katie's patient, taking in the tourniquet and his overall condition. "I'd take him directly to surgery, but Williams is already in there."

"What happened?" Katie motions to the full waiting room. People are coughing, sneezing, and blowing their noses. I instantly feel like I'm in a petri dish.

"Nothing good." Jacquie shakes her head. "It started last night. Williams's patient was coughing so hard that she passed out. She slipped down the steps, broke the handrail and her leg bad. We were already overwhelmed, so Dr. Wolff called in Williams. Let's get your guy set up. I'll let Dr. Wolff know."

Katie turns toward me. "I guess my shift is starting early. I need to talk to Leo and have him take Gerry home. He'll probably come back."

I give a nod. "I'm on tonight, too, so I might as well get at it. We'll be here for the duration."

Katie scurries toward Leo, touching his arm while they talk. She bends down and rubs her dog behind the ears. I help my young patient to a chair, then tell him someone will be by shortly to get him taken care of.

Once I'm changed into my hospital clothes and washed up, I find Jacquie and ask how best I can help. "Can you help Katie with triage? If Nettie needs to remove the arm, I'll assist her."

I'm taking the temperatures of a new family that's arrived for treatment when the front door sounds again. I glance up to see Leo, Bowski, and a couple of men from the ranch. Despite my efforts to control it, a faint smile plays on my lips.

Bowski lifts his hand in greeting. "I had no idea you were so busy. Opal said they need stitches. Since it's on their faces, she figured it'd be best to have a pro. Maybe we should go back?"

A symphony of coughs interrupts us. I inform the family I'll be right back and swiftly approach Bowski so I can assess the two men. One of them requires stitches above the eyebrow, while the other has a cut near his lip.

"I doubt we'd get to you guys any time soon. Truth is, whether Opal stitches you up or one of us does, you'll probably end up with a scar. Besides, you might encounter more than stitches if you stay here." I gesture to the crowded room. Katie appears by my side and agrees it'd be best if Opal could handle it.

"Yep." Bowski nods. "Leo, Katie, I'll see you two later." He turns to me. "Your mother-in-law is in the wagon. She wanted a ride back home."

"Thank you. Could you let her know I'm starting my shift now and won't be home until . . . " I let out a sigh. "I'm not sure when. At least tomorrow morning. Did you see Shawn? He left a few minutes ago."

"I met his wagon on the way in. What a day, huh?"

Leo leans closer to Bowski. "Has there been trouble like this with the neighbors before?"

Bowski shakes his head. "Not that I know of. There's been a few tiffs but never an actual fight. Hayward used to be a good guy. Lately, he's gone a little off the rails. Things are tense between him and Kevin Maher now. The wives are still friends, though. They try to keep things from getting too crazy. But after today . . . who knows. I'll take these guys back to Opal. Is this serious enough you'll need Hugo?"

I shake my head. "I'm not sure yet. One of the men we brought in will have to have his arm amputated."

Bowski furrows his brow. "I'll stop by later and see how things are going. I'd like to give Hugo a break if possible."

After Bowski leaves, Leo changes into his hospital attire and heads to the surgical suite. Katie and I continue attending to the sick patients. As we work, Dr. Wolff emerges from an exam room and signals us over. I excuse myself from my patient, assuring them I'll return shortly. Katie does the same with her patient.

"How'd it go?" Katie asks.

"Not great. He's alive, but . . . " Dr. Wolff shakes her head. "That was from a dog? A pet dog?"

Katie and I share a glance before she responds, "Trained dog. I saw them. They looked fine. Not wild or anything. Very well behaved. Did Jacquie tell you they killed another man? And there's one more waiting to be seen—a boy."

"I heard. I'm going to check on the boy, and then we'll continue attending to the sick people. There are a lot more people here now. I think we need to open up the med school. This situation looks bad." She gestures toward the coughing individuals. "It's going to spread, just like last winter. As if we don't have enough troubles. Has Williams come out of surgery yet?"

I shake my head, while Katie says, "I haven't seen him. Leo went in to assist."

"I'll poke my head in and make sure he's okay with using the school. I'm also sending for Chastity." She raises her eyebrows. "Not that I want to." She mutters the last sentence under her breath and walks away.

Within ten minutes, we begin the process of converting the med school into a secondary treatment center. We still have cots set up in a couple of rooms from the day of the explosion. This building, which used to house several businesses, offers ample space.

When it was first repurposed as a school, Williams only prepared one business suite for use. However, after the attack on the ration building, he realized the need for expansion. Clearing out the rooms wasn't a problem; they had already been organized in the past. The challenge was gathering the necessary supplies to transform the multi-suite office building into a functioning clinic—woodstoves for winter heating, treatment tables, beds, and more. Additionally, we had to stock up on medical supplies to avoid constant back-and-forth trips.

Williams managed to gather a small crew of workers, and they made significant progress before the explosion at Camp Rapid. Although the situation has improved, with the building now equipped with heat and basic supplies, there's still a long way to go before it becomes fully functional.

Our main obstacle is the lack of personnel. With only three doctors and a handful of nurses and medics, we don't have enough staff to efficiently run two buildings. As aspiring doctors, we understand the urgency of learning our skills quickly and thoroughly. As soon as Williams is able, he'll start training more nurses. He's even considering adding a few additional janitors, who play a crucial role beyond cleaning.

With fires burning in several woodstoves at the med school, I conduct quick examinations of those waiting in the hospital triage area. The least severely ill will be selected to move to the second building once it's heated up and Chastity Morrow arrives. Fellow med student Kerry Hendricks has gone to fetch her. They should return soon. Williams also asked Kerry to visit the remaining med students' homes and call them in for duty.

I work with Katie, checking in patients and determining who should be directed across the parking lot and who needs to remain in the main hospital. As we attend to a new family of sick individuals, the front doorbell rings and another family comes in. I instruct them to have a seat in the last of our four chairs.

The back door chimes, and I breathe a sigh of relief. I glance down the hall and spot Kerry and three other med students stomping the snow off their boots. I keep my eyes on them, waiting to see Dr. Morrow. After Kerry hangs up her coat and moves to a bench to remove her snow boots, our eyes meet. She shrugs her shoulders and shakes her head.

My brow furrows. What is she trying to tell me?

I return to the family of four and inform them I'll be with them shortly before making my way down the hall to Kerry. Along the way, I'm stopped several times by people inquiring about when they'll be able to see the doctor. My response is always the same: "As soon as they can attend to you," accompanied by the most pleasant smile I can muster.

After exchanging greetings, the med students inform me they're going to change into their scrubs and find out where they're needed.

"You might want to hold off on that for a moment," I suggest. "We're converting the med school into a clinic." I motion to the multitude of people filling the hospital halls. "Maybe keep your street clothes on and take your scrubs over there to change? It's going to be chilly walking patients back and forth. We're waiting for Captain Williams to finish surgery before we begin the transition."

They nod and indicate they'll organize their belongings before returning promptly.

Once they've stepped away, I ask Kerry about Chastity.

"She wasn't home. I left a note on her door."

"She did have the day off. Maybe she had plans?" I speculate.

Kerry snorts. "Who knows? Chastity doesn't talk to me about her plans. We're not friends. Not anymore, anyway."

I respond with a slow nod. Same here. I don't actually know the woman. She was friendly to me when I first started here, but I noticed a change in her when she started dating Geoff Landers.

"Stella will be here shortly," Kerry says. "She's gathering a few herbs she thought may be helpful for this flu, or whatever it is. Did they mention where they want me? Should I go to the med school and assist Rand with the preparations?"

"You should check with Katie. She's managing triage."

Kerry nods and strides down the hall toward Katie.

Dr. Wolff emerges from the surgical suite. "Are we ready?" she asks.

"I think so. More people have arrived. They're ambulatory and don't look terrible. Katie is checking them. Kerry's back. She didn't find Chastity but left a note on her door."

"Chastity wasn't home?"

"I guess not. She didn't answer her door."

"Great. Even with as wishy-washy as she's been lately, we could use her help. I can't wait until all you students are better trained."

I choose not to remind her Captain Williams expects it to be a couple of years before we're fully functioning doctors . . . if we make the cut. The rest of us will act as nurses or medics instead of full-fledged doctors. "Should we try and get some of the nurses from the care centers to come in?"

"Let's see how we are once we get people moved. Are all the students here?"

"Stella hasn't arrived. Kerry talked to her, and she's on her way."

"She knows what we're dealing with? Maybe— "

"Kerry told her. She's bringing some herbs."

The door to the surgical suite opens, and Williams and Leo join us in the hallway. "Are we ready to move?" Williams asks.

"Waiting on your okay. Chastity wasn't home," Dr. Wolff says.

"We'll make do."

"Would you like me to take the med school?" Dr. Wolff motions in the direction of the other building. "You stay here?"

"Let's have Jacquie handle the other building. She'll take Katie, all the med students, and Rand. We'll keep the rest of the staff here with the sickest. How's your arm guy?"

She scrunches up her face. "Not doing as well as I'd hoped. Jesse is in with him."

Williams looks at me. "Change of plans, Merissa. You'll monitor the amputee for now. We'll have Jesse help move people to the school building. Only ambulatory people, but I want them escorted. Let's clear the hall and waiting room as best we can."

I nod, fully aware of the gravity of the situation unfolding before me. I square my shoulders and take a deep breath as I mentally prepare for the duties ahead. So much for a relaxing New Year's Day.

Chapter 22

Katie

With a frazzled expression, Stella adds kettles of water infused with herbs to the woodstoves in the med school waiting room. As she pours more water, she says, "Every time you walk by, check and make sure it has enough water. Okay, Sergeant Burnett? Add a scoop of herbs from this jar whenever you add water."

"Okay, sure," I acknowledge with a nod.

Stella shakes her head and leans closer to me. "Katie, this is terrible. There are so many sick people. We need to get things organized."

While I understand Stella's concern, I believe we're fairly organized given our situation and location. Unlike the hospital, which boasts an open layout with ample sunlight from the setting sun, this section of the converted office complex feels more enclosed. It used to be a computer-based business, back when computers were still a thing. Originally, it had a small waiting area, a receptionist area, a couple of offices, and numerous cubicles.

The first step was removing the cubicles. Williams kept the waiting area intact and expanded it to include the receptionist space. He had the private offices transformed into treatment rooms, and a wall was knocked down to annex the adjacent office space, converting it into a large dormitory-style sleeping room for patients requiring overnight stays.

Currently, we have people resting on cots while they wait to be seen, and we've added many chairs to accommodate both sick individuals and their accompanying family members. Even those who claim not to need treatment are coughing and sniffling.

In the waiting room and sleeping area, the woodstoves provide warmth, while the kettles of herbal-infused water introduce humidity to the dry air and create a pleasant aroma.

Jacquie enlisted Stella to assist her in examining each patient. Despite Stella's anxious demeanor when speaking with me, she remains composed and calm when attending to the sick. They've provided patients struggling to breathe with bowls or pots of steaming water and blankets to create steam tents.

As day transitions into night, we move from one patient to another. The process is slow and further impeded by the continuous influx of new patients. Our triage system shifted from conducting examinations at the hospital to conducting a preliminary assessment at the guard station.

Kerry is stationed there to determine whether the new patients need to be sent to the hospital or the clinic. If she cannot make an immediate determination, she's instructed to err on the side of caution and direct them to the hospital. Some clinic patients initially deemed not severely ill in the initial triage have ultimately been transferred to the hospital following their examination.

It is almost 2300 hours when Nettie approaches to check on our progress. She appears utterly exhausted after being on duty since 0600.

"We're okay," I respond. It isn't entirely truthful but not entirely false either. "How's the man with the arm?"

She shakes her head. "We lost him about an hour ago. I'm sorry."

I sigh in response.

"You did everything you could, Katie. Your treatment was the best possible. He was already unwell before the attack. Did you see how skinny he was?"

I lift my shoulders. "Still, I hate this part of it."

"We all do," she says with a sad smile. "Chastity still hasn't shown up. Williams sent Jesse to her house to check again. The note was still in place, and she didn't answer her door."

"Weird. Maybe she's out of town? Or staying with a friend?"

Nettie steps closer to me. "Or maybe she ran off with Geoff Landers. Have you heard he went to Custer?"

"Custer? I heard he went to Deadwood. Does anyone even know for sure if he left Rapid City?"

Nettie grimaces. "I don't even know who started the rumor he left town. Williams told me he heard that one of the drayers gave him a ride. But I don't know if he spoke to the drayer. Seems Williams heard it from Shaw who heard it from someone else. The Black Hills grapevine is alive and well."

"For sure."

"I'll go check with Jacquie to see if she needs anything. I'm glad to see Stella has set up the steam tents. She also left us an herbal blend. We've created a similar arrangement over there. It certainly adds a pleasant scent. I can't imagine what we'd do without her and her herb garden."

Working throughout the night, my official twelve-hour shift is ending. Even so, it's unlikely I'll be leaving anytime soon. Jacquie, who's been on duty for over forty-eight hours, is taking a nap in one of the offices down the hall. Kerry is currently on a half-hour break from the guard station triage and is warming up by the fire.

"What a night."

I stretch and twist my back. "I don't think the day's going to be much better."

"No. Did you hear Williams tried to get us another doctor?"

I shake my head. "We only have the handheld over here. Jacquie and Stella keep it in case they have an emergency. I'm out of the loop."

"This sickness is widespread. All the districts are heavily affected, including the surrounding towns. Even the doctors and nurses are falling ill."

I bite my top lip. "Do you think Chastity is sick? Maybe that's why she isn't answering her door?"

Kerry shrugs. "That's a good question. Maybe? She's had a cough since Christmas, but she never seemed truly sick, you know? I should get back out there. It's so warm in here, though. It makes me want to curl up and nap."

About twenty minutes later, Leo shows up. I haven't seen him since I transferred to the clinic. Since Captain Williams had his partial amputation, Leo's stuck pretty close to his side. We shared a laugh about it—a pair of invalids teaming up. I believe it's less about Williams needing Leo due to his foot problem and more about their comfortable teaching relationship at the med school. Leo acts as Williams's aide more than anything.

"Feel like stretching your legs?" Leo asks after saying hello and asking about how things are going.

"Meaning?"

"Kerry suggested Chastity might have this flu. Williams wants us to check on her and get inside the house. Deputy Shaw will meet us there and unlock the door."

I wrinkle my forehead. "He has a key to her house?"

"Apparently locks aren't much of an issue for him."

"Can you give me a minute to check in with Jacquie and let her know?"

After updating Jacquie and putting on my warm jacket and boots, Leo and I head out. "Brr. I wish I would've gone to the hospital and changed into my street clothes."

"We can do that," he offers, motioning toward the building.

I tighten the hood of my insulated sweater and pull my stocking cap lower over my ears. "Let's just walk fast."

"At least it's close by." Leo reaches for my hand, and we intertwine our gloved fingers. "How're you holding up?"

"Tired, but this walk should wake me up."

"No doubt."

Shaw is already waiting for us in front of Chastity's house, accompanied by his dog, Tank. I drop to my knees to greet the pup. He has grown huge and lives up to his name, his tongue lapping across my chin.

"He needed a walk," Shaw says, motioning toward the dog.

"How's the training going?" Leo asks. Shaw plans to train Tank for police work, though the specifics remain a mystery.

Shaw snorts. "Lots of energy. Short memory."

That sounds like the Tank I know. When he and the others were still living with us, Tank was always the most rambunctious and the hardest to train. Potty training, leash walking—everything was a challenge. We had warned Shaw, but he was smitten with the dog from the first meeting. My guess is Tank may be more of a pet than a working dog.

"Williams mentioned you're overwhelmed with sick people. How many?"

I shrug. "We have seventy-seven in the clinic."

Leo shakes his head. "We have about double that number in the hospital. It's insane. Did you hear we tried to call in another doctor from one of the other district hospitals?"

"Yep. It seems everyone is affected. We had a similar situation last year. Many deaths occurred. Williams said it was because they were already weak. We didn't have the rationing system in place then, and everyone had to work to survive, coupled with poor hygiene. Hopefully, it won't hit as hard this year."

"Poor hygiene is still an issue." I shake my head. "I can't count how many times I've had to remind people to cough into their elbow and avoid touching their faces. We're using hand sanitizer liberally."

"We didn't have that last winter—the hand sanitizer, I mean," Shaw clarifies. "They were making it in Deadwood, but there was so much snow they couldn't get it to us. You have a good stock of it?"

I bob my head. "Decent. And at least the weather isn't as harsh as last year." A shiver runs through me. "But it's still cold. Can we go inside and check on Chastity?"

Leo and I follow Shaw and Tank up the walk. I point to the chimney. "No smoke."

"Might be a wasted trip," Shaw says. "Oh well, the dog needed the exercise anyway."

We wait on the large porch while Shaw knocks sharply on the door. The note is still in place. I press my face against the window. The curtains are closed, but there's a slight opening where they meet. I cup my hands around my eyes, trying to get a glimpse inside.

The room is dark. As evidenced by the lack of smoke, the woodstove shows no sign of flames. As I'm about to pull away from the window, something catches my eye. I squint, trying to make out the sight. It's one of Chastity's shoes. The angle is odd, not like a shoe sitting on the floor but more like a shoe on a foot lying on the floor.

I step away from the window and try to make sense of what I'm seeing.

"Bingo," Shaw says as he opens the door.

"Wait a minute." I motion toward the door. "I think something's wrong." My hand rests on the butt of my gun as I lean against the house.

Chapter 23

Katie

Following my lead, Leo and Shaw both draw their weapons and move away from the door. Shaw gestures with his head and asks, "Katie, what'd you see?"

I release a breath, trying to calm my pounding heart. "I'm not exactly sure. I think she's on the floor. I don't know."

"Is there an intruder?" Leo interrupts.

"Maybe?"

Shaw scrutinizes me briefly before nodding. "All right. You two know how to slice the pie?"

"We do," Leo affirms.

Shaw points to Leo's gun. "You can handle that? Are you trained to shoot weak-handed?"

"Yep. I'll take the middle?"

Shaw agrees, instructing Tank to sit and stay. He then assigns me the right, saying he'll take the left. I've never been in Chastity's house, but judging by the porch and the exterior, Leo and Shaw will likely handle the living room and main living areas. There's probably a room to the right of the living room, but it might be closed off instead of having an open floor plan. This means I'll only have a small area to cover.

Setting up takes us mere seconds. The door, already unlocked thanks to Shaw's lock-picking skills, remains closed. He asks me to turn the knob while Leo kicks the door open. The execution is flawless, and we swiftly enter the house. As expected, my area is mostly wall and empty space. The smell inside hits me hard—a scent I've unfortunately become too familiar with since the beginning of the apocalypse.

Shaw has moved into the living room. "Chastity's down. Katie, take care of her. Leo, let's finish clearing the house."

I move quickly to where Shaw is and drop to my knees next to Chastity. Her eyes are open, staring vacantly at the ceiling. I don't need to check her pulse to know she's gone, but I do it anyway. Her skin is cold, just like the house.

My nose burns, and my throat feels scratchy. I squeeze my eyes shut and try to suppress my emotions. When I believe I'm in control, I open them to assess the scene. Chastity's head lies in a pool of vomit, and there's more around her mouth. I don't see any obvious signs of injury.

Shaw calls from another room, declaring the house is clear.

Leo steps into the living room. "Dead?"

"Yeah. Is anyone else here?"

"No."

I point to the coffee table. "There was. Look . . . two glasses and an empty bottle."

Leo lets out a sigh as Shaw joins him. "Let me fetch my dog, then we'll figure this out."

After standing up, I take a throw blanket from a side chair and cover Chastity with it.

"What do you think? Overdose?" Shaw asks.

"Seems likely." Leo motions to the coffee table. Even though Chastity's drug use isn't common knowledge, Williams told Leo and asked Leo to let me know he'd been informed. "Although, the only thing I see is a bottle that looks like it had either wine or some sort of spirit in it."

Shaw approaches the table and picks up the bottle with his gloved hand. He sniffs it and grimaces. "Wine, I think. Or something too sickly sweet to actually drink."

"You think Geoff Landers was here?" I ask, scanning the room. Like most places these days, her house lacks decoration or anything requiring extra maintenance.

"Hard telling." Shaw shakes his head. "Considering how much time he spent with her, I'd expect there to be more evidence of his presence. I'll inform Hugo. Will you two inform Williams?"

"Yeah." Leo nods. "This is a blow. Chastity may have been going through a rough patch, but she was a good doctor. We needed her." He turns toward me. "Are you all right?"

I release a raspy breath. "Not really."

Shaw uses his radio to call Hugo. Since his channel differs from the hospital's or police's, the news will be kept discreet for now. However, as the Black Hills grapevine demonstrates, it won't remain a secret for long. At least Leo and I can return to the hospital and inform Williams before word spreads too far.

Hand in hand, we walk back to the hospital. The cold feels even more biting, and our pace slows. Tears stream down my face as we go, increasing my chill. Chastity and I were friends—or at least I thought we were until the incident with Landers. I was still angry at her for slapping me, but I thought maybe we could work things out and become friends again. Hearing that Landers moved away gave me a glimmer of hope.

But now . . . she's dead. I'm also seriously questioning whether Landers is truly gone. Two glasses strongly suggest she had company. Was it Landers or someone else? Did she have a small New Year's celebration with someone? I furrow my brow, trying to recall when her last shift was. New Year's Eve, I believe.

I pull a handkerchief from my coat pocket and blow my nose loudly. "What'll we do without a third doctor?"

Leo shakes his head. "I'm not sure. Eventually, they'll probably send someone from the main hospital, though not until this sickness is over. It's going to be a challenging time until then. Williams has been trying to put on a brave face, but it's obvious he's struggling. His foot, the med school, his regular physician shifts . . . it's too much. I don't think Nettie's faring much better."

"Is that why Williams has you by his side so much?"

"Probably. This incident with Chastity and the drugs only added to his stress and workload. He had to rearrange everything so she always had someone watching over her. I suppose there's no way to keep this problem a secret now. Not that it was much of a secret anyway. The med students were already whispering about it."

"Yeah, I know. You heard Merissa in the wagon . . . was that yesterday?"

He chuffs. "Yep, just yesterday when we attended the church service at Opal's. Feels like a lot longer."

I dip my chin. "Merissa was asking about Chastity. It was obvious she'd been struggling."

He lets out a sigh. "Was she a Christian?"

I shake my head. "I don't know, but my guess is no. She once came into the break room while I was reading my Bible and told me she wasn't a churchgoer. I wish I had taken the time to talk to her, to share the gospel." Tears well up again. "I've been so angry at her, I never considered how much she might need the Lord, with the troubles she was facing and how horribly she treated people. I never prayed for her or anything. Just . . . " A cough interrupts my words.

Leo motions me to stop walking and wraps me in a hug. He whispers soothing words in my ear, and I break down even further, melting into him as tears flow uncontrollably.

We remain in our embrace for several minutes until he says, "It's too cold to be out here like this."

Finally, we reach the hospital and enter through the back door, with Leo using his key to let us in. We used to leave the back door unlocked, but that changed when we received a threat against the hospital. In the midst of the apocalypse, even making keys is a tedious task. The owner of a local hardware store had a vintage key-making machine he managed to get working. He replaced the lock and crafted enough keys for the hospital staff, including spares in case of loss.

Williams is tending to a patient when Leo pokes his head into the exam room and requests a moment of his time. Williams emerges into the hallway and notices me. He shakes his head and gestures toward his office with one of his crutches. Once we're inside the privacy of the room, he sighs and says, "Tell me."

I try to be stoic and fail miserably, suddenly overcome with emotions.

Leo rests a hand on my shoulder, and he delivers the news. "Chastity's dead, sir."

Williams gives a slow nod as he visibly swallows. When he finally speaks, his voice is shaky. "Was it the sickness or the drugs?"

"We aren't sure, sir. She was in a puddle of vomit. Looks like it happened yesterday, maybe earlier."

"So, the drugs?"

"There was a bottle of wine or something," I add, my voice sounding scratchy.

"I should've done more for her." He sinks into one of his chairs, allowing his crutches to fall to the floor.

"Deputy Shaw is calling Hugo," Leo says. "Does she have any family?"

"Not nearby. They're back east somewhere. Was Landers involved in this?"

"Unknown, sir."

He scrubs his face with his hands. "We lost two of the sick patients while you were away. The elderly woman you assisted me with, Leo, and the little girl."

Leo's jaw clenches as he nods in understanding.

"Yeah. I don't think they'll be the only ones." Williams gives a weary sigh. "I'd better get on the horn and see if they'll send me another doctor now. There's no way Dr. Wolff and I can handle this on our own."

"I'll return to the clinic, sir," I say, stepping toward the door. "Unless you need me for something else?"

"No, that's where I need you. Make sure you arrange a sleeping rotation with Jacquie. We'll all be here longer than any of us would like." He looks at Leo. "You should do the same with the staff here. Do you need to go home and check on your dog?"

"He's with the neighbor." Leo glances at me and offers a small smile. "I'll see you later."

I dip my chin. "Should I let the others know, sir? About Chastity, I mean."

"Might as well. I'm sure people are wondering why she isn't here."

In the hallway, I lean against the wall and close my eyes, letting out a long breath. *Please, Lord. Help those who are sick. Help us help them.* I exhale another sigh, which transforms into a cough—no mere delicate cough, but a massive, rib-racking cough.

Chapter 24

Katie

I'm still hunched over, gasping for air, when Leo emerges from Williams's office. "Katie?"

Raising my head, I signal with my index finger to give me a moment. Finally able to breathe, I stand up, only to be seized by a sneeze. I barely manage to position my elbow in time to contain it. "Ugh. Gross." I mutter, my voice raspy.

"When did you start feeling sick?"

"I don't feel sick. At least . . . I didn't. It just hit me."

He wrinkles his face.

I tilt my head. "My throat felt slightly scratchy at Chastity's. But I thought it was . . . you know, emotions? Finding her and all. Are you okay?"

He shrugs. "We'll find out soon enough. Williams mentioned Jacquie sent a note with Rand while we were away, saying one of the med students was now coughing. She doesn't feel sick yet, so she's wearing a mask and doing what she can without touching patients."

"I don't feel sick." As I speak, a wave of exhaustion washes over me. Whether it's due to the illness or simply being awake for too many hours, I don't know. "I'll grab a mask and head back to the clinic. Will you inform Williams?"

"You could go home."

"We're already short-staffed."

His lips tighten. "If you start running a fever, you need to lie down, okay?"

"I'm sure Jacquie will have someone checking me regularly."

Leo exhales and closes his eyes. When he opens them, he reaches for my hand. "Be smart, Katie. Don't run yourself into the ground."

"I'll be smart. You'd better go wash up. I don't want you to get sick." I shake my head, recalling the embrace we shared on our way home. As husband and wife, we've already exchanged plenty of germs with each other. Did I catch this in the short time I've been at the hospital? If so, it's certainly a fast-acting illness. Or maybe I contracted it somewhere else? Perhaps during the few hours we spent at Opal's ranch?

Since right before Christmas, we've had sick individuals at the hospital nearly daily. I've worked several shifts since then. Most of the time, they weren't severely ill, and we sent them home with a portion of Stella's homemade cough syrup.

The syrup, a blend of wild honey and a few herbs or spices, tastes so good it's almost a treat. Stella even admitted it's tempting to use more than necessary, but it isn't always the best choice.

Often, the best option is to forgo cough syrup altogether and let the body heal naturally. Rest and ample fluids are Stella's preferred remedies. Unfortunately, those aren't always easy to come by. There's little time for rest when we all have so much to do just to make it through the day.

Leo heads to one bathroom to wash up, while I make my way to the break room, equipped with a sink. We also keep a supply of cloth face masks there. I put one on and stash two more in my pocket. Unlike previous occasions when our hospital was overwhelmed with injuries, the break room is devoid of patients. Opening the clinic to care for those who appear less ill was a wise decision.

The cold air seems to have intensified since Leo and I walked back from Chastity's place. I wrap my jacket around myself and hurry across the parking lot to the med school turned clinic.

Checking in with Jacquie, I first inform her about Chastity. She shakes her head and lets out a sigh. She points to my mask, inquiring about the reason.

"I started coughing. And sneezing."

"Oh, no. Do you need to go home?"

"I don't think so. I don't feel terrible. I'll keep you posted."

"Let's check your temp. We'll go from there."

After a quick examination, which reveals a normal temperature, Jacquie agrees with my plan of assisting without direct patient care unless absolutely necessary. She informs me things seem to be slowing down. Since I left for Chastity's house, we've only had two new patients.

Jacquie, who had worked closely with Chastity like I had, mourns her passing. We both distanced ourselves from her recently due to various issues that arose in our budding friendships.

My responsibilities include monitoring the water containers on the stove, as well as janitorial tasks, which have been challenging to keep up with. As the hours pass, I continue to cough and sneeze, but no fever develops.

Jacquie has implemented an hourly check of not only my symptoms but those of the entire staff. By late afternoon, I'm not the only one wearing a mask due to coughing and sneezing. Rand Hendricks is even running a fever. In anticipation of more staff catching this sickness, we've opened another room specifically for our needs.

Before falling ill, Rand built a fire in the small woodstove, and I set up a stockpot of water and herbs. Stella also makes sure all the staff has some kind of antiviral herbal concoction, which is a hot and spicy apple cider vinegar. Those of us with a cough are being administered one of her cough syrups. Not the tasty one we'd been giving patients, but one heavily infused with garlic.

With numerous staff members now sick, we've had to reevaluate the tasks we can and cannot perform. I'm back to treating patients but making every effort to minimize contact while frequently sanitizing my hands and changing my face mask as needed. We don't have an on-site laundry; it's all done in a nearby house and delivered daily. When the wave of illness began, Williams informed the laundry workers. They've regularly been picking up our soiled linens and items—including face masks—and delivering fresh ones.

Food is also prepared off-site, so the cooks have been called in, along with the crew responsible for our water supply. Despite having ample firewood in our stockpile and even in an indoor storage room in the hospital, a team is delivering additional wood to the clinic. It truly is a community effort. Unfortunately, some of the workers vital to sustaining operations have also fallen ill, much like the hospital staff.

During the next hourly illness check, Stella asks how I'm feeling.

"About the same." I shrug. "I don't feel terrible unless a coughing fit hits me. Then it's not fun."

"Is the cough syrup helping?"

I make a face. "Maybe?"

After confirming I have no fever, she administers another dose of the unpleasant concoction. When I shudder after my dose, Stella gives a light laugh. "It'll treat what ails you. Jacquie said you're to take the next four hours off. Go get some rest."

"What are we hearing from the hospital? Are they starting to slow down?"

"New patients have decreased, but like us, the staff is also falling ill. It's going to be a long few days."

Chapter 25

Merissa

"Merissa?" There's a gentle tap on the door. "Are you awake?"

I shift in the narrow bed, unsure if I actually slept. "Is it time?"

"Ten minutes," Stella declares.

Suppressing a sigh, I resist the urge to question the early wake-up call. "I'll be right out." Most likely, Stella is next in line for the call room and wants to ensure I vacate on time. While Stella is a valuable asset to our medical program, she's strict about following rules and maintaining schedules. While admirable, Captain Williams has emphasized she needs to be more flexible. In hospitals, there are unpredictable events that cannot be controlled by a set schedule.

Rolling onto my back, I stretch, awakening not only myself but also the baby who gives me a solid kick. I sit up and twist my neck, attempting to alleviate the tension. Aside from an hour-long break when I went home to change clothes and check on Mother Pearl, I've been at the hospital since we brought in the men mauled by Hayward's dogs.

Two of them didn't survive, while the boy is recovering at a care center. I'm uncertain what will happen to him when he's released from there. He lost his parents, and the men he was with were his father's friends. Making their way from Minneapolis, they had planned to settle in the Black Hills based on rumors of opportunities.

His mother passed away the year before the attacks, leaving only him and his father. In the spring, they left Minneapolis, aiming to reach here before winter. However, they fell behind schedule and his father became ill along the way, eventually succumbing to the illness. The friends kept the boy with them and promised to help him. It seems unjust for these men, who went through so much, to be killed upon reaching their destination.

I'm not fond of Hayward training his dogs to kill. I understand his need to protect his property, but it feels morally wrong. The dogs don't know any better; they're simply following what they were taught.

Opal mentioned Hayward used to be different. Although they weren't close friends, they worked together on projects and collaborated to survive during the early days of the troubles. However, something changed last winter. He snapped. Even his wife is perplexed and concerned about the transformation.

The wife convinced him to see the district doctor for a medical evaluation to rule out any underlying issues. Then, their satellite hospital was attacked. Although the doctor survived, they lost a nurse and other staff members, along with the building. They're currently in the process of setting up operations in a new location.

The doctor asked Opal if she'd be willing to work at the hospital since she has filled in during emergencies. Opal found it amusing, considering she lacks proper medical training and has treated more animals than humans.

She informed him she'd be available for emergencies but couldn't be added to a regular schedule. Privately, I know she doesn't hold the doctor in high regard and disapproves of how he runs the hospital.

When Mother Pearl and I first arrived, Opal took us to the Guard District Hospital instead of her local one, citing staffing issues. Through subtle remarks and gestures, I've realized her concerns run deeper. Additionally, the doctor is perpetually short-staffed, given the number of patients he sees daily.

I let out a sigh. Now we're also severely understaffed. Geoff's termination—although losing him wasn't a significant loss—and the death of Dr. Morrow mean we'll all have to work longer hours and more days. Captain Williams has issued a call for a replacement physician, but that will have to wait until this flu surge subsides.

At least things are starting to calm down. The med school turned clinic still has a small staff, but they're gradually closing it as patients recover enough to go home. Good thing. I don't know how much longer we can keep going.

This surge started on January 1st, and it's now the fourth. Four long days of exhausting shifts broken up only by the occasional retreat to the call room or sleeping in the break room. I've been doing my best to rest when I'm able. Fortunately, I haven't been afflicted by the illness. Other than being tired, I'm perfectly well.

In some ways, it's good I'm working so much. I worry about taking this illness home to Mother Pearl. When I went home to change, I wore a mask and kept my distance. As a courtesy, Alice Williams has been stopping by my house daily to make sure Pearl is well. She doesn't go in, only knocks on the door and calls out. So far, Pearl has also avoided the illness. I just pray that continues.

After composing myself, I step out of the call room and into the hallway. I nod at Stella as she heads straight for the now-vacant room. With only one room, no bigger than a closet, and a single bed, she'll be hot racking—slipping into a still-warm bed. Knowing Stella, she might change the sheets first, and I can't blame her. Personally, I don't bother with it; rearranging the bed requires more energy than I currently have and cuts into precious sleep time.

"Guess who just walked in." Jesse Talbot wiggles his mustache at me.

I start to ask who but stop midway. "Don't tell me. The Ebrights?"

"You got it."

"Haven't seen them in a while. I thought they might have found a new hobby. Did they notice how busy we are? Did you tell them we don't have time for their shenanigans?"

"They claim to be sick too. But their illness also involves seizures. The older one had a seizure right in the entryway."

"Again?"

"Yep. This time she managed to knock over a few chairs while her younger sister coached her through it."

"Coached her?"

"Mm-hmm. She'd say something like, 'At home, she flopped over on her stomach like a fish.' Two seconds later . . . " Jesse raises his hands.

"And she flopped over on her stomach?" I chuckle. "They're something."

"They seem to like you, so Doc Nettie asked if you could take them into exam room three and work your magic."

I shake my head. "I don't know why they like me. I'm not nice to them."

"Maybe they see you as a challenge?"

"Doubtful," I scoff.

Elaine and Marilyn Ebright are special cases. They're spinster sisters who, somehow, have not only survived but also managed to thrive since the power went out. These two women are regular visitors with almost exaggerated complaints.

In addition to the Ebright sisters, there's also a man in his sixties whose daughter frequently brings him in. The daughter usually whispers to us he's pretending, and he usually is. However, on one occasion, he was complaining of pain in his foot. After an exam, Dr. Wolff determined he likely had a stress fracture. While not a life-threatening situation, it reminded us we need to thoroughly investigate all patient complaints, even if they have a history of theatrics.

I should wake up Stella and ask her for some remedy to convince the Ebright sisters they're fine and can resume a normal life. If only such a treatment existed, then we could truly start turning this apocalypse around.

Steeling my shoulders, I approach the sisters in the waiting area as they engage in a casual chat, seemingly carefree. Marilyn, the younger of the two, notices me and nudges her sister in the ribs.

Suddenly, Elaine slides down in her chair, all the way to the floor, and promptly begins her fish-like flopping, this time on her back. With her previous obesity, Elaine's excess skin adds to the flopping sensation as it slaps against the tile.

Suppressing the urge to laugh at their antics, I tighten my mouth.

After a few seconds, Elaine opens one eye. Upon seeing me watching her, she resumes her performance.

"Make sure you don't hit your head," I caution. "I'm not in the mood to stitch you up."

Marilyn narrows her eyes at me before shifting her gaze to my stomach. "What happened to you?"

I rest my hand on my hip and purposefully emphasize my protruding belly. "I've been drinking a lot of beer."

"Elaine, get a look at her. She's going to have a baby."

Elaine ceases her shenanigans and pulls herself into a sitting position without using her hands. Despite being in her late sixties and previously overweight, she exhibits surprising agility. "I didn't even know you had a boyfriend."

Marilyn mutters, "Didn't even know you liked the fellas."

I blink several times, uncertain whether to laugh or cry. "I was married."

Marilyn crosses her arms. "Did he leave you?"

Elaine shakes her head. "He died, didn't he?"

"When did the seizures start?" I interject.

"Just this morning. Came out of nowhere. I think it's part of this flu going around."

"You know, this flu is a serious matter. There are many sick people here, and people are dying. It's probably a contagious virus."

Elaine shrinks within herself. "Are you saying we shouldn't be here, even with my troubles?"

"I'm saying being here could make you sick."

"Aren't you worried about your baby?"

I rub the back of my neck. "I am. But I have to be here. You don't. Now, if you're genuinely ill, Elaine, I want a doctor to see you. But if you're not . . ."

"Of course she's sick. You saw her." Marilyn nudges her sister, subtly pointing to the floor.

"Do you have any idea how dirty the floor is?" I ask. "I mean, we mop and do our best, but this sickness has various components, including vomiting. Not everyone makes it to the toilet or trash can."

"She's too sick to care."

Elaine grabs her sister's arm. "I'm feeling much better. Let's go home."

"But . . . but . . ."

"Seriously. Let's go."

Elaine practically drags her sibling toward the front door. As they exit, someone enters. It takes only a fraction of a second for me to recognize Bowski's towering figure. I start to turn away, but his deep voice stops me.

"Well, hello, Ms. Ebright and Ms. Ebright. I hope you two aren't here because you're ill."

"Elaine's under the weather, but— "

This time, Elaine pokes her sister to silence her. She beams at Bowski. "We're fine, Ritchie. And you?"

"I'm well, thanks for asking. Is your wood supply holding up okay?"

I swear Elaine blushes when she tells him it is and how kind he is to always ensure they have wood and other things they need.

"Please." He raises his hand. "It's my pleasure. You two were also very helpful when I needed a permit or assistance with figuring things out."

I take a step closer and consider this information. I knew the sisters had some sort of office job but never took the time to ask about it. From what I gathered, they may have worked for either the city or the county.

Bowski, among other things, was a building contractor. He never explicitly mentioned it, but I've heard it through the semi-reliable grapevine. It does make sense, considering his skill set and his apparent familiarity with everyone in the area.

"Well, Ritchie, you've certainly repaid us for anything we ever did for you," Elaine gushes. "If it wasn't for you, I'm not sure we'd even be standing here today." She glances in my direction before turning back to him. "You're sure you aren't sick?"

"No, ma'am." His shoulders drop. "I'm on mortuary detail."

Both sisters shake their heads. Marilyn places a hand on his arm. "Bless you, Ritchie. You're always the one doing the terrible jobs."

She motions for me to come closer. "Do you know Merissa? She always helps Elaine when she comes in with one of her episodes. Today was a bad one. She was having convulsions. But Merissa made us realize being here right now isn't smart. It's better for Elaine to recover at home."

Bowski meets my gaze. "I think Mrs. Weaver's right. Staying at home and waiting until this subsides is the best plan. Do you two have plenty of sewing to keep you busy?"

"Oh, heavens yes." Elaine chuckles. "More than enough. Especially since you brought us those things to make." A strange expression crosses her face as she looks from Bowski to me. Her face contorts into a smirk. "Well, then. We'd best get back home."

"Mind if I stop by and check on you in a few days?"

"Please do," the women respond in unison.

Once the Ebright sisters have gone, Bowski turns toward me. "I've heard they come in here a lot."

I tilt my head. "You've known them for a while?"

"Years. They're quite a pair. Nice enough in their eccentric ways."

"You're here for the remains?"
"Hugo said someone called."
"Sadly, yes. We lost someone overnight. Just one, thankfully."
"Maybe we're on the tail end of this?"
"I hope so. It's been . . . challenging."

Chapter 26

Katie

Both Leo and I coughed and sneezed but didn't get too sick. I had a slight fever at one point, but it disappeared within a few hours.

Rand Hendricks was admitted to the hospital with a lung infection and suspected pneumonia. He's now recovering at home. One of the med students also fell seriously ill and spent several days in the hospital before being transferred to a care center for recovery.

Today, January 8th, is my first full day off since it all started. I'm finally feeling like I'm getting better, with only occasional sneezes and coughs. Leo is also improving and is working today.

The hospital is still receiving sick people, though at a slower rate than those chaotic first days. The death toll has been alarmingly high. Many people didn't seek treatment at the hospital and tried to recover on their own, often with fatal consequences. They didn't show up for work, and someone discovered them dead.

Classes at the med school have been suspended as the students are now part of the hospital rotation. With the loss of Chastity, Captain Williams and Nettie are working even longer hours than before, which were already excessive. Monument Hospital assures us they'll do their best to provide another doctor, but it'll have to wait until the flu subsides since everyone's overworked and understaffed.

Gerry and I are snuggling on the couch. I'm trying to read a medical book on the history of the Spanish Flu, given to me by Williams to further my education, when there's a firm knock on the door. Gerry and I jump up, the dog giving a small whine but otherwise remaining silent.

My holstered sidearm sits on the side table next to me. I grab the gun and hold it alongside my leg. I move toward the entryway, staying close to the wall. "Who is it?" It wasn't long ago I laughed at Leo, thinking someone would come knocking on our door with ill intentions. After what happened with RJ Kittleson, my perspective has changed.

"Katie? It's Opal Maher. I've got Pearl with me."

Their unexpected arrival instantly brightens my day. Opal's presence is like a burst of sunlight, spreading joy wherever she goes. Her sister Pearl is a different sort, but I still enjoy her company.

"Opal, give me a minute," I call through the still-closed door as I place the gun on a high shelf in the entryway. I direct Gerry to stay and mind his manners. I don't want him jumping on the older women. Once we're ready, I open the door and usher them in.

"I brought you a pot of soup." Opal smiles, lifting the container in her hands. "Let me just put it on your woodstove. I heard how crazy things have been at the hospital." She shuffles from the entryway to the woodstove in the living room. With her hands now empty, she points at her feet. "Sorry about the mess."

"That's nothing. I'm so glad you're here." She reaches to hug me, but I step back.

"I've been sick. I got a mild case of the flu." I mentally kick myself for not thinking about wearing a face mask before the women came into the house.

"At least you're not wearing one of those terrible masks." Pearl clicks her tongue. "Merissa won't come near me without one on. Looks silly as all get out. Seems to me they're as useless as a screen door on a submarine."

I let out a laugh. "I guess it helps me keep my spit to myself." I motion at the book on the coffee table. "There's some evidence suggesting mask-wearing prevented the spread of the Spanish Flu. So, I don't know."

"Humph," Pearl scoffs.

"Pearl." Opal raises her eyebrows and gives a shake of her head.

"I'm just saying . . . "

"Let me put one on," I say.

"It's fine, dear." Opal waves her hand dismissively. "We'll keep our distance."

I respond with a nod. "How'd you know I was off today? Do you want to hang up your coats?" I gesture toward the hooks by the door.

"Merissa," Pearl says in her gravelly way as she unbuttons her coat. "She finally came home. Wearing that mask and— "

"Yes, sister. You said plenty on the way over here when talking about Merissa wearing her mask. I'm sure Katie has heard it all too."

I maintain a smile as I listen to the two women bicker. Opal is right; I have heard it all.

"Would you like to sit?" I motion to the couch as I take the chair farthest from them. "I'll heat some water for tea. And I have bread."

"Tea sounds wonderful." Opal dips her chin. "I brought snacks." She reaches inside the large bag slung over her shoulder, pulls out a covered container, and places it on the coffee table. "Well, Gerry. I think you've grown since I saw you last."

Gerry thumps his tail on the floor but remains still. Opal looks at me with a questioning look on her face. I give Gerry permission to approach, and his tail wags stronger until Opal motions for him to come to her.

After spending ample time giving the dog attention, she looks at me. "Quite a rough time you've all had. I heard about Chastity Morrow. That's a terrible blow."

"It really is." I refrain from mentioning our uncertainty about the cause of her death. I'm certain there are rumors circulating, and Opal or Pearl must have heard their fair share.

Opal scans my little house. She's visited us several times, but not since the incident with Kittleson when I was essentially held hostage. She doesn't acknowledge the new furniture but does notice our bed now occupying what used to be the dining area. "Too cold in the bedroom?"

"Much too cold. We only use this space now. It's easier to heat. It still isn't particularly warm, as you can tell."

"I think it's fine. Your garden looks like it's growing nicely." Opal gestures toward the shelves in front of the window, adorned with containers of lettuce and other easily grown items. It may not be much, but it provides us with a small supply of fresh food. Leo started a mason jar of radish sprouts yesterday evening to give us additional fresh greens. They'll be ready to eat in about a week.

"It's doing okay. We were at the hospital for four days straight. Everything dried out, and it got cold in here. I'm surprised the plants didn't freeze."

"What do you do with your dog when you're working?" Pearl asks as Gerry turns toward her. She scratches him under the chin.

"Sometimes Leo is home. If we're both absent during a regular shift, we leave him alone. For emergencies and long shifts, he stays with the neighbors. They have a young boy and girl who adore Gerry." Upon hearing his name, he turns his head in my direction.

"Sometimes I wish we had a dog." Pearl lets out a sigh and affectionately pats Gerry. "Yes, I do. A cute little pup like you." Her voice takes on a high-pitched falsetto as she coos at my dog.

The kettle begins to steam. I excuse myself to fetch the tea components. Opal offers her assistance, but I dismiss it. Before retrieving the plates, I wash my hands with the hot water stored in a cooler near the sink.

"Merissa washes her hands so frequently they're starting to crack," Pearl calls out. "Are you experiencing the same problem?"

I examine my red, dry hands. "I am. I've been putting some elk tallow on them. I know I should save it for cooking, but . . . " I shrug.

"Better than that awful alcohol stuff. Goodness, it reeks like an old drunk. I don't like Merissa using it. All the booze seeping into her skin might harm the baby. And that martial arts stuff you all are doing . . . I hope she's cautious."

"She's careful, Pearl," Opal says. "Merissa's smart. Besides, they haven't really started their training. Right, Katie?"

"Not yet. We were supposed to, but with the illness, everything is on hold. Lieutenant Paul did find us a couple of mats to use in the training room. Merissa will be assuming more of an instructional role than anything else. She'll be extremely careful."

Upon my return to the living room, carrying a stack of plates, mugs, and tea enclosed in reusable muslin bags, I arrange everything on the table. "I don't have any cream or milk. We didn't get any this week. I do have honey, though. Let me grab it."

After pouring the tea and Opal distributing the generous portions of gingerbread, I take my tea and treat to my chair.

I ask how things are going on the ranch. Opal remarks that things are fine, but they're still encountering some issues with their neighbor. "Kevin tried to talk to him and asked him to use a different approach with trespassers. Two men dead . . . " She shakes her head. "It's awful. And now, with the boy on his own . . . "

"Forcing those dogs to be killers is what's awful," Pearl interjects before taking a sip of her tea. "This is good. What's in it?"

"Mostly mint, I believe. Along with a few other ingredients. It's something Stella gave me. She calls it her apocalyptic winter wellness blend."

"I'll have to ask Merissa if she can get us some of this. I miss my coffee, but I could get used to this."

"I'm sure she can get you some," I respond. After taking a sip of my tea, I say, "We were talking with Bowski when he brought the other men in that day, the ones you ended up needing to stitch up?"

Opal nods. "When Ritchie told me about the hospital being full up, we decided staying home and hunkering down would be smart. I wish Pearl hadn't gone into town with him. Thought she'd be safer on the ranch. Today's the first day I ventured out."

"Did anyone get sick at your place?"

"A few did. Nothing too serious. What were you saying about Bowski?"

"Bowski said he knew Mr. Hayward. Said he was a nice guy before."

"Nice enough, I suppose. A little crotchety." Opal glances toward her sister. "Moreso as he ages. His wife, though, has always been wonderful. I know she's having a hard time with the changes in her husband."

"So, his actions are new?" I ask, wondering if there may be a medical explanation. I only briefly saw him, and I certainly didn't do any sort of examination, but paranoia—which it sounds like he has—could be medically related. Or it could be because of our environment. There are plenty of reasons to be paranoid in the apocalypse.

"New enough. I'm sure he's merely doing what he thinks is best to protect his land. And his wife. They never had any children. It's always just been the two of them, and he's always done all he could to keep her comfortable. Not that she's some delicate flower. She's a ranch woman through and through. Why, in some ways, she might be tougher than him. I know she's not at all happy about the dogs.

"They had a couple of old ranch dogs when this all started, and still have one of them who hangs out at home. After we heard about the killing of all the pets in Black Canyon, Hayward went looking for more dogs. Said it seemed smart to give them a good home. He didn't tell his wife he was training them to be killers." Opal shudders. "She never would've gone along with such an idea. Watchdogs, sure. That's fine. We use our pups as watchdogs." She glances at Gerry. "I didn't hear him bark when we knocked on the door."

"We've tried to train him not to bark for knocks. But he does bark at other times. It's been interesting to see how Gerry seems to know when it's a friend visiting or a problem." I swallow as I remember how he was barking and whining when Kittleson broke in.

"It's good he can stay quiet when needed." Pearl nods. "He's exactly the kind of dog I'd want. Of course . . . " A dreamy look crosses her face, smoothing out her wrinkles. "With the baby coming soon, we don't really need the added burden of a dog. Did Merissa tell you I'm working at the daycare? Figured it'd be good training for when we have our own little one. My son's child." Her eyes fill with tears. "She told you about how my boys died?"

"Some, yes."

"Terrible. It's terrible to lose your children. You planning on having kids?"

"I, uh . . . maybe?"

"Leave her alone, Pearl." Opal shakes her head. "She and Leo have enough on their plate right now. I told you how they're supposed to join the National Guard." Opal looks at me expectantly. "How's that coming, Katie?"

"Good. I think it's good. We're waiting to see about Leo's arm. The plan was to go for an exam with Dr. Bollinger shortly after the new year. However, due to the outbreak, we've had to put it on hold. Monument Hospital's been hit even harder than we have. They can't spare him right now."

"What does it mean for your husband?" Pearl asks.

"He's doing fine . . . we think. Just ensuring everything stays clean and being cautious." While I hope what I'm saying is true, I must admit I wish Bollinger could conduct a thorough examination to ensure Leo's arm is healing properly. Leo has already endured so much. His arm not healing right and permanently having troubles . . . I don't even want to think about that possibility.

Chapter 27

Katie

"Can I get anyone more hot water?" I ask, swallowing my concerns about Leo's healing.

Once the tea's been refreshed, we chitchat about nothing much for several minutes until Pearl interrupts with a clearing of her throat. "I heard about that neighborhood, about all the deaths there. Why didn't they go to the hospital?"

I release a breath and shake my head. One of the neighborhoods in our district was hit particularly hard, the same neighborhood where Jack and Bonnie Turner reside. It turns out the midwife in their neighborhood, Addison, who also practices herbalism, is not as skilled as Stella.

Addison managed to convince the neighborhood to seek her services instead of going to the hospital. As the sickness spread through the community, she even started making house calls. It was Jack Turner who eventually brought his severely ill wife to the hospital and alerted us to the dire condition of several of their neighbors.

Although Jack was also sick, Bonnie's condition was far worse, with her lungs so congested she struggled to breathe. Despite our efforts to treat her with all the medicine and different positioning techniques, her weak body, already strained by pregnancy, gave out. We lost her shortly after her arrival.

At that point, grief-stricken Jack willingly divulged everything he knew about Addison and her treatment methods. According to him, Addison had no prior knowledge of herbalism or childbirth before the EMP. She used to work as an office manager and moved to the area from the other side of Rapid City after her home was destroyed in a fire.

Recognizing the opportunity, she presented herself as a trained medical professional. To be fair, she did amass numerous books on the subject from the library and other sources after the EMP, but she lacked practical experience.

Concerned by the information shared by Jack Turner, Williams requested Deputy Shaw investigate it. While Shaw agreed to talk to Addison, he acknowledged there wasn't much he could do. Ration chips are closely monitored, and the black market is discouraged, but there's no specific law against Addison's actions. Williams countered, arguing her actions could be considered close to murder.

When Deputy Shaw reported back to Williams, he revealed Addison had disappeared. Her house had been emptied of essential items, and she was nowhere to be found. During a door-to-door search, many extremely sick or dying neighbors were discovered, revealing the true extent of the trouble in the neighborhood.

I lift my shoulders and shake my head. "I believe they thought they were receiving proper treatment."

"Sad thing for sure," Opal adds, also shaking her head. "How many died?"

"At least a dozen," I respond, choosing not to elaborate further. We prioritize patient privacy, and Pearl doesn't need to hear about the death of a pregnant woman. Merissa kept her pregnancy quiet for as long as possible to avoid raising Pearl's hopes. The poor woman has already endured enough loss. I lower my gaze to the floor, my eyes welling up. We've all experienced more than enough loss.

Our visit continues for a while, allowing us to enjoy a third cup of tea. When Opal suggests it's time to leave, I offer to accompany them out. Gerry could use some time outside. As the women put on their coats, I retrieve my boots and attach the leash to Gerry. Once I'm ready and bundled up, I ask Opal about the soup pot she left on my woodstove.

"Just give it back to me next time I see you. We have plenty of cooking pans. Come for Sunday service again. If you can get me a message, I'll pick you up."

"That'd be wonderful. I had no idea Shawn was such a wonderful preacher."

"The Lord has truly blessed him."

Upon opening the front door, we're greeted by a blast of cold air. Pearl tightens her jacket around her neck. "It wasn't this cold when we got here."

I glance toward the dark sky in the west. "Looks like another storm's coming in." I look down the road. "Where's your wagon?"

"Shawn is meeting us at Pearl's house. We thought the walk would do us good."

"Gerry and I can walk with you."

We allow Pearl to set the pace, which turns out to be brisker than expected for a woman in her seventies. She mutters about the weather several times. Not only is it cold, but gusts of wind make it feel even colder.

Pearl points to my backpack. "Do you always wear your pack?"

"Pretty much," I confirm, realizing that while I put on my daypack, which contains what I consider essentials for survival, I forgot to grab my pistol. It's still sitting on the shelf in the entryway. However, I do have a backup gun tucked inside my backpack.

Although I don't anticipate needing a firearm on this short walk, it's reassuring to know it's there. I should take it out of the pack and put it in place. I glance at Opal, who carries a large revolver on her hip. Pearl also has a gun, possibly a Glock, but it's difficult to determine from the glimpses I've caught.

When we reach Pearl and Merissa's place, I don't see the wagon. Anticipating my question, Opal gestures toward the driveway. "It's in the garage. Shawn wanted to keep the horses inside." I follow her finger and spot a large, detached garage at the end of the driveway.

"Can I help you with anything?" I ask.

Opal opens her arms to give me a hug. "Not a thing, dear. Let me know when you can come visit again. We're praying for you and Leo."

I tell Pearl goodbye and let Opal know we'll try and visit soon. With a wave, Gerry and I turn back toward our house. While he was happy to walk alongside Pearl and Opal, now that it's just the two of us, he starts lollygagging, stopping and sniffing everything. "C'mon, Gerry. Hurry up. It's freezing out here."

Instead of retracing our steps, which tends to prolong Gerry's sniffing, I decide to turn down a street that loops around the back of our house and leads to the alley. The last time I was on this street was the day we found Chastity. She lived only a few houses down.

As we continue, I notice a man walking toward us on the other side of the street. I keep my eyes on him, and Gerry, sensing something, stops with his hair raised.

"Let's go," I whisper, giving a gentle tug on his leash.

"Burnett?" the man calls out, turning toward us.

Squinting against the cold wind, I strain to make him out. He's bundled up, making it difficult to recognize him. As he crosses the street, I can now see him clearly.

It's Geoff Landers.

I haven't seen him since the day he stormed out of Williams's office after the revelation of his and Chastity's drug use. Although we worked together for several weeks during his time in med school, we were never friendly. He always seemed to go out of his way to create difficulties for me . . . and everyone else, really.

"Where's Chastity?" he asks as he nears the sidewalk.

I release a puff of breath, watching as the condensation resembles smoke. If he's unaware of her death, I don't want to be the one to break the news. "Um, you should go to the hospital and speak with Williams."

"Is she on duty? I asked one of the guards, a new guy. He claimed he didn't even know her. He said Williams is working today."

I glance down at Gerry, who stands at attention with his gaze fixed on Landers. "Really, Geoff, go talk to Williams." I step backward to create some distance between us.

He moves closer. "Tell me where she is," he snarls, his lip curling.

Instinctively, my hand reaches for my waist as I take another step back. My throat tightens when I remember I don't have my gun. Gerry positions himself between Landers and me and releases a low but fierce growl.

"Better keep your dog under control, Burnett." He points at Gerry, who appears more ferocious than ever.

"Step back and he'll be fine." My voice is shaky.

Landers narrows his eyes, shifting his gaze between me and Gerry. He raises his hands. "Whatever. I'm here to see my girl. Now tell me where she is."

I lower my chin and continue to step backward. Landers is not to be trusted. The incident where he and Jesse argued, and Landers reached for his weapon, remains fresh in my mind. While I forgot my sidearm, his is clearly holstered on his hip. If I inform him about Chastity, will he shoot me? I wouldn't put anything past him.

I keep moving backward, relieved Landers remains in place instead of pursuing me. When there's approximately twenty feet between us, I once again urge him to go to the hospital and talk to Williams.

"She's gone, isn't she? He transferred her to a different hospital."

I shake my head and take another step backward, abruptly stopping as I bump into something. Gerry spins and growls. My heart sinks as strong hands grab hold of my arms.

"Easy there," the man holding me says in a low voice. "Now . . . Mr. Landers politely asked you to tell him where his girl is. It's about time you provided an answer. And control your dog."

Gerry's teeth remain bared, his body taut as a wire. "Gerry, sit."

He emits a low growl before settling on the ground. Although he may be sitting, he remains alert.

The man releases his grip on me, stepping around to stand next to Landers. He's dressed warmly for winter, sporting a heavy camouflage coat and a brown beanie pulled down to his eyebrows. His brown beard obscures the rest of his face. I scrutinize him but fail to recognize him.

Landers gives him a nod. "Where'd Williams send Chastity?"

I shake my head. "He didn't. She . . . " I clear my throat nervously. "She died. The flu, we think."

Landers stares at me, his disbelief evident. "What?"

"I'm sorry."

The man beside him places a hand on his shoulder. "Sorry, buddy."

Landers shakes off the gesture. "I don't believe you. Where'd he send her?"

His friend motions toward me. "I think she's telling the truth."

"Don't bet on it," Landers snorts. "She's in cahoots with Williams. Part of the group that set me up to fail."

I swear I see Landers's friend roll his eyes. "C'mon, man. Why would she lie about your girl dying?"

"She would. I'm telling you, she's out to get me."

"I'm not, Geoff. I'm truly sorry, but Chastity died."

Landers narrows his eyes. "If she's truly dead, which I doubt, Williams killed her. He knew she was going to get him out of the hospital. He killed her." Landers spins on his heel. "I'm going to get to the bottom of this. If you're telling the truth, Williams will pay." He points his finger at me. "You'll all pay." Landers strides away.

The friend shakes his head, silently mouthing an apology before chasing after Landers.

Gerry and I remain there for a few moments, trying to gather ourselves and comprehend what is unfolding. Whatever it is, it certainly isn't good.

Gerry and I turn in the opposite direction and briskly make our way toward the hospital.

Chapter 28

Katie

Gerry and I make good time reaching the hospital. When we reach the back door, I realize my key is hanging on the hook inside the house. I opt to knock instead, hoping for a response. Surprisingly, a voice calls out, "Yes?"

"Merissa? It's Katie Burnett. I forgot my key."

She opens the door with a smile that quickly fades. "What's wrong?"

Glancing behind me, I have a sense of being watched. I should've informed the sentry about the threat from Landers. Now that I'm here, we can use the radio. "I just saw Geoff Landers. He threatened to make Williams pay for Chastity's death."

"What? That doesn't even make any sense."

"He thinks Williams killed her." My words rush out as Gerry and I hurriedly enter the hospital.

Merissa wrinkles her face. "I don't understand."

I exhale and slow my words. "Landers thinks Captain Williams murdered Chastity. He mentioned something about her trying to get Williams out of the hospital."

"Landers is a crazy dude."

"No doubt." I shake the snow off my boots and instruct Gerry to sit.

"He's not here."

"What?"

"Captain Williams. He and Leo left for their rounds."

"Leo? Is he pushing the wheelchair?"

She shakes her head. "Mrs. Williams is. The captain asked Leo to join them."

"Do you know which care center they'll visit first?"

"I'm not sure. I've never accompanied him on rounds, only Dr. Wolff."

"Did they go out the front or the back?"

"The front, I think. I was in a room, but I'm sure I heard the front door. Jacquie might know for sure. He took the radio."

"Of course!" I gesture toward the radio on her belt. As the on-duty medic, she handles communications with other hospitals and our law enforcement. "Will you call?"

She's already removing the radio from her belt. "Base to Williams, come in."

I hold my breath as the radio emits a squawk. Gerry whines while I lean closer to Merissa. Following the squawk, silence ensues.

"Let me try again." The second transmission is followed by several seconds of silence before a voice comes through.

"Base, this is Josiah at the front guard station."

Merissa furrows her brow. "Go ahead, Josiah."

"Williams mentioned he forgot to charge his battery. He told me to inform you when he left. I got held up with a visitor."

Merissa shakes her head and thanks Josiah.

"Wait a minute. Can you ask him who the visitor was?"

"You thinking it was Landers?"

"Maybe. There was another man with him."

Merissa asks Josiah if it was a patient at the guard house. He confirms it wasn't and describes the visitor as someone looking for Dr. Morrow.

Merissa's eyes go wide. "Was it Geoff Landers?"

"Not Landers. Someone else. I didn't recognize him, and he didn't provide a name."

I motion for the radio. Merissa hands it over. "Josiah, it's Katie Burnett. Can you describe the guy?"

"Around my height, maybe slightly shorter. He had a beard, dressed in winter clothes. You know, like everyone else."

"Brown stocking cap?"

"Yeah. And a camouflage jacket. You know him?"

"I'm on my way out. I'll talk to you shortly." I hand the radio back to Merissa. "I'm taking Gerry down the hall and going out the front door."

"Should I call Deputy Shaw?"

I'm already moving, so I call over my shoulder. "I'll talk to Josiah and see what he says."

"Who's the other guy?"

"I'll tell you later." I give a wave and fast walk down the hall. Jacquie steps out of a room asking if everything's okay.

"I hope so," I reply without stopping. Once we exit the hospital, our pace quickens. I'm nearly jogging, as close as one can get on the slippery ice, when the guard station comes into view.

Josiah walks toward me. "What's going on?"

I give a quick recap of my run-in with Landers and his friend wearing the brown beanie. He scratches his beard. "So, you think Landers will go after Captain Williams? And that guy was confirming Chastity is dead?"

"Did you tell him she is?"

He lifts his shoulders. "Yeah. Didn't see any reason not to."

"Landers didn't believe me at first. His friend convinced him I was likely telling the truth. Landers suggested Williams probably did it."

He wrinkles his forehead. "Did what?"

"Killed her. Killed Chastity. Because she was part of the group who wants the National Guard to lose control of the hospital."

Josiah shakes his head and waves a hand dismissively. "This doesn't make any sense."

"Do you know which care center Williams is visiting first? Can you have Shaw meet me there?"

"He didn't say. Probably Poppy Gardner's place since it's the closest. Leo's with him, you know. And Mrs. Williams."

"I know. Call Shaw." I motion to the radio on his collar.

"Do you truly believe Landers . . . scratch that. We've both witnessed him lose control. I wouldn't put anything past him."

I purse my lips and nod. "I'm going to find Williams and Leo."

"Want me to keep your dog?"

I glance down at Gerry. He looks up at me and gives me a doggy smile with his tongue lolling to one side. I could leave him with Josiah, but then I'd have to return for him. If there's an issue where Josiah is needed, it'd be inconvenient. I release a sigh. "I'll keep him with me."

The crunch of the ice and the sound of my breathing break the silence of the apocalyptic afternoon as Gerry and I cautiously traverse the frozen ground like penguins. I'm well aware of how slippery this section can be, having walked it back and forth to work.

I inhale deeply, hoping to calm my rattled nerves. The scent of wood smoke, one of the aromas I associate with winter, fills the air. In the distance, there's a loud crack and the buzzing of voices, possibly the firewood or water crews making their daily rounds. I try to focus on these sensations, grounding myself in what's tangible. The cold. The smell of wood fires warming houses and providing comfort. The sounds of the workers.

I let out a breath. Focusing on the physical things helps keep my mind from drifting toward the uncertainty. While I need to relay the threat made by Landers, I don't need to create a scenario worse than it is. The man accompanying Landers didn't seem unhinged. He appeared normal, even sympathetic. If he's friends with Landers, he might have enough influence to calm him down.

Poppy Gardener's care facility comes into view. It's a medium-sized home on Plum Tree Lane near the tennis courts. The care center, run by Poppy and her husband, offers the highest level of care among all our long-term facilities. Some residents still reside here from the ration center explosion in November. These are individuals with little chance of returning to their own homes and families. The current objective is to prepare them for a transfer to a less acute facility.

After ringing an old-fashioned doorbell, Gerry and I wait on the front porch. I reach up to ring again but hear a rustling behind the door.

"Yes?" a man calls. "Are you here for a visit?"

"Um, no. I'm one of the nurses from the hospital. I'm looking for Captain Williams."

The door cracks open. The man—possibly Poppy's husband, though I can't confirm since I've only met her—states Williams hasn't been here today. "Did you try the apartments? He usually goes there first." He glances down at Gerry. "Cute dog."

Gerry responds with a wag of his tail. "Thanks. The apartments on Dakota Drive?"

"Mm-hmm. He starts there and works his way back. We're usually last. Dr. Wolff sees us first. Those two are creatures of habit. Now Dr. Morrow, she liked to mix things up. Too bad about her. She could be abrasive, but we still liked her. Have you heard anything about getting a new doctor?"

"No, not yet. If you see the captain, can you tell him I was here? Katie Burnett. If I don't find him, he has an important message at the hospital guard station."

"Oh, I'm sure you'll find him. All the care centers are together in these few blocks. You won't miss him if he's on his rounds."

I nod appreciatively. While I haven't accompanied Williams or Doc Nettie on their rounds, I know the locations of all the care facilities, thanks to a map in Williams's office and leisurely walks with my husband and dog. Leo pointed them out during our strolls.

I thank the man for his help and continue on my way. Back on Canyon Lake Drive, heading east, Gerry tugs on the leash.

A smile spreads across my face, and I wave a hand. Half a block ahead, I spot Williams in his wheelchair, with his wife pushing and Leo walking beside them.

Leo waves back before picking up his pace. When we're about ten yards apart, he calls out, "What's wrong? Did something happen at the hospital?"

I shake my head and hurry to meet him. "Not the hospital. Geoff Landers. I saw him. He said he's going to make Williams pay."

"Pay?"

I explain how Landers holds Captain Williams responsible for Chastity's death. By the time I finish, Captain and Mrs. Williams are near us.

Leo turns toward the couple. "Geoff Landers is back in town. He believes you're responsible for Chastity's death."

Chapter 29

Merissa

I relay Katie's message to Dr. Wolff, along with the conversation via the guard station and how Captain Williams's walkie-talkie is dead.

"Great. More drama from that whole Chastity thing," Dr. Wolff responds.

My eyebrows shoot up at her response.

She makes a few incoherent noises before saying, "What I meant is . . . oh, never mind. Just ignore me, Merissa. You don't need to hear about my issues." She gives a weak smile. "Please call Josiah at the guardhouse. Find out what, if anything, he wants us to do."

Josiah gives a nonanswer, saying the supervising deputy will be around shortly. The back guard is aware of the threat, and they're both on high alert.

Dr. Wolff rolls her eyes. "Sounds about like the norm. Let me know when the deputy shows up."

We're still seeing way too many sick people, especially with our limited staff. Dr. Wolff has taken up residence at the hospital. I don't believe she has left for more than an hour or two since the outbreak began. Captain Williams also works incredibly long shifts and spends more time here than at home. Alice Williams is also working here.

I recently discovered she was Williams's first office nurse when he established his private practice. Although she claims her skills are rusty, she excels at handling the extra tasks no one else seems to have time for, particularly keeping the hospital records organized.

Janitor Rand Hendricks has yet to return to work after recovering from the flu, and one of my fellow med school students is also recuperating. Rand's wife, Kerry, reports her husband is improving, but he's still weak and fatigued. I'm truly grateful to not have caught the virus, and I'm doubly grateful Mother Pearl has remained unaffected. I also hope, perhaps even pray, this virus will run its course before my baby is born.

We don't have to wait long for the deputy on duty. I'm mildly surprised to see a man wearing a campaign hat and donning a neatly pressed uniform. I'm more taken aback by his youthful appearance and impeccably smooth-shaven face. Being clean-shaven is uncommon in today's world.

He introduces himself as Trooper Schroeder. From the introduction and uniform, I deduce Schroeder is one of the South Dakota Highway Patrol officers assisting the county deputies.

After briefly exchanging pleasantries and confirming my name and hospital position, he asks me to share what I know. As I recount Katie's arrival and her words, he jots down a few notes.

"Anything else?"

"That's all."

"All right. Do you know where the doctor makes his rounds?"

"I'm familiar with all the care centers, but I've never shadowed Captain Williams on his rounds."

"I'll need you to accompany me and show me where you think he might be."

"We'll need to clear that with Dr. Wolff. We still have a lot of sick people here, and we're shorthanded."

Dr. Wolff is less than pleased with the trooper's request for me to accompany him, but she agrees finding Captain Williams and ensuring his safety is important. I take a few minutes to change into my regular clothes and put on my boots. We received a couple of inches of snow overnight, so I also wear a neck gaiter, gloves, a beanie, and a heavy coat.

We head out on foot and stop at the guardhouse. The trooper instructs Josiah to ensure anyone approaching the hospital has legitimate business. Josiah acknowledges this while conveying his understanding of his duty. The trooper thanks him and suggests we get moving.

"You said your name is Weaver?"

"That's right. Merissa Weaver."

"And you're one of the nurses?"

"I'm a medic."

He raises his chin. "When's your baby due?"

I pause before answering. Apparently, my silence makes the trooper uncomfortable. He clears his throat. "I'm sorry to be so nosy. My wife's expecting too. She's due in early May."

"Does she come to our hospital for prenatal care?"

"We live in the Main Street District, right on the dividing line, actually. She's going to the hospital in our district . . . it's closer. I divide my time between both districts, assisting their deputies."

As we walk about half a block, I inform the trooper the first care center is approaching.

"Are you the one who was with McKay when he was murdered? I recall hearing it was a pregnant woman."

I do my best to tamp down the memory of watching McKay die. "Y-yes." My voice cracks on the word.

"Terrible business. We're actively searching for the shooter. We've issued an all-points bulletin to the best of our ability in today's world. I must say, the holidays tend to drive people mad. It's always been that way. The period between Christmas and New Year's is particularly volatile. People start evaluating their lives, and sometimes they snap. I heard he beat his woman pretty badly."

"Bad enough."

"We're going to find him, just like we found the guys who killed Raymond Harrington. We also have promising leads on the perpetrators of the explosions. It's only a matter of time. We're adopting the Mounties' motto: we always get our man. The apocalypse is no excuse for the issues we've been having."

While I admire the trooper's passion, I suspect some of his enthusiasm stems from his youth. "How long were you with the highway patrol before everything fell apart?"

"Two months."

There it is. Still, considering the state of our world over the past year and a half, I expected a touch more cynicism. I assume this man has witnessed and endured the same horrors as the rest of us. I contemplate asking him about it but decide to let it pass.

"Hey!" a woman from a nearby house yells, frantically waving her arms. "Are you a cop? I need help!"

Trooper Schroeder mutters something less than enthusiastic under his breath. Perhaps he does possess a healthy dose of cynicism. He adjusts his hat and straightens his posture. "Want to wait here?"

"Whatever you prefer."

"Might as well come with me. Make sure you do as I ask."

"Naturally." My reply is tinged with sarcasm. Does he assume I'm incapable of understanding our roles?

The woman stands on her porch, clad in a long robe and slippers. As we approach the stairs, the trooper signals me to wait here. My hand slides under my coat, resting on the butt of my gun. I'm still wary after the assault that resulted in McKay's murder.

"Ma'am? What seems to be the problem?" the trooper asks, his voice tired and uninterested.

She glances around nervously before stage whispering, "There's someone in my shed."

I find it amusing that she's suddenly whispering after yelling to get us over here.

"Someone's in your shed?" Schroeder questions, his voice loud and booming.

The woman cringes. "Yeah."

"You saw them?"

"Nope. But there are tracks after last night's snow."

"You've gone out to the shed?"

"Of course not. I saw them from my kitchen window. Come in, I'll show you."

Schroeder glances back at me. "Might as well come in, too, instead of waiting out here in the cold."

I consider telling him I'm fine, but I decide I'd rather be indoors with him than out here alone, especially considering the possibility of someone lurking about. I wonder if Schroeder suspects it's Gordon Cummings, the man who beat his girlfriend and shot Patroller McKay. That's certainly my first thought.

I follow him and the woman into the house.

"What's your name?" Schroeder asks.

"Cindy." Her slippered feet pad along while Schroeder and I clomp in our boots. Neither of us questions whether we should remove them, even though several pairs of outdoor shoes are by the door.

"No work today?" he asks.

"Finally got a day off. I work at the auto shop up on Main. I think we've met before." She pauses, gazing at him expectantly.

"Is that right? I was in there a few weeks ago checking on—oh, yes." His head bobs up and down. "You're the scheduler."

She beams. "That's right. My husband is one of the mechanics. My oldest boy too. When you were in the shop, I asked you about shaving."

"Right. I remember."

"I think it's sweet your wife helps you shave. I can't even imagine my husband trusting me enough to use a straight edge on him. We watched *Sweeney Todd*, and it made quite an impression." She widens her eyes before covering her mouth. "I mean . . . I wouldn't kill him. It's a joke between us."

Schroeder waves his hand dismissively. "My wife and I have a similar joke. I'll admit, though, I've never seen the movie. She's a few years older than me and insists the music is excellent."

We continue our short walk to the kitchen, and she points out a large picture window with a table in front of it. The disturbed snow and footprints are clearly visible.

"You're sure your husband or son weren't out there?" Schroeder asks as he steps closer to the window.

"I can't imagine they would be. They both left early this morning . . . well, the usual time anyway. They'd have no reason to go to the shed."

"What's in the shed?"

"Nothing much now. We used to keep garden equipment and stuff in there. But with the way things are, we moved anything we didn't want to lose inside. The old lawnmower is still out there. It even works. Jim's been talking about turning it into a vehicle for us somehow, though I can't really imagine how that would work. It's not like it's a riding lawnmower, just a push one." She shrugs.

"Can I use this door?" He motions to a door near the table.

"Sure."

"Want me with you?" I ask.

He looks directly at my stomach instead of making eye contact with me; it takes all my restraint not to tell him to look me in the face. "Nope. You can wait here. I'm not completely sure, but it looks like the tracks go in both directions."

"Do they?" Cindy steps closer to the window, placing her hands on either side of her eyes before pressing them against the glass. "You may be right."

"Is the shed locked?"

"Not anymore. We used to keep it locked, but there's no need now. If somebody wants to get in, they'd break the lock anyway, so why bother?"

Schroeder slips out the back door, his weapon cautiously held against his leg, despite stating he believed everything was fine.

Cindy continues her running commentary, describing his actions and expressing her hope he doesn't think she really wants to slit her husband's throat. She flits to the subject of her work at the auto shop.

I mainly tune her out, occasionally adding appropriate comments as I see fit.

When Trooper Schroeder finally reaches the double shed door, I suggest to Cindy we step back from the window in case things go south. I position myself to one side where I can still see, while she moves to the other side. She finally falls silent as she stares out.

Schroeder raises his sidearm and swiftly pulls the door open. It takes only a few moments for his actions to indicate the shed is empty. He closes the door and returns to the house.

Back inside, Schroeder says, "There's a pile of bedding in the shed."

"There shouldn't be bedding in there."

Schroeder informs her he'd like to arrange for someone to watch their place and find out who's been using the shed. He asks her and her family to avoid the building until the situation is resolved.

She clutches her throat. "Are we safe in the house?"

He assures her they should be and asks for a couple of hours to make the necessary arrangements. He asks when the rest of her family will be home. When she tells him, he says he'll be back after they return home and advises her to keep her doors locked.

Outside again, I ask Schroeder if we're still going to search for Captain Williams.

He sighs. "I'd better focus on this. I'll walk you back to the hospital and inform the guard of the situation. I'll catch up with Williams as soon as this is sorted out."

"You think it's him? Gordon Cummings?"

"Could be. Or it could be a transient."

"In the dead of winter? There are shelters and plenty of housing."

"I guess we'll know soon enough."

Chapter 30

Katie

It's been a little over a week since Landers threatened the captain. When I told Captain Williams about what Landers said, he shrugged but didn't seem particularly surprised or concerned. In fact, he even said he could understand Landers's desire for answers regarding Chastity's death.

We were all shocked by her death and don't know what happened. For the most part, Chastity appeared healthy. Her short foray into drugs shouldn't have debilitated her to the extent the flu could claim her life so rapidly. However, this flu strain has been peculiar, causing fatalities even among those who should've been able to combat it.

It is now mid-January, two weeks since the worst wave of the illness hit us. While we continue to encounter patients on an almost daily basis, the numbers have stabilized to the point where we only require the use of the hospital, rather than the medical school clinic as well. Other hospitals are also reporting a decline in cases, to the extent they have assured us of a new doctor within the week.

Despite Landers's threats of revenge, security measures at the hospital have remained largely unchanged. The limited number of police and military personnel prevents any significant modifications to the existing arrangements.

We still have a guard stationed at the entrance to screen hospital visitors as well as a second guard at the rear. Previously, we had a third guard responsible for roving patrols, but the position was eliminated after the explosion at Camp Rapid. Currently, the second guard leaves his post to patrol the perimeter of the hospital and med school grounds at least one time per hour, which Captain Williams believes is better than nothing.

Leo proposed assigning a guard to Captain Williams's house, but the captain dismissed the notion as unnecessary. Nevertheless, Deputy Shaw has taken steps to increase foot patrols in the neighborhood.

However, like the military, the sheriff's deputies and Civilian Patrols are stretched thin.

One piece of very good news from the last few days involves young Elliot Tillman, who was believed to be paralyzed following the Camp Rapid explosion. He's now regaining sensation and movement in his lower body, leading Captain Williams to believe he might experience a substantial recovery.

Elliot's father, who was injured in the blast at the ration center, has also improved enough to leave the halfway care facility and return home. Although he still faces some weakness and lingering issues, he has joined the delivery crew providing meals for the hospital and care centers.

I've encountered him several times as he delivers food for our patients. When he isn't too pressed for time, we spend a few minutes chatting. As expected, he's incredibly optimistic his son will make a full recovery.

The medical school has resumed operations, although in a modified manner until the arrival of the new doctor. Classes are scheduled either before or after Captain Williams's hospital shift. Occasionally, two hours of classes begin at 1830 hours, after Williams completes a day shift. At other times, classes commence at 0630 after he finishes an overnight shift.

Alice Williams has also increased her presence at the hospital and medical school. The official explanation is the staffing shortage and the influx of patients, but Leo believes it's primarily due to Landers.

Mrs. Williams's presence at the hospital brings a sense of reassurance to the captain, knowing she's nearby and beyond Landers's reach. However, we cannot definitively establish whether Landers was involved in anything more than mere conversation. No reports have surfaced of anyone sighting Landers or the man accompanying him since I encountered them last week. The identity of the second man remains a mystery.

"I'm ready for winter to be over." I express, snuggling closer to Leo on the sofa with a throw blanket draped over us. Gerry snoozes by my side, his head resting on my leg.

Leo's studying a book for the med school lesson they're working on. Although my husband is an instructor, he continues his own learning journey alongside the students. Captain Williams has expressed confidence multiple times that Leo will make an excellent doctor. While nothing is official yet, we suspect the captain intends to declare Leo an official student soon.

Williams has even dropped hints he wants me to join the medical school as well, to become a Doctor of the Apocalypse. Although I find the idea intriguing at times, I'm mostly content with my current role.

While Leo studies, I continue adding to my letter home. The Christmas letters were a delightful surprise, but with our busy schedule at the hospital, I have yet to complete my replies. Not that it matters much. Given the harsh weather conditions, it's unlikely any mail will be sent out soon.

A knock at the door startles Gerry and me, with Leo closely following suit. I release a sigh. "I'm so jumpy."

I grab my sidearm from the table and approach the entryway. "Who is it?"

"David Paul. I know it's late, but I was hoping you'd both be home."

I glance back at Leo, who has his pistol in his hand. He smiles and places the gun on the side table.

"Just a minute," I call out before placing my gun on the high shelf in the entryway. Opening the door, I invite Lieutenant Paul inside. He shakes off the snow from his boots and removes his jacket. "Should I take them off?" he asks, gesturing toward his feet.

"No. It's fine. Come in by the fire and get warmed up. I can't believe how cold it is out there."

"You're not kidding. It's brutal."

Leo and the lieutenant exchange handshakes before Leo asks about the reason for his visit on such a bitterly cold night. Stepping closer to the fire, Paul says, "I'm on call tonight. There's an operation I can't go into. Figured I'd take advantage of the time to chat with the two of you. With the explosion and all the troubles, we haven't had a chance to discuss the paperwork sent to you from Wyoming." He casts a glance in my direction.

I nod in acknowledgment. "We understand how chaotic things have been. And with Leo's arm . . . " I motion to my husband, his slinged arm still held tight at his side. "It isn't like there's a rush for answers, not until Bollinger releases him."

"Any updates on when you'll see the surgeon?" Lieutenant Paul removes his stocking cap and crumples it into a ball, stowing it in a pocket on his shirt. Despite shedding his outermost layers, he's still clad in several warm garments. He takes a seat in the chair closest to the fire.

"Now we're waiting until the new doctor arrives. Should be by next week. Then we'll radio the main hospital and schedule a time with Bollinger," Leo says. "Or worst-case scenario, we wait until Bollinger does his scheduled rounds. That's mid-February."

Paul flicks his eyebrows. "That's about the same timeline I relayed to the general. You know, thanks to Captain Williams, you'll hold your current Volunteer ranks when joining the National Guard."

I frown, feeling a sense of disappointment. I had hoped the college records Jake provided would enable us to obtain officer commissions. While it may not hold significant importance in the present circumstances, it could make a difference if a sense of normalcy returns in the future.

Eventually, we may have some form of currency again, and being an officer would result in higher pay compared to enlisted ranks, as it was in the past. Furthermore, there is a chance, a slim chance, I might find fulfillment in the National Guard and choose to pursue a full career, as Captain Williams and Lieutenant Paul have done. In such a scenario, an officer's commission would prove advantageous.

"The college records didn't help?" I ask.

"They're fine and provide the needed proof. The issue is we're currently adding enlisted personnel, not officers. But once you have your clearance— " He points to Leo's arm. "We'll see. Captain Williams has been championing both of you, saying it should be his choice in the end since you'll continue to work at the hospital and med school with him. He also wants to ensure the hospital remains under Guard control and is pushing for other doctors and nurses to join the National Guard."

Leo nods solemnly, seemingly unsurprised by Williams's desire to expand the Guard.

I turn to Leo and ask, "You knew about this?"

"He started pushing for it when there were rumors about Sheriff Melvin Cabal wanting to demilitarize the hospital," he replies.

"Demilitarize? I never felt like we were militarized in the first place." I shake my head.

"You're not," Lieutenant Paul says. "It's Cabal's talking point to bring about change. He's trying to portray the hospitals as military installations. Captain Williams is fighting back by encouraging his peers to accept direct commissions. If Melvin wants to call the hospitals military, then let's make them military."

I struggle to grasp the logic behind the plan. "Why does Sheriff Cabal care if the hospitals are military or not? Shouldn't that be up to the governor?"

"It is. The governor prefers things the way they are and believes our system is running smoothly. In fact, it's being replicated across the state."

Leo smiles and adds, "I've heard about that. Captain Williams thinks it's a great idea. There are plans to duplicate his med school concept as well. Once the weather improves, doctors will be coming here to observe our school with the intention of replicating it in their own counties or towns. It's a good thing. Too many people have been in denial about our situation for too long. And to think South Dakota is a leader in the rebuilding effort. What does that say about the rest of the country?"

"It is a good thing," Paul agrees. "Too bad Cabal doesn't think so. He's so against it, he's stirring up the civilians and is trying to convince them they're somehow being wronged."

"What do you mean?" I ask. "I haven't heard anything about this other than outside the hospital." I don't add I never really go anywhere but to the hospital, but still, the rumors usually get back to us.

"Cabal. He had what was essentially a press conference yesterday, with that lady—you know, the one who's trying to get a newspaper up and running?"

Leo and I nod our understanding of who he means.

"He read a statement about the National Guard, the hospitals, the ration system, and how we'd all be better off with a different setup. He avoided saying anything to directly call out the governor for bad leadership, but it was certainly implied. The press conference had a fair number of people at it and was very well received."

"Yikes." Leo shakes his head. "I can't imagine that went over well with the Office of the Governor and the National Guard."

"Nope. Not well at all. I haven't heard if the governor is planning a response or hoping it fades away."

I lean forward in my seat. "The governor can't really just let it go, right?"

"Unknown. Those aren't discussions I'm included in."

Leo motions to the radio on the lieutenant's belt. "Is this part of your operation?"

With a dip of his chin, Paul says, "In a roundabout way. You know how Cabal has been dragging his feet on finding the person or persons responsible for the attacks and explosions?"

"What do you mean dragging his feet?" I ask. "I thought it was a joint effort between law enforcement and the Guard?"

"It is now, after they attacked Camp Rapid. But up to then, Cabal took the lead. It's widely believed if he'd done his job in the first place . . . " Lieutenant Paul slams his mouth shut. The volume of his voice had increased substantially, to the point Gerry is even staring intently at the man.

Paul releases a sigh. "Forgive me. I'm a little worked up tonight. Cabal's speech brought up a lot of anger."

The lieutenant sits back in his chair, looking like he's trying to relax. Even so, there's still an edge to him that isn't usually there. He brings up the subject of how even after more than eighteen months of the lights being out and our world turned upside down, many people are still in denial.

The people of South Dakota, like those in Wyoming, were a self-sufficient bunch before the lights went out, and that's made it easier to adapt in many ways. Hunting and fishing were normal activities and a part of ordinary life. And truly, those still alive should be the toughest of the tough or blessed in some manner.

Even so, there's still a segment of the population who thinks things could change overnight and go back to what it once was. He doesn't say it, but he implies these are the main people behind Melvin Cabal.

He and Leo begin discussing news from other areas. With the Ham radio transmissions increasing, we know there were some areas with a death rate of around 90 percent. South Dakota got off easy with about 50 percent overall, though the number was higher in the cities of Sioux Falls and Rapid City. Most city folks weren't as equipped to survive as the ones in the smaller towns and rural areas.

The death toll would've been higher if not for Camp Rapid, Ellsworth Air Force Base, and people like Bowski organizing the way they did. The hospitals going under military control were part of that organization. And contrary to what Melvin Cabal believes, these aren't exactly military hospitals.

Besides, it's not really up to the sheriff. The governor of South Dakota is the one who wants things the way they are, and according to Lieutenant Paul, the Office of the Governor is happy with the way things are. Cabal really shouldn't be stirring the pot like he is. What does he even hope to accomplish with the press conference and statement?

"What do you know about what's happening in Lead?" Leo asks Lieutenant Paul.

When Leo and I were walking home from work today, he said Deputy Shaw had gone to the hospital for a meeting with the captain. At first, Williams wanted Leo to join them, but Shaw said it was top secret and involved the underground research facility in Lead.

Sandford Underground Research Facility is located in a former gold mine and used to do a variety of neutrino research. After the EMP, they've been doing other things since their deep underground location protected their sensitive equipment.

Exactly what they're doing is a mystery, but we're told it's something to help the rebuilding efforts. The research facility is one of the main reasons the Black Hills has a reputation as one of the leaders in the reconstruction of the United States.

Paul opens his hands. "Very little. What I do know is a staffing request has arrived from the governor. Staff we don't have. While the explosion and our death toll have been reported, sometimes I think the Office of the Governor doesn't quite understand how deeply we've been affected. Losing so many of our enlisted people took a toll not only on our numbers but on morale. That combined with the fact we're continually looking over our shoulders, waiting for another attack . . . " He lets out a sigh.

"There's not much we can do until things change. We're rearranging things and have pulled people from patrolling Mount Rushmore, Pactola Dam, and the other dams in the area."

"Is that smart?" I ask. "I thought there was concern about the dams being weaponized. Blow up the dam and flood Rapid City—how many people would die?"

"In the Black Hills Flood of 1972, there were over three hundred deaths and three thousand injuries. Things have changed since then, but the death toll could still be substantial."

"And?" I urge. "Is this not a concern?"

"It's a concern, but not enough of a concern to deter the newest plans." Paul takes his stocking hat out of his pocket before shoving it on his head and standing. "I wanted to let you know we're reviewing your paperwork. We'll have a decision by the time you're released for duty."

"Is the biggest concern the commitment time?" I ask. "I mean, if I understand it correctly, if we go in as enlisted, you can tell us how long we have to stay. But if you decide to make us officers, we can negotiate our time?"

"That used to be the way it was. But things are now different. Everyone is in for the long haul. It's wartime. So, no . . . that's not the issue."

"Then what?"

"Katie," Leo warns under his breath.

I let out a sigh. "I'm sorry. I don't mean to seem disrespectful. I'm only trying to understand."

Leo puts his hand on my arm. "I think maybe they're trying to determine the validity of the documents?"

Paul tilts his head. "People who don't really know you did wonder about that. Those of us who do know you aren't concerned. It's a process we're following in this noncomputerized world."

Though a commission would be nice for when things do start going back to normal, in the end, it doesn't matter much. We'll do what we need to do, working at the hospital and helping to train new doctors and nurses. Leo may even become a doctor himself.

All of this feels right. Whether as part of the United Volunteers, officers in the South Dakota National Guard, or even as just regular Katie and Leo Burnett, God brought us to the Black Hills to help save lives.

Chapter 31

Katie

As we're saying our goodbyes, the radio on Lieutenant Paul's belt emits a squawk, followed by a voice saying, "Elkhound, Black Bear, over." He swiftly moves the radio to his mouth and replies, "Go ahead, Black Bear, over."

Black Bear instructs Paul to switch to a different channel, and once they make the switch, he provides the rendezvous coordinates.

"The information was good?" Lieutenant Paul asks, his gaze fixed on Gerry.

"Correct," Black Bear responds. "Are you still with the Burnetts? Over."

He looks up at Leo and me. "Correct."

"Bring them both as medics. Give them rendezvous coordinates. Meet in thirty mikes, over."

"Confirm, bring the Burnetts to the rendezvous point, meet in thirty mikes, over."

"Correct, over."

"Wilco, over."

"Roger, out."

"We need five minutes to get dressed," Leo says as Paul returns the radio to his belt. "Do you want to wait or have us meet you?"

"I'll wait," Lieutenant Paul says. "I would've given you a heads up, but no one told me you'd be involved in this."

"Is this about the explosions?" I ask.

"Five minutes, Burnett," the lieutenant responds with a curt nod. I'm slightly taken aback by his more formal demeanor. He has always been warm and patient with me, calling me Katie and acting friendly.

"Um, yes, sir," I answer before hurrying away.

In the bedroom, Leo gives me a smile. "Got to earn our United Volunteer ranks."

Once we're dressed for the winter evening and Gerry is dropped off at the neighbor's, we briskly walk to the rendezvous point, which is only a few blocks from Camp Rapid. There's no chitchat or conversation between us and the lieutenant during the walk. He is all business.

When we reach the rendezvous spot, there's already a sizable crowd gathered, including Jesse Talbot and Merissa Weaver, each with two large duffle bags by their side. Even from a distance, I know the bags are filled with medical supplies we may need.

"Wait with them until you receive your orders," Lieutenant Paul gestures toward the medics before striding toward a huddled group.

"Leo, Katie," Jesse acknowledges. Dressed in combat gear, he reaches for Leo's hand. "Quite the shindig."

Merissa, clad in the same type of gear as Jesse, nods before remarking, "I was mildly surprised when the radio call came in. Not only did Williams send Jesse and me, but they also suggested you two join us. Seems odd to have all four of us."

I nod. "Lieutenant Paul was at our house. I was surprised when he was asked to bring us along. It must be big."

"The people behind the explosions, that's what we think." Merissa jabs her thumb in Jesse's direction. "Why else would they want all of us? The hospital is preparing too. So is the Main Street District Hospital."

Jesse gestures at Leo's broken arm. "Not sure what the actual plan is and how you can be in combat."

Leo gives his friend a determined look. "I'll manage."

"Hey, buddy, I know you will."

I choose to remain silent. While Leo and I have made significant progress in our marriage, the memories of those difficult times when our relationship was strained are still fresh in my mind. During those times, I didn't dare mention my concern for Leo's health for fear of him snapping at me.

Although, like Jesse, I have no idea how Captain Williams thinks Leo can keep from reinjuring his arm in a combat situation—and truthfully, I question Merissa's attendance in such an event. We all know the Guard is stretched thin, so maybe they're taking any warm body available.

I give a quick glance around, looking to see if they've enlisted the help of the sheriff's department and Citizen Patrol, but discover the units to be suspiciously absent. "Deputy Shaw isn't here?" I ask.

"We noticed that too," Jesse says in a low voice. "Whatever this operation is, it's National Guard only. Well . . . and us."

It's only a few minutes until we're given our orders. Even though the lieutenant wouldn't tell us if this was regarding a tip they have on the preacher and his group, he now confirms that is exactly what's happening.

He also informs Jesse and me we'll be at the casualty collection point in the general area of the operation. He says he needs us combat-ready and confirms with each of us we can handle the assignment.

My stomach bubbles. I had combat training in Bakerville and with the United Volunteers, but I've been strictly a nurse since being assigned to the Guard District Hospital six months ago.

Jesse, Leo, and Merissa were at least put through some basic training and instructions with the National Guard as part of their role as medics and the expectations they may need to operate in the field either with the Guard or with the sheriff's department.

"Burnett?" The lieutenant looks at me expectantly.

"Yes, sir. I'm ready."

"Good. Mrs. Weaver and the other Sergeant Burnett will be at the secondary location, which will be a backup base. If things go south, this is where we'll have law enforcement meet us. Mr. Talbot and Sergeant Katie Burnett will come with us. They'll hang back at the CCP, ready to assist as needed, both as medics and potentially combat personnel."

He turns to Merissa. "Weaver, give your body armor to Burnett. I want both her and Jesse fully ready. We'll have rifles for you too." He motions to someone in the distance, who responds with a nod before scurrying over with two rifles.

It's a whirlwind as the private makes sure both Jesse and I know how to operate the weapons. I swallow my nervousness as I realize they're some sort of AR-15, which I've become very familiar with since the world fell apart. The private reminds us to conserve ammo and only fire if necessary.

When he's gone, Paul says, "I know this is less than ideal. The plan is for you two to simply be there to provide medical aid, but we all know how plans can go."

Leo looks at me with slightly raised eyebrows.

I give a brief nod as I respond to Lieutenant Paul with another, "Yes, sir."

"Make yourselves ready. We're moving out in five minutes."

Though we walked to the rendezvous area, assorted trucks will take us closer to where they believe the preacher and his people are living. The goal is to apprehend the entire organization without weapon fire, but the four of us are here in case things don't go as planned.

Huddled in the bed of a pickup truck, along with Jesse, Merissa, and four from the Guard, I ask Leo if he's been on an operation with so many medics before. I'm sure he hasn't because I'd have heard about it, but my nervousness has me talking and wanting to hear his calm voice of reassurance.

He rests his hand on my knee. "You know what to do, right?"

"As a medic or in combat?"

"Both."

"Mostly do what I'm told and don't get shot?"

He chuckles. "That's mainly it."

Our eyes meet, and even in the darkness, I perceive his love reflected in his gaze. He lifts his hand from my knee to tenderly caress my cheek.

I tilt my head slightly and press my lips against the inside of his wrist, my bottom lip grazing his skin beneath the glove.

He rewards me with a small smile. "Definitely avoid getting shot."

As the truck rumbles through the dimly lit streets, tension hangs heavy in the air, each of us silent and staring into the distance. Leo maintains his hand on my knee. I sense his grip tighten as the truck decelerates, bringing us closer to our target area.

When the truck comes to a stop, Leo gives my knee a final squeeze before disembarking alongside Merissa and two of the guards. Jesse, the remaining guards, and I remain seated. Lieutenant Paul, who rode in the front seat, steps out.

"You four are assigned to Bravo group." He motions to a second truck stopped in the parking lot of what used to be a fast-food restaurant. Half a dozen soldiers are by the truck.

"The rest of you stay put. We have approximately five minutes. Remember, our objective is to apprehend without resorting to violence. However, remain prepared for any scenario." Lieutenant

Paul's voice exudes firmness and authority, a stark departure from the social encounters I've had with him.

As Paul returns to the front of the truck, I raise my hand toward my husband, offering a small wave.

He silently mouths the words, "I love you," as the truck speeds away.

I take a deep breath. My mind is racing with a mixture of anticipation and fear, along with determination. I focus on the feel of the cold metal I'm sitting on as I inhale again. Exhaling, my gaze shifts to Jesse, who's again staring off into the distance.

As the truck slows to a halt, we pile out and join the rest of the team in a hastily organized formation. My heart pounds in my ears, and my gloved hands feel clammy. I remove the gloves and tuck them in my pockets.

Lieutenant Paul, accompanied by a few seasoned soldiers, briefs us on the plan. They outline the operation's specifics, assigning roles and responsibilities. Jesse and I are tasked with establishing a forward medical station, ready to provide aid as needed. We proceed silently on foot for the remaining few blocks.

Jesse and I position ourselves near the rear. We move forward, cautiously navigating the dimly lit streets. A silent hand gesture halts our progress. Jesse and I are singled out, and Paul motions for us to move toward the driveway of what appears to be an abandoned house. I guess this is the spot we'll use as our triage location. The two soldiers who rode with us in the truck will act as our guards.

Other than opening our duffle bags and making sure everything is where it should be and within easy reach, there's not much to do to prepare. The soldiers tell us we can sit near the edge of the house and, if there's any shooting, to keep our heads down unless they tell us otherwise.

I scuff the snow away from the edge of the house to clear a spot to sit when there's a shout in the distance. One of the soldiers mutters, "Here we go."

Adrenaline surges through my veins, heightening my senses as I choose to remain standing, pushing into the wall. Jesse, who spent several years in the Army, appears almost relaxed as he leans against the house.

He gives me a nod. "Remember to breathe."

The shouts continue, though I can't make out much that's being said. Most of it sounds like, "Keep your hands where I can see them." Thankfully, there's yet to be any shooting.

I realize one of the sounds I hear is a baby crying. Closing my eyes, I focus on the sound. Is it a baby living nearby simply awakened by the shouting? Or does the preacher's group have a baby with them? I guess that's certainly possible. I don't really know anything about the preacher and his group other than seeing him at the festival before the attack.

Bryson Young is the one who told me the preacher was behind the explosions. Since then, there's been plenty of speculation concerning not only the man but his followers. The popular opinion is he's something resembling a cult leader, convincing his people God wants us to be an agrarian society, and it's up to him and his church to ensure this happens through any means necessary.

Within mere minutes, Lieutenant Paul arrives at our impromptu medical clinic. With a smile, he tells us we can stand down. "This was a peaceful surrender. There are no apparent injuries." He turns to Jesse and me. "There are a few children in the group. They seem healthy enough, but we'd like you to go in and check them out before we move them. There's a pregnant woman too."

The lieutenant takes Jesse and me into the house. There are probably thirty people in the large living room. All are sitting on the floor with their hands bound either in front or behind them. None of them seem concerned about their situation. A few even have their eyes closed . . . either praying or sleeping, it's hard to tell.

In the master bedroom, there are five children ranging in age from a few months old to eight or nine. A very pregnant woman is holding the infant in one arm with a toddler on her lap. While her hands aren't bound, she looks considerably more nervous and uncomfortable than her friends in the living room.

I tell Jesse I'll start with her and the children she's holding. He nods before walking toward a boy of about five.

"I'm Katie," I tell the woman as I set my medical bag on the floor. "I've been asked to check you and the children before we move you."

She wrinkles her nose and wiggles in her chair. Her eyes go wide, and her mouth forms an *O* as she looks down at her lap. "I think . . . I think my water just broke."

Chapter 32

Katie

My eyes widen in surprise as the pregnant woman's words hang in the air. I blink several times and run through the implications of what she said. While her water breaking is important to know, it doesn't necessarily constitute an emergency.

"Stay calm," I reassure her, my voice sounding less calm than I'd like. "Are any of these your children?" I motion around the room.

She looks at the toddler in her lap. "Shawna's mine." She lifts her arm slightly. "This is Zach. His mom is— " She slams her lips shut and shakes her head.

I look at Shawna and give the girl a smile. She curls into her mom, hiding her face. "Shawna was born before the EMP?" I ask.

"A few months before, by cesarean."

I keep a smile on my face while my heart pounds harder. "What's your name?"

"Kemeera."

"Do you remember the reason for the c-section?"

"Uh . . . failure to progress or something." The woman squirms again as a look of discomfort crosses her face.

"Are you having contractions?"

"My back hurts. Maybe . . . could you take Zach?" She raises her arm, offering me the infant. His eyes are open, and he's sucking on a pacifier.

I cradle the tiny baby in my arms. "Jesse?" I call out, while focusing my attention on Kemeera.

"Yeah? Is everything . . . Oh." Jesse quickly appears by my side, carefully avoiding the expanding puddle of liquid on the carpet. "Ma'am." He gives her a nod.

We exchange a quick glance, our silent communication conveying the shared understanding that this is beyond our initial expectations.

"I think we're still in the early stages of labor," I say. "Kemeera's having some back pain." I motion to the carpet. "And her membranes have ruptured. We need a truck to take her to the hospital."

She shakes her head. "Not the hospital. I don't want another surgery. I want— " She tightens her face. "Please." She pants out a breath.

Jesse gives me a nod and slips out of the bedroom.

Holding the small baby in one arm, I rub her shoulder with my free hand. Once she's relaxed, I give her shoulder a squeeze.

She lets out a sigh. "I suppose, with the way things are, the hospital is my only choice. What about the children?"

"We'll take care of them, and you're going to be okay," I say softly. "We'll do everything we can to ensure a safe delivery for both you and your baby."

Returning to the room, Jesse's gaze meets mine. "We're all set." He returns his attention to the boy he was examining before. His voice takes on a higher pitch as he chats with the children.

Within minutes, the roar of multiple engines fills the quiet of the night. Lieutenant Paul appears at the bedroom door. "We'll take everyone from this room first. Burnett and Weaver should arrive shortly." He nods in her direction. She's staring at her lap while her hand rubs her daughter's back.

"Her name is Kemeera," I say. "Are we waiting here for Leo and Merissa?"

"I want them to help with Kemeera and the children." Paul glances around the room. "Might as well start moving out. Is Kemeera able to move?"

"I can move," she says, her voice quiet but determined. "Just give me a minute and I'll . . . "

As she rides out the contraction, I check my watch. It's been almost four minutes since the last one. Less than a minute later, she relaxes and gives a nod, indicating she's ready to go.

Paul moves from the doorway and asks one of the female soldiers to help us move everyone. I hand off the baby to her while I hold Kemeera's daughter Shawna and offer the woman my arm. She gives a slight shake of her head. "I can manage."

Jesse carries the young boy he was examining, while the two older girls walk behind him. Lieutenant Paul follows our little procession.

We leave the hallway and reach the living room where the preacher and his followers are being held.

"*Be strong in the Lord and in his mighty power. Put on the full armor of God, so that you can take your stand against the devil's schemes,*" a booming voice says, filling the room.

I glance in the direction of the voice to see the man that was preaching on the lawn of the festival. He lifts his chin in my direction, his shoulder-length dirty blond hair moving as he continues with the Bible verse.

"*For our struggle is not against flesh and blood, but against the rulers, against the authorities, against the powers of this dark world and against the spiritual forces of evil in the heavenly realms. Therefore, put on the full armor of God, so that when the day of evil comes, you may be able to stand your ground, and after you have done everything, to stand.*"

Several voices call out amen. One of the soldiers says, "Keep quiet."

As I near the front door, the preacher continues, "*Stand firm then, with the belt of truth buckled around your waist, with the breastplate of righteousness in place, and with your feet fitted with the readiness that comes from the gospel of peace. In addition to all this, take up the shield of faith, with which you can extinguish all the flaming arrows of the evil one. Take the helmet of salvation and the sword of the Spirit, which is the word of God.*"

Out the door and on the front porch, his voice begins to fade, but it's loud enough to hear as he continues with the armor of God chapter from Ephesians. Listening to the familiar words, delivered in his confident tone, almost has me yearning to hear more.

If this man is indeed the leader of a murderous cult, I can almost grasp why people were drawn to him. Even people like Kemeera who appear entirely ordinary. There's no denying the man possesses a certain charisma when he speaks.

Headlights and engine noise from down the block suggest Leo and Merissa are arriving. When the truck pulls to a stop, Leo hops out of the bed with a couple of Guard members while Merissa gets out of the passenger's side of the cab.

We take only moments to relay the medical situation of Kemeera. Lieutenant Paul asks if we're okay to take the pickup and go directly to the hospital. They'll take care of everyone here, and he'll meet us there when he's done.

Right on time, Kemeera whispers, "It's starting again." She leans against the pickup until the contraction passes. It's decided I'll drive the truck and she'll ride in the passenger's seat. Merissa says she's fine in the bed of the truck with Leo, Jesse, and the children.

"Try to take it easy, okay?" Merissa suggests with a smile as I hand her the infant. "Boy, he's light," she says with the baby cradled in one arm.

"Very light." I glance at the snow-covered road, the light of the moon showing patches of ice that I'm sure are slick.

"Do you know how to get back to the hospital?" Leo asks.

"Yep. I know where we are."

Cautiously navigating the snow and ice-laden streets, it takes just under twenty minutes—or four of Kemeera's contractions—before we reach the guard shack. Having received notice from Lieutenant Paul that we were on our way, the night guard waves us through. Nurse Jacquie Haley and Dr. Wolff are both waiting in the roundabout.

As I pull to a stop, another of Kemeera's contractions start. I let out a sigh of relief, knowing we've made it to the hospital where Nettie and Captain Williams can take care of the laboring woman.

I signal Nettie to wait a moment before opening the door. Once the contraction subsides, I ask Kemeera if she's ready to get out.

"Will you stay with me?"

"Sure, I can if you'd like." Although I keep my voice even and a soft smile on my face, fear churns my stomach. The last time I was at a delivery, neither the mother nor the infant survived.

"Thank you." She sighs. "I had a midwife. She promised she'd be here to help me, but when I went to see her for my last scheduled appointment, she was gone."

My eyebrows shoot to my hairline. "Addison? Is your midwife Addison?"

She nods. "Did you work with her? She told me she was friends with a few people from the hospital. One of the women doctors."

The discomfort in my stomach increases. Was Addison friends with Chastity? My gaze travels toward Nettie, now holding the infant and looking expectantly into the front of the cab. Could Nettie know Addison, the pseudo midwife and herbalist? Surely, she would've said something about knowing her when Captain Williams sent Shaw to find the woman.

"Do you feel like you can get out of the truck and make it inside now?"

Kemeera gets out of the truck and moves to a waiting wheelchair. I push her into the hospital and, at Dr. Nettie Wolff's request, take her into our smallest exam room. All the children are taken to one of the other rooms. Within a few minutes, there's a knock on the door, and Nettie strides in followed by Merissa.

"How's my daughter?" Kemeera asks.

"She's fine," Nettie replies. "They're all fine. Now let's take a look at you."

Following a noninvasive examination in which she experiences two contractions, there's a subtle shift in Nettie's calm demeanor when the previous c-section is mentioned.

"We'll keep a close eye on you. Katie isn't on duty right now, but you'd like her to stay with you?"

Kemeera looks toward me before giving a firm nod. "I would . . . if that's okay?"

"I'll stay," I respond, stepping closer to the woman.

"I'm going to have Merissa stay with you for a moment while I take Katie to Captain Williams. He's in charge of the hospital and will need to hear her say she's willing to work when she's not on shift, okay?"

Kemeera shrugs as her entire body seems to tighten. I check my watch to see the contractions are now closer to three minutes apart. Once she's relaxed again, I step out of the room with Nettie.

"What's wrong?" I ask, knowing the captain doesn't need me to agree to work when I'm off shift.

"Hopefully nothing. Just because she had a c-section before doesn't necessarily mean she'll need one this time, but it's possible. I want someone with her continually, monitoring both her and the baby. The baby's heartbeat sounded strong, and the contractions felt solid. I'm hopeful we'll have a natural delivery. After she changes, we'll do an internal exam and see how she's progressed."

"All right. That all sounds good."

"Let's hope it goes as planned."

Back inside the exam room, I let Merissa know I'm going to help Kemeera change. After Merissa leaves, the expectant mom says, "The doctor is worried about having to do a c-section, isn't she?"

"Worried? No, not worried. We're going to monitor you closely, you and the baby. If a c-section is necessary, it'll happen immediately. You're going to be okay." I place a reassuring hand on her arm.

With slightly shaking hands, I assist Kemeera into a gown and then into a comfortable position. When Nettie returns a few minutes later for a more thorough exam, she declares the labor is progressing nicely.

"I don't think it'll be long until you're holding your baby," she says with a smile.

Not long ends up being about four hours. She never screams. Even when the labor pains become intense, she quietly works her way through them, her lips moving possibly in prayer.

While I hold Kemeera's hand and tell her how wonderful she's doing, Merissa stands nearby with a bassinet for the baby while Jacquie assists Nettie in the delivery.

As the final moments of labor approach, a hushed reverence descends upon the room. Kemeera pants a few times before whispering, "Now?"

"Now, Kemeera."

And then, with one final push, the room is filled with the cry of a newborn. A symphony of emotions run through me—relief, joy, and a profound sense of gratitude. "You did it, Kemeera! You did it!" I say as she rests her head against the pillow.

She lifts her head slightly "Is she okay?"

"He's fine," Merissa responds, moving the now mewing infant toward his mom's chest. Tears of exhaustion and elation stream down Kemeera's face as she cradles her newborn son in her arms.

Chapter 33

Merissa

True to his word, Trooper Schroeder returned to the hospital to provide me with an update on the situation regarding Cindy's shed. They surveilled the area for several days, but no one ever appeared.

Schroeder himself checked again, but there were no fresh tracks. After meeting with Cindy and her husband at their workplace, they decided to suspend the operation. It remains unknown whether Gordon Cummings—McKay's murderer—or someone else was involved.

Kemeera and her baby, along with the majority of the children, have been relocated to one of the long-term care centers. While she is willing to discuss matters concerning her baby or her older daughter, she adamantly refuses to talk about the preacher and the others from his group.

Similarly, none of them are cooperating. At this point, aside from the infant Zach, we have no knowledge of who the parents of the children are. The five-year-old boy mentioned his mom's dead and his father's name is Danny, but none of the prisoners respond to that name. The slightly older girls refuse to disclose their names or the names of their parents.

The mother of Zach came forward. Both she and the baby are being held separately from the rest of the preacher's group. A makeshift jail has been set up in our district using an old junk storage business after the holding cells at Camp Rapid were destroyed.

The cult members were held there overnight before being transferred to the main jail the following morning, except for the mother and baby Zach, who are still held in our district.

Sheriff Melvin Cabal was reportedly speechless when the National Guard apprehended the group. Rumor has it he insisted they shouldn't have carried out such a significant operation without his involvement, and he remains disgruntled about the entire situation. It took the governor's intervention once again to persuade the sheriff of his role in this matter.

Although it's suspected the preacher and his group are responsible for the explosions, their silence prevents any confirmation. To say the least, the past few days have been eventful.

Even the relocation of Kemeera and the children presented challenges. Initially, Poppy Gardner, who oversees the care centers, refused to accommodate them. She expressed concerns about the potential danger if the preacher is indeed behind the murders, as it could put her other patients at risk. Her fear is that not all of the preacher's followers were apprehended during the raid.

Kemeera refuses to disclose the identity or whereabouts of either of her children's fathers, or even acknowledge her affiliation with the preacher's congregation. Similarly, none of the detainees claim to know Kemeera or any of the children. It's a rather perplexing situation.

On my one precious day off, after concluding a study session, I find solace in catching up on my journal. I can hear Mother Pearl moving around in the living room, and it won't be long before she either knocks on my door or calls out for me.

While my elderly mother-in-law values her independence, I'm aware of her loneliness. I often ponder what would be best for her—should she stay here with me, or would she be better off at the ranch with Opal?

Opal is wonderful about visiting town as frequently as her schedule permits. Nevertheless, Pearl spends most of her time alone. She does work at the childcare center two or three days a week, depending on their needs, and I know she enjoys it. Once my baby arrives, or as Pearl fondly refers to him, *our* baby, things will likely improve for her.

However, I do wonder if Pearl has the necessary energy to assist in caring for him. Despite the fact babies primarily sleep, eat, and soil their diapers, she already returns exhausted from her work at the daycare.

I spoke with Captain Williams regarding what Katie said about the baby accompanying me to school. He reassured me it would be acceptable on classroom days. Additionally, he suggested converting one of the unused rooms into a daycare where Pearl could watch my baby. He believes it makes sense to allocate the space for the next group of students. In the next few weeks, he plans to initiate nurse training, and those students may also have childcare needs.

Poppy Gardner will assist with the training, allowing Williams to concentrate on future doctors while she focuses on recruiting new nurses at various levels. Similar to our hospital, her care centers operate with limited staff resources.

The new doctor for our hospital is expected to arrive next week. Once he settles in, we'll resume our regular medical school classes. Currently, we're following what Williams refers to as an abbreviated school schedule. I currently work around three shifts as a medic per week, in addition to three shadow shifts and the classroom days. I'm unsure how this will change when we revert to our regular schedule.

One piece of good news is the addition of another medic. Dr. Wolff met the man last month when his mom was in the hospital for a blood pressure issue. At that time, he revealed his prior service in the Navy and his basic medical background. There are still a few loose ends to be tied up from his current job, but Williams said we should expect him to start at the hospital within the week.

Leaning back in my chair, I close my eyes. How much longer can I maintain this schedule? I'm exhausted, not only from work but also from the lack of sleep. Finding a comfortable position has become challenging, and I've been experiencing severe heartburn. Moreover, I make far too many trips to the bathroom.

Stella gave me some digestive bitters, which alleviate the heartburn, but she merely laughed when I asked about anything to reduce the frequency of bathroom visits. Realistically, I understand these discomforts are due to the presence of the baby, but it's still quite bothersome and terribly annoying.

Dr. Wolff examines me weekly now. It seems my advanced maternal age, over thirty-five, has her concerned. I guess I've always known this would be an issue, but I've chosen to ignore it. There's not much that can be done. Thirty-six and pregnant does come with risks to both me and the baby, but here we are. I don't think my age matters much, though. Having a baby in today's world is a risk at any age.

A smile covers my face as I think about Kemeera and the birth of her baby. She named him Caleb, and he was truly perfect. She was absolutely amazing during the entire labor. Somehow, I doubt I'll be as composed as she was. My guess is my days from the Coast Guard will come rushing back, and I'll embarrass myself by remembering all the colorful sailor words.

I lean forward and close my journal. It's time to visit with Pearl. Although we had our differences in the past, things have improved between us. I know she feels indebted to me for staying with her. My sister-in-law Courtney would've been the logical choice, given her excellent relationship with Pearl since the day Tomas brought her home; I was always the outcast.

I don't entirely blame Pearl, though. I understand I'm not the easiest person to get to know. Even here in Rapid City, working at the hospital, I find it challenging to make friends. I'm content with my colleagues, but we don't exactly share a warm and affectionate bond. Although I must admit a few, like Katie, make an effort to be friendly.

It's easier with the men, particularly since most of them have a military background. There's good-natured banter about me being a Coastie. It feels normal to me. However, sharing my emotions with women isn't something I'm accustomed to. I'm fairly certain, once they get to know me and my awkwardness, they won't want to befriend me.

Currently, I'm the new pregnant girl, which brings some intrigue. I have never fully understood why it's challenging for me to form and maintain friendships with other women, but it's an aspect of my life I can't seem to shake.

In the living room, Pearl stands by the woodstove, stirring the pot. She turns toward me. "Opal's beans. Hope they soften up a sight better than the last batch. Those beans must have been old. It was like eating rocks."

I'd shared the batch of beans with her, and she complained throughout the entire meal. While I agree they weren't as tender as they could've been, I believe it was more a matter of undercooking. Pearl has never been much of a cook, and mastering woodstove cooking requires skill.

Aware of her sister's culinary limitations, Opal is kind enough to bring us pots of already prepared stew and beans. These beans were precooked by Opal, only needing to be reheated, so I'm confident they'll turn out fine.

"You get your studying done?" she asks, turning her attention back to the bean pot.

"For now. I don't think I'll ever truly be done."

"I worry about you. Working so hard. Studying so much. You and the baby." She keeps her gaze fixed on the pot, unwilling to meet my eyes.

"I'm fine," I assure her.

Pearl emits a noise that falls somewhere between a snort and a groan. "I'm just saying . . . " She lets out an exaggerated sigh. "Never mind."

I move to the bench next to the woodstove. The elaborate exhaust system has warmed the rocks nicely. Placing a pillow behind my back, I lean against the wall. "Could you sit with me for a minute?"

Pearl gives me a surprised look. "Well, okay."

She's getting around without her cane today, which is quite common inside the house. I believe it's more of a security measure than anything else, especially given how the cane's grip digs into the snow. I support her use of the cane if it prevents her from falling and getting hurt.

Instead of leaning back on the bench, she perches on the edge, exactly as I would expect from my formerly affluent mother-in-law. She was accustomed to a life of luxury. It's not that she lacks toughness; she possesses it. The way she has persevered through everything we've been through is truly remarkable. Witnessing her resilience and determination has brought me to a new level of understanding with her—love, even.

As I exhale deeply, the movement I've been waiting for begins. "May I have your hand?"

Pearl starts to inquire why, but a smile spreads across her face. I take her hand and place it against my belly. Immediately, the baby responds with a firm kick.

Mother Pearl's eyes light up. "He's amazing."

"Indeed, and very active. He seems perfectly fine. I didn't mention this before, but the doctor examined me yesterday and believes everything is progressing well. She still anticipates his arrival around the end of March or early April."

"It could be a girl."

"It could be," I agree with a nod.

"Do you have a preference?"

"I don't. Do you?"

She gives me a wry smile. "I'm rather fond of little boys, you know. A little boy who resembles Braedon would be . . . " Her voice trails off as she chokes on her words.

After taking a few moments to regain her composure, she continues, "I miss him so much. The both of them. Braedon would be immensely proud of you, not only because of the baby but for everything you're doing. He always believed you were destined for greatness."

I let out a laugh. "Is that so? I'm not entirely sure greatness is happening here."

She meets my gaze with a serious expression. "It is, Merissa. The things you're doing, *becoming a doctor*, it's an accomplishment to be proud of. I know I'm proud of you."

I can't hide my surprise. While Pearl has occasionally said kind things to me, she has never explicitly expressed her pride in me. Before I can respond, the baby kicks again, capturing all of Pearl's attention.

We spend several minutes with her hand on my belly as she coos and talks to the baby.

Our baby.

Braedon and I may have created him or her, but Pearl will pour all her love into this child. In this chaotic and uncertain world, Pearl's love and devotion are something I can rely on.

Chapter 34

Katie

"It won't be long now. Leo will be home from work soon," I say, tossing a chunk of limp carrot to Gerry, who skillfully catches it before it reaches the ground. "Good job. I bet you'd be a great frisbee dog."

Gerry perks up his ears, seemingly intrigued. "Does that sound fun? Catching a frisbee?" He sneezes. I let out a chuckle. "Or do you only catch food?"

Gerry's food is nothing like what dogs used to have before the EMP. As far as I know, dog food isn't being manufactured anymore. Even if it were, we lack the systems to transport it. When we first brought Gerry and his littermates home, they were so tiny their eyes weren't even open yet. We fed them with a bottle, giving them cow or goat milk whenever we could obtain it; otherwise, we resorted to a homemade broth-based formula.

Through radio communication with a vet, we managed to acquire a crude recipe for milk replacer, as cow's milk alone lacked sufficient protein. Eggs would've been ideal, but they were hard to come by. However, during hunting season, we could find liver and other organ meats more easily, so Opal made sure to regularly bring those for Gerry.

More than once I heard it was a miracle all the puppies survived. A miracle, yes. And lots of work too. Now that Gerry's on a regular diet, we feed him food that closely resembles what we eat. The vet provided us with a basic formula to ensure he gets enough protein, carbohydrates, fiber, and fat. Ensuring he consumes enough calories is always a concern, not only for our dog but also for us.

Although we still receive our weekly rations of meat and winter-hearty vegetables, I've noticed quantities seem to be decreasing. Leo brought it up with Williams. According to him, they faced several issues during the peak of the flu outbreak. While the crops had been harvested for winter, the transportation system faced challenges, causing delays in supplies reaching their destinations.

The hunters, who now mainly provide migratory waterfowl, were also affected and couldn't hunt. Additionally, the ranchers couldn't slaughter the cull cattle without people to assist. Now that the illness seems to be subsiding, everyone hopes our rations will return to their previous quantities.

Although the captain's explanation seems plausible, I'm still concerned there might be more to it. What if the food grown and stored for winter doesn't last as long as expected? We experienced a population surge during the summer, with people moving here for a better life after hearing the Black Hills was thriving. Others attempting to head south for the winter ended up stranded here for various reasons.

Opal took in several transient families at her ranch, as they were unable to continue their journey. Thankfully, their stories ended better than the three men who were attacked by Hayward's dogs. Opal assured the surviving boy that when he's well enough, he's welcome at their ranch.

With a thin stew simmering on the woodstove, I move on to handwashing our undergarments. I'm truly grateful our hospital clothes are washed by the laundry crew, along with the bedding, towels, and other items we use. The hardworking men and women who manage the laundry make my life much easier.

A few times a week, either Leo or I wash our socks, underwear, long johns, T-shirts, and other garments. Our regular clothes—the pants and shirts that don't directly touch our skin, thanks to our extra layers—don't get washed as frequently as they should, and our coats and insulated snow pants haven't been washed since we obtained them. It's simply too labor-intensive.

I hate to admit even our bed sheets aren't cleaned as often as they used to be when we had electric washing machines. With our busy schedule and the amount of work involved, we usually go several weeks between washes. However, since I had the day off today, I took the opportunity to change the bed sheets first thing this morning. I put on the extra set of sheets and started the laborious task of cleaning the dirty set.

The clean sheets and pillowcases are now freeze-drying in the unheated extra bedroom, hung on the clothesline we set up. Once I finish with the undergarments, I'll move them there to dry as well.

It's been a busy day for both me and Gerry. Sometimes I feel like my days off are more demanding than my shifts at the hospital. I glance down at the little dog, sitting patiently at my feet. It has been a day of work, but still a good day overall.

Several hours later, the laundry is done, and the stew is ready. The sun has set, and it's almost 1900 hours, about half an hour later than when I expected Leo to come home. I keep myself occupied with various tasks around the house.

Even in our new minimalist world, it's astonishing how things can become disorganized. However, I will say the absence of paper is helpful. Other than the heartfelt letters from home and a couple of sheets of scrap paper I use for my to-do lists, our home is practically paper-free.

This house originally belonged to a young couple, slightly older than Leo and me, according to our neighbors, the Harringtons. The couple was out of the country when the attacks began. Crystal Harrington mentioned the wife is from Germany, and they were visiting her family.

While we're aware of troubles in other countries, and many people believe we're essentially in an undeclared World War III, there are places we don't hear much about—at least, I don't hear much about them. Leo and I assume people like my sister Calley who monitor the radios have a far greater understanding of current events than we do. She probably knows more than what she shared in the letter we received.

Calley only revealed what she considered to be the most interesting news, focusing on concerns emerging from the West Coast and the Wastelands. I don't know if there's any truth to it. I suppose it's likely people are discontented about being forced out of the Wastelands and their homes. If I lived in a place I loved and didn't perceive imminent danger, I wouldn't want to leave either.

There has been some debate about whether the president even has the authority to declare the Wastelands uninhabitable. Well, I guess he can declare it, but can he truly prohibit people from living there? That's the question many people have been asking.

This question arose back in the spring when Leo and I first joined the United Volunteers, thinking we'd assist with evacuations. The official story at the time was people welcomed the Volunteers. They needed the help.

But now I'm not so sure that's the case. After Calley's letter, we started asking around. Both Lieutenant Paul and Captain Williams acknowledged the situation was being kept quiet, but they had also heard about strong resistance to leaving. The demarcation line is becoming a skirmish line, with Americans fighting Americans.

This news makes Leo and me profoundly grateful we decided to stay in Rapid City and join the National Guard instead of leaving with the rest of the Volunteers. I can't even fathom the idea of fighting someone, shooting at them, simply because they want to stay in their own home.

The low rumble of an engine interrupts the eerie silence. I glance out the window and spot a single headlight. In the darkness, it resembles one of the snowmobiles used by the sheriff's department and the Citizen Patrol, likely dropping off Oscar Harrington from his patroller shift. There's enough light to make out a figure stepping off the back of the machine. Within seconds, the snowmobile speeds away.

I move to the window to close the still-open curtains. Oscar Harrington, at least I assume it's him, is on the sidewalk talking with another man. The stature and stance of the other man brings a wave of happiness over me.

Leo. With a happy smile, I complete the task of closing the curtains and then transfer the stew to the hottest spot on the stove, ensuring it becomes delightfully warm. Afterward, I proceed to the kitchen, where I slice bread to accompany our dinner.

When we converted our dining space into our bedroom, we moved the table and chairs out, and now we eat all our meals in the living room. Surprisingly, I've come to enjoy this arrangement. The crackling fire and the gentle glow of an oil lamp provide the perfect amount of romantic light.

Leo and I went through a difficult time in the weeks following his fall from the horse, but we're better now. We still have our moments, as any married couple does. But with God's guidance, we're making it work. Working at the hospital remains challenging. Although I love my job, it's far from easy. Dealing with sickness, injuries, and the inevitable deaths are things I don't know if I'll ever fully get used to.

Warmth fills my heart as I think of Kemeera and her baby Caleb. His birth has brought me much happiness, serving as a healing salve for the grief I've carried. It's a vivid reminder of the natural cycle of life God has ordained, where both death and birth coexist in harmony.

Another unexpected bright spot is the women's self-defense training we were finally able to start. We've held a few classes, and it's going well. Finding a convenient time for everyone has been difficult, so we offer multiple options throughout the week, and whoever can make it attends.

In addition to Merissa and me having some knowledge in self-defense, Kerry Hendricks brings her expertise in martial arts. She practiced Taekwondo during her high school and college years, even achieving a 2nd Dan Black Belt and working as an assistant instructor.

After marrying Rand and moving to Rapid City, her formal training ceased, but she has continued to practice on her own for fitness. When we schedule class times, we ensure at least one of the three of us is available to lead.

I'm delighted by the enthusiasm displayed by everyone eager to learn. I believe Chastity's death has heightened the interest. While it's assumed she died from the flu, rumors of foul play persist. Without an autopsy, we simply don't have answers. Additionally, with Geoff Landers's threat against Captain Williams, we all recognize the importance of being able to defend ourselves.

Beyond the practical survival skills we're acquiring, it's the incredible camaraderie within our women's self-defense group that truly elevates our learning journey, infusing it with a remarkable sense of unity and support.

As the aroma of the stew permeates the air, mingling with the warm glow of the crackling fire and the soft light of the oil lamp, I can't help but feel a sense of gratitude for the new friendships we've managed to carve out in this chaotic world.

Chapter 35

Katie

The table is set with bread and a soft cheese spread, accompanied by small salads made from our miniature window shelf vegetable garden. I diluted some of the cheese spread to create a salad dressing.

This morning, the sprouts were ready for harvest. After giving them a final rinse, I diligently removed as many hulls—the outer coating of the seeds remaining after the sprouts emerged—as possible.

The instructions provided by Jake, and originally written by my mom, emphasized that removing the hulls and ensuring the sprouts were as dry as possible would help prolong their freshness in the refrigerator.

Of course, our refrigerator is merely a picnic cooler we replenish with ice or snow from outside. The best part about winter is having the means to keep our food fresh. The picnic cooler serves as our fridge, and the entire world becomes our deep freeze.

I'm about ready to step outside and inform Leo supper is ready when I hear his key turning in the lock. Both Gerry and I make our way to the entryway.

"Hey," I say as he steps inside. "Long day?"

My husband releases a heavy sigh. "Wasn't bad until the last few hours. There was an accident at one of the water facilities."

"An accident?"

"Yeah," Leo replies, removing his coat as he speaks. "Someone slipped while trying to break the ice for the ram pump. They broke their leg. Another guy fell while trying to assist the injured one off the ice, resulting in a dislocated shoulder."

"That's terrible. Are they keeping them overnight?"

"Just the broken leg." He takes a deep breath. "Something smells good."

"Stew—of course."

He laughs. "I like your stew."

I offer him a smile. "Take off your boots and get comfortable. I'll dish up our bowls." As I make my way to the woodstove, I continue the conversation. "I saw you with Oscar. That's nice he got a ride home on the snowmobile."

"He had a rough day too."

"Oh?"

"There was some sort of trouble. You know, the usual fight over something stupid." Leo pads across the floor in his stocking feet. "As Oscar tells it, he spends more time breaking up fights than anything else. But today was different."

"Different how?" I ask, holding both bowls as I approach the coffee table. "Do you want to change before we eat?"

"Sure. Give me a minute." Leo disappears into the cold bedroom. Despite his arm still being in a splint and the external fixation device in place, he has become adept at dressing and undressing, at least from the waist down. I help him with his shirts in the morning and at night.

It only takes a few minutes for him to return, now dressed in sweats after exchanging his heavily lined pants. His feet are adorned with insulated slippers. "That room is cold. I'm beginning to think we might as well move our clothes out here, too, and just ignore the bedroom altogether. The temperature really dropped today. Oscar said it was about ten below when he left the patroller's building. It's so cold they're suspending roving patrols tonight."

I shake my head. "I've kept the fire going, so it's been all right in here. But when I took Gerry out earlier, he did his business quickly. What kind of trouble did Oscar have today, aside from the cold?"

"The fight today. Usually, he and his partner will break it up and everyone goes on their way. But today, one of the troublemakers turned on Oscar and tried to land a punch. Oscar managed to avoid the worst of it. They arrested the guy and took him in. Which, you know, doesn't really do much good since they can't hold someone for something minor. He was given a stern talking to and then released, but he threatened Oscar and told him he knows where he lives."

"Really? That's scary."

"Oscar said he has no idea who the guy even is. A lot of people know Oscar since he grew up here, but this guy's a stranger." Leo moves toward the couch. "The sprouts look good."

"Thanks. I think they turned out all right. They're the radish sprouts again, so they're a little spicy but not too bad. I'm just happy to have something green and fresh during these dark days of winter, plus they're supposed to be a good source of folate and one of the B vitamins . . . I forget which one. I'm going to give some to Merissa. It should be good for her baby. Did they end up keeping the troublemaker for the threat, or did they let him go?"

"They let him go. The holding cell setup isn't great now. Besides, they only hold people for severe offenses. You know, like murder. Fighting, even threatening a patroller, isn't serious enough."

"How'd the guy know Oscar?"

Leo shakes his head. "Maybe he doesn't really know him. He might have been trying to intimidate him through empty talk."

We continue discussing our day and make plans to fully close off the bedroom. We hope that with January coming to an end, the weather will start to warm up. However, winter in the Midwest often only begins around this time, and we can expect cold temperatures and snow well into March or April. It was the same in Kansas, where Leo and I both went to school.

Though Wyoming isn't typically considered part of the Midwest, it can experience incredibly harsh winters. I truly hope this cold snap will be short-lived. Negative ten degrees Fahrenheit is no joke, especially when accompanied by strong winds. I pray people stay indoors and keep warm.

Last winter, many lives were lost due to the cold. They didn't have the systems in place that we have now to provide wood for heat. Currently, all occupied homes have some sort of woodstove. Many are homemade, like the one we have, while others are commercially produced, like the stoves found at the hospital.

I can't even imagine how we would get through a winter in South Dakota without wood heat. With the cold and snow we experienced last year, the deaths we witnessed were considered normal for most of the country. According to the reports we've heard, the winter was harsh nationwide. Even snowbird states like Florida and Arizona were heavily affected, with substantial loss of life.

Of course, it wasn't just the cold; starvation and violence also took their toll. In many ways, South Dakota and Wyoming were easier to survive in compared to Arizona and Florida, primarily due to the lower populations.

Before the EMP, the entire state of South Dakota had fewer than nine hundred thousand residents, and Wyoming had fewer than six hundred thousand. Combined, these two states have a population similar to that of Phoenix, Arizona.

"Katie?"

"Yeah?"

"Did you get lost in your own little world?"

Snickering, I raise my hands. "I guess I was just thinking about the cold and hoping people are staying warm tonight."

After we finish eating, I swiftly wash our few dishes using the pot of water that's been simmering on the stove. I move the soup to the back porch to cool before placing it in the cooler. Even the brief moments it takes to get the soup outside sends a chill through me.

"Come sit with me," Leo beckons, pointing to the couch.

Once Gerry and I are on the couch, covered with a blanket, Leo grabs the Bible. Captain Williams gave Leo a devotional Bible designed for couples, featuring daily devotions, scripture passages, and marriage-building questions for couples to read together. We try to engage in daily reading whenever our work schedules allow. We're also trying to attend church services.

We enjoyed Shawn Maher's sermon and would love to return to the ranch for a Sunday service. Leo also heard there's a daily church service being held in a building on Main Street. One of the members from Leo's men's Bible study group has attended a couple of the services and said they were quite good.

Leo opens the Bible and reads a passage from Isaiah. The focal point of the passage is Isaiah 5:4. *What more could have been done for my vineyard than I have done for it? When I looked for good grapes, why did it yield only bad?*

The devotional reminded me a lot of the troubles Leo and I have faced. We were turning away from each other and God instead of turning toward Him and each other. When we should've been tending to our marriage, we were both suffering separately in silence.

While we've made progress, passages like this remind me we can't take our relationship for granted. We need to continue nurturing our marriage, just as the farmer tends to the vineyard, and take steps to improve and bear good fruit.

After reading, we hold hands and pray, thanking God for helping us through our difficulties and allowing us the opportunity to grow through His Word, both individually and as a couple.

We sit in comfortable silence, listening to the crackling fire and savoring the peacefulness of the evening. After a while, Leo announces he's going to get ready for bed.

"I'll stay up for a bit, maybe move my chair closer to the fire and read. I'm on night shift tomorrow, so . . . " I raise my hands, indicating my schedule allows for a later bedtime.

Leo kisses me on the nose. "I'll take Gerry out to do his business."

"I'll handle it. He'll stay up with me and be ready to go out when I'm ready for bed. You know how he is."

We both glance over at our little dog, who wags his tail in response to the attention. "I know how he is." Leo squats to rub Gerry's ears. "Trouble for your mama, huh?"

"Never," I reply with a chuckle. "He's an angel." Gerry wags his tail in agreement.

After telling Gerry goodnight, Leo turns his attention to me, giving me a tender kiss and telling me not to stay up too late.

Leo heads off to get ready for bed, and I settle into my chair, drawing it nearer to the fire.

We may be in the midst of an ongoing war for survival, battling both external threats and the internal demons that haunt us, but together, we're steadfast. Together, Leo and I will forge ahead, navigating this shattered world with determination, love, and an unwavering belief that brighter days are yet to come.

The adventure continues in Deceptive Mayhem: Dakota Destruction Book 4.

Is their world finally safe now that the preacher and his followers are behind bars?

Surviving the apocalyptic winter in the Black Hills of South Dakota is hard enough. But when sinister forces shatter Katie's world, her fight for survival reaches a whole new level of intensity.

With all the unknowns surrounding the attacks, the preacher's group, and the drug overdoses, Katie and Leo aren't sure who they can trust…or who is out to harm the people of Rapid City.

Can the perpetrators be caught before they claim even more lives? Or will their next attack be the deadliest one yet?

Thank you for spending your time on our new South Dakota adventure.

If you have five minutes, you'd make this writer very happy if you could write a short review on Amazon, Goodreads, Bookbub, or your favorite review site.

I appreciate you!

Join my reader's club!
As part of my reader's club, you'll be the first to know about new releases and specials. I also share info on books I'm reading, preparedness tips, and more.

Please sign up on my website:
MillieCopper.com

Also by Millie Copper

The Havoc in Wyoming Series

When a series of coordinated attacks devastate the United States, the people of Bakerville, Wyoming, must come together to survive. Unfortunately, not everyone has the town's best interest at heart. Some are striving for personal gain during the apocalypse.

The Montana Mayhem Series

A group from Bakerville, Wyoming strikes out on their own while searching for the desires of their heart. Unfortunately, the road will not be easy, and sometimes the heart is hardened and deceitful.

The Dakota Destruction Series

After a series of coordinated attacks devastate the United States, Katie and Leo sacrifice everything to help their country. But some things aren't as they seem. Is it time to go home and start fresh, or can something good come out of this terrible situation?

Wyoming Fall Series (In The October Fall World)

In the blink of an eye, an EMP changed everything for Lauren and her family. Now they are in a fight for survival, trying to keep their loved ones alive as society collapses around them.

Nonfiction Books

Millie has penned seven nonfiction, traditional food focused books, sharing how, with a little creativity, anyone can transition to a real foods diet without overwhelming their food budget. Many of her books also include preparedness and food storage tips.

Find these titles at:MillieCopper.com

Acknowledgments

Thanks to:

Ameryn Tucker, my editor, beta reader, and daughter wrapped in one. I had a story I wanted to tell, and Ameryn encouraged me and helped me bring it to life.

Dee from Dauntless Cover Design.

My husband, who gave me the time and space I needed to complete this dream and was very patient as I'd tell him the same plot ideas over and over and over.

Three more adult daughters and a young son, who willingly listen to me drone on and on about storylines and ideas while encouraging me to "keep going."

My amazing Beta Readers! Thanks to Barbara, Christy, Glen, Ilona, Judy, Melonie, Tonya, Tammy, and Tracy for your help in creating the final story. Your insights and abilities to see the things I miss are very much appreciated!

A special thank you to Kristy who gave me a peek inside the world of the Coast Guard and Forest Service. And also a special thank you to Tim, a specialist in all things that go boom, for always answering my questions and pointing out things I wouldn't even think about.

And to you, my readers, for spending your time on our new South Dakota adventure. If you have five minutes, you'd make this writer very happy if you could leave a review. I appreciate you!

About the Author

Millie Copper, writer of Cozy Apocalyptic Fiction and preparedness mentor, was born in Nebraska but never lived there. Her parents fully embraced wanderlust and moved regularly, giving her an advantage of being from nowhere and everywhere.

Millie Copper lives in the wilds of Wyoming with her husband and young son, tending chickens and attempting a food forest on their small homestead. After living off the grid for several years, they've recently gone back on the grid. Four adult daughters, three sons-in-law, and five grandchildren round out the family.

Since 2009, Millie has authored articles on traditional foods, alternative health, homesteading, and preparedness-many times all within the same piece. Millie has penned seven nonfiction, traditional food focused books, sharing how, with a little creativity, anyone can transition to a real foods diet without overwhelming their food budget.

The twelve-installment *Havoc in Wyoming* and six-installment *Montana Mayhem* Christian Post-Apocalyptic fiction series use her homesteading, off-the-grid, and preparedness lifestyle as a guide. The adventures continue with the *Dakota Destruction* series.

Find Millie at www.MillieCopper.com
Facebook: www.facebook.com/MillieCopperAuthor/
Amazon: www.amazon.com/author/milliecopper
BookBub: https://www.bookbub.com/authors/millie-copper

www.ingramcontent.com/pod-product-compliance
Lightning Source LLC
Chambersburg PA
CBHW020804190726
48285CB00006B/2158